The Wedding Soup Murder

◇◇◇◇◇◇◇◇◇◇◇◇◇◇◇◇◇◇◇◇◇◇◇◇◇◇◇

An Italian Kitchen Mystery

◇◇◇◇◇◇◇◇◇◇◇◇◇◇◇◇◇◇◇◇◇◇◇◇◇◇◇

Rosie Genova

AN OBSIDIAN MYSTERY

OBSIDIAN
Published by the Penguin Group
Penguin Group (USA) LLC, 375 Hudson Street,
New York, New York 10014

USA | Canada | UK | Ireland | Australia | New Zealand | India | South Africa | China
penguin.com
A Penguin Random House Company

First published by Obsidian, an imprint of New American Library,
a division of Penguin Group (USA) LLC

First Printing, September 2014

ISBN 978-0-451-41515-8

Printed in the United States of America
10 9 8 7 6 5 4 3 2 1

Also by Rosie Genova

The Italian Kitchen Mystery Series

Book 1: *Murder and Marinara*
Book 2: *The Wedding Soup Murder*

For Adam,
who sees wonderful things—with love and pride

Acknowledgments

As always, I am indebted to Sandra Harding at New American Library and Kim Lionetti of Bookends for being good listeners, clever problem solvers, and staunch supporters of my work. Once again Ben Perini has proven that he is not only a gifted artist, but also a mind reader: His cover is everything I imagined and then some.

I also owe many thanks to my brother, Joseph Genova, whose work in environmental claims inspired a key plot element. He read pages, directed me to the necessary research, and shared professional anecdotes. I am grateful for his expertise and patience. It seems unnecessary to add that any errors are entirely my own.

To my cousin by marriage and musician by trade, Jim DiBattista, who answered my questions and helped me get the ball rolling on Facebook—literally and figuratively, you rock!

To the fellow writers, librarians, book bloggers, book club members, readers, students, colleagues, and friends who've helped spread the word about the Italian Kitchen Mysteries—I am forever grateful.

And finally, to my very own Jersey Guys—AP, Adam, John, and Anthony—you're loved more than you know.

Chapter One

"What are you doing in here, Vic?" The deep, familiar tones of my ex's voice still had the power to set my heart pounding. But I didn't look up.

"What does it look like I'm doing, Tim?" I released the scoop, gently dropping the thirteenth meatball onto the sheet pan. That left a mere 987 to go. At the rate I was going, I'd be spending my thirty-fourth birthday in the Casa Lido kitchen, still scooping ground meat from this bottomless aluminum bowl.

He stood with his hands on his hips, frowning. "Who said you could make the meatballs?"

"I'm not *making* them." I tried to keep the impatience out of my tone. "I'm forming them." I held up the scoop, covered in flecks of raw meat. "Nando mixed them up."

"Good." Tim strode over to the stockpots, lifted the lid of the nearest one, and sniffed. Then he stuck a spoon into it, blew on it, slurped its contents noisily, and nodded. He pointed the spoon at me. "You didn't make this stock."

I slammed the scoop down on the worktable. "No, I

didn't make the stock. My grandmother started it and Nando finished it." I gestured to the simmering pots of stock. "But it will probably be my job to pick every piece of edible chicken from those bones, right after I finish making—sorry, *forming*—a thousand tiny meatballs for the Wedding Soup." I imagined tray after tray of meatballs, lined up until the crack of doom, and shook my head. "It's like some mythological punishment Nonna dreamed up."

"You wanted to learn the business." His voice was terse. "That's why you came back, wasn't it? I mean, it sure wasn't for me."

I tried to concentrate on the task in front of me. I had to make these quickly, while the meat was still cold. Aside from health reasons, if the ground beef, pork, and veal mixture sat out too long, I'd get misshapen *polpetti.* And then there would be hell to pay, extracted by my eightyish but still formidable grandmother.

But even fear of my nonna wasn't enough to take my mind from Tim's powerful presence a few feet from my elbow. I'd come back to Oceanside Park to learn the family business and research a new book, a departure from my mystery series. Instead, I'd stumbled into a murder and briefly back into Tim's arms. But my role in the outcome of the investigation had left him furious with me. I glanced up and met his cold gray stare.

"Yes," I said, "That's why I came back." It was only a partial truth, and we both knew it. I'd been in love with Tim Trouvare for more than half my life, and trying to push away those feelings was about as easy as fighting a riptide. "Look, Tim, I'm sorry about the way things turned out in May. But it could have been much worse."

"Right," he sneered. "I could have been arrested for murder."

I sighed. "Can't we just get past this?"

"Oh, I'm past it, sweetheart." He patted me on the shoulder and I jumped. "I'm past it all." With that, he swept out the kitchen's swinging door.

"Ohhhh-kay." I stuck the scoop back into the meat and tried to focus. I could work only in one-hour intervals, as Nonna was strict about how long the meat could stay unrefrigerated. I looked down at the raw mixture, catching whiffs of fresh parsley and garlic. Once the stock was skimmed and strained, it would be brought to a simmer, and the *polpetti* would be dropped in quickly to cook. But that was only the last step of the process. There was still the escarole to be cleaned and blanched, another job that would likely fall to me. And the whole thing had to be done in stages. I dropped another meatball onto the sheet pan and counted. Again.

As a favor to an old friend of my dad's, we'd agreed to make our special Wedding Soup for his daughter's reception. With two hundred guests, we needed God knows how many gallons of soup. My grandmother had specified five meatballs per bowl—hence the thousand count. But while we could make the stock ahead of time, we needed to complete the last steps at the reception, just before serving. That meant making up all the meatballs and freezing them. Prepping the stock and greens. Transporting all of it to the Belmont

Beach Country Club a couple of hours before the service. And Nonna had put me in charge.

"You wanted more responsibility," she'd said with a shrug. "So now you're responsible."

"But, Nonna," I told her, "Belmont probably has its own staff. You know Chef Massimo——he'll want to oversee the prep and service. And we'll never keep Tim out of there. How will we do this with two kitchen staffs butting heads?" The panic rose in me as I imagined all those culinary egos clashing in one small space. "Can't we just make it here and drop it off?"

"No." She crossed her arms, frowning over the top of her glasses. "The *polpetti* and greens must be cooked just before service." She shook a knobby finger at me. "Not one moment sooner."

I could still hear her voice in my ears as I shook out the last tiny meatball. At fifty per tray, I'd need twenty sheet pans. Each would have to be double-wrapped in plastic and set carefully into the freezer. How would we get it all there? How many trips in my little Honda would it take? Not to mention the soup itself: How would we transport all those gallons of chicken stock down Ocean Avenue?

"God," I moaned. I stared down at the tray of tiny pink spheres. "How did I get myself into this? If I never see another meatball again, it will be too soon."

But as it turned out, meatballs were the least of my troubles.

*   *   *

"Now, darling," my mom said, fluttering around me in the Casa Lido kitchen like a stiletto-wearing butterfly. "When you go over there, make sure you clear everything with Elizabeth Merriman. She's very particular about how things are done." Mom smoothed the collar of my cotton blouse. "Would you like me to give this a quick press before you go? It is the Belmont Country Club, after all."

I looked into my mother's freshly bronzed face. Her long curls, now a purple-tinted auburn, brushed her shoulders, slightly bared by her lime green boatneck top. The combination of colors was blinding. "Mom, I'm fine. I'll be spending most of my time in a hot kitchen. Once that soup is made and served, I'll be hightailing it out of there."

"No, you won't." Like an avenging ghost, my grandmother materialized out of nowhere, pronouncing her words with a finality that sealed my fate. And whatever it was, it wouldn't be pleasant. But it was a price I was willing to pay. I'd even left my East Village apartment in Manhattan to come back to the Jersey shore. Because I was working on a new book based on my family's history, I planned to spend a year learning about our restaurant business. But thus far, things hadn't quite turned out as I planned.

"You will stay until the end of the reception," Nonna said, setting a tray of cookies down on the butcher-block worktable. I stared at the pale, plump pillows edged in golden brown, each perfectly formed. The licorice scent of anise wafted upward, pulling my hand toward the tray like a magnet. And then the sound of my grandmother's slap resounded across the kitchen.

"Hey!" I rubbed the back of my hand. "Why can't I have one? You know your ricotta cookies are my favorites."

"They are for the reception. You'll put these out on the dessert table." She crossed her arms, pressing her lips together in a tight red line of warning. It was a line I knew better than to cross.

Oh, no. Waiting for the dessert service meant I'd be stuck at that wedding all night. I'd hoped to be back at my cottage and at my computer by seven to put in a couple of hours of work on my novel.

"But why?" I wailed, sounding like the ten-year-old who'd helped my grandmother set tables in the restaurant more than two decades ago. "Aren't they having some overloaded Venetian table filled with cannoli and éclairs and napoleons? Do they really *need* more cookies?" The second the words dropped from my mouth, I realized how foolish they were. This was an Italian wedding, after all. We always needed more cookies. Then a sense of dread overcame me like fog over the ocean. "Nonna," I said slowly, "these aren't iced."

"Of course they aren't. You'll ice and decorate those two hours before service, not a minute before or after." She produced a plastic container of what looked like silver BBs. "One teaspoon of icing per cookie and three silver balls on top. No more, no less."

My mouth gaped open like one of my brother Danny's fresh-caught tuna. "I . . . but . . ."

"But nothing, Victoria." Nonna glared at me from behind her bifocals. I turned an imploring look on my mother.

"Now, Mama," my mom said, "we can prep these ahead—don't you think?"

Nonna turned her stony gaze on my mom, who, despite forty years' acquaintance with her mother-in-law, still flinched. "Nic-o-lina." My grandmother pronounced each syllable separately and crisply, a sure sign of danger. "The Casa Lido has a reputation to uphold," she said. "I will not be sending out dry cookies that are imperfectly iced." Nonna trained her laser-beam stare back on me. "Especially after what happened a couple of months ago."

St. Francis, give me patience, I prayed. "Nonna," I said gently, "what happened then was no one's fault." But I knew that on some level, she held me responsible. "And we've recovered."

"Thank God," my mom said. "In any case, Mama, can you really expect Victoria to make all that icing as well as oversee the soup service at the club? It seems like an awful lot to ask."

"No. Tim will make the icing." My grandmother's tight lips curved into either a smile or a sneer. With her it was hard to tell. But Tim had been in her bad graces ever since that little mishap in the pantry, and this was her version of revenge. Tim saw himself as an up-and-coming chef de cuisine, not an assistant baker. It was bad enough we'd have to work together all night, but now he'd be in a fouler mood than usual.

I exchanged a look with my mom, who gave a small shake of her auburn extensions that spelled it out for me: *Give it up.*

"Okay," I said. "So, fill me in on how all this is going to work."

My grandmother rested her palms on the worktable in a war-room pose. Any minute now she'd get out a wall map and pushpins. "All right," she said. "The *polpetti* will remain in the freezer until the moment we are ready to load the van. The stockpots are sealed. The escarole is prepped. Both are in the walk-in. Nando will load the van and drive; Chef Massimo will follow."

"And Tim's driving me in my Honda." *Oh, goody.* Forty minutes alone in the car with my ex-boyfriend. "And when we get there?"

"By all the saints, have we not gone over this?" My grandmother shook her head at my obtuseness. "You set the stock to simmer, adding the greens in bunches. At the very last, you add the *polpetti*, and you cook them only until they are no longer pink inside, understand?" She spread her fingers wide. "And when you plate, only five meatballs per bowl. As far as the cookies—"

"I know. Ice before service, and only three silver balls per cookie. I get it."

She narrowed her eyes at me. "Remember that you are representing the Casa Lido, Victoria."

"I will, Nonna. Speaking of which, what about our dinner service here tonight?"

"Nando will drive back for prep, and Massimo will return after the soup is served at the reception. You and Tim will stay for the dessert service and bring back our stockpots."

"I probably have to wash them, too," I muttered.

"What was that, Victoria?" my grandmother asked sharply.

"Nothing, Nonna." I said with a sigh. "I just don't see why we're doing this," I grumbled. "We're not even getting paid."

"Now, hon," my mom said. "Dr. Natale is an old friend. And he wants Roberta to have a special day."

"Ugh, Roberta," I said. "Is she still a brat?" The Roberta Natale I remembered was a pampered princess with big hair and an even bigger ego.

My mother frowned. "Now, that's no way to talk about the bride, Victoria. You just bear in mind that Chickie is a friend of your father's. And look how he's taken care of our teeth all these years."

"That's reason enough *not* to help out," I said, remembering how Dr. Charles Natale, affectionately known as Dr. Chickie, had outfitted me with a monstrous set of braces when I was thirteen. "He tortured me for two years. I was known as Brace Face all through middle school."

My mom grasped my chin in an Italian love hold and shook it from side to side. "And look how beautiful that smile ended up."

I peeled her fingers from my face. "If you say so, Mom. Hey, how come Danny never got braces?"

"*Daniele*'s teeth were straight," my grandmother called over her shoulder. "You had a gap you could drive a truck through."

"Thanks a bunch, Nonna." My grandmother made no bones about her preference for my older brother, a detective in the local police department. As Nonna's only grandson, he was subject to a different set of rules than I was—that is to say, no rules at all. Basically, all he had to do was show up and eat. "Hey, speaking of my big bro, what's going on with him and Sofia?"

My mother's perfectly groomed brows met in a winged arch over her nose, and she gave a little sniff. "I have no idea. Your brother chooses not to share details of his personal life with me. And I'm not entirely certain they belong together anyway."

"*Zitto*, Nicolina! For shame." My grandmother crossed her arms in classic battle pose. "They are married, legally and in the eyes of God. And they will stay that way," she pronounced. "This is nothing more than some life troubles. They will get past this and start their family."

"I hope so," I said, setting the tray of cookies carefully in a plastic bin. "They've seemed pretty close lately." Though my brother and sister-in-law Sofia were officially separated, I knew that Danny was spending more time at the house. He hadn't yet moved back in, which had us all wondering. And my sister-in-law, with whom I was pretty tight, had been uncharacteristically silent on the subject of my brother. I figured she'd fill me in when she was ready.

"I'm sorry," my mother said, shaking her head, "but I blame Sofia for that mess you got into."

I exchanged a look with Nonna. We both knew very well who had gotten me into "that mess" back in May, and she was wearing bifocals and red lipstick. But Sofia, who had hopes of entering law enforcement, *had* relished her role in solving a murder. "I got myself into it, Mom, but it's over and done with." I wedged the container of silver balls down next to the cookie tray. I planned to hold these on my lap; there was no way I was letting my grandmother's famous cookies ride in the back of the van. When my phone buzzed, I didn't even have to look at it to know who it was.

"Well, ladies, my prince awaits." *Where the hell are you???* his text read. "And as impatient as ever for my company." I lifted the container of cookies, holding it close to my nose to inhale the anise scent. The minute I was in that car, I planned to stuff one in my mouth.

Nonna, who besides being a restaurateur was also a mind reader, narrowed her eyes at me. "Don't get any ideas, Victoria. I know exactly how many are on that tray. And don't be surprised if I come and check on you over at the club."

I nearly dropped the plastic bin. "Why? I can take care of things." I struggled to keep the panic from my voice; if Nonna sensed weakness, she'd zero in for the kill.

She raised her eyebrows over her glasses. "That remains to be seen."

A loud honk from the parking lot startled me into action. "I'll be fine, Nonna. Don't worry about anything."

I struggled at the back door, trying to ease it open with my elbow without jarring the precious commodity I was holding, all while Tim grinned at me from inside the car.

"Thanks for the help," I said. Settling the cookies

next to me on the seat, I slammed the car door for emphasis.

He lifted a broad shoulder. "C'mon, Vic, you don't need my help. You're the girl who's got it all under control, right?"

"Right," I said through my teeth. But I couldn't have been more wrong.

Chapter Two

*T*he summer season was in full swing as Tim and I headed out of our small beach town of Oceanside Park. It was a Saturday in July, and thousands of families had begun their yearly pilgrimage to the shore. Ocean Avenue, the coastal route along our section of beaches, was crawling with weekend traffic. The boardwalk and beaches were packed, and no doubt the Casa Lido would do a brisk business this evening. I found myself wishing that I'd be waiting tables instead of working a wedding reception.

"Do we do this a lot, Tim?" I asked, breaking the silence of the last seven miles.

He leaned close to the steering wheel, eyeing the line of cars in front of him as if he could will them all to move faster. "Do what? Sit in traffic on a Saturday in July?"

"No. I mean the Casa Lido making the soup for this wedding—since when are we caterers?"

"We're not. This is just a favor. And I'm not any happier about it than you are."

He stared straight ahead, his lips in a tight line. He

already had his bandanna tied around his head, and I noticed the faint furrows over his brows and the lines starting around his eyes. If I looked in a mirror, I'd see the same on my own face. When had we stopped being kids? Was it when we'd gone away to college? Or the day Tim came back and broke my heart? I blinked, both in surprise that it still had the power to hurt and at the tears that started gathering. Tim glanced at me once, and his voice softened. "You okay?"

"Fine."

"What are you thinking about, then?"

"Well, if you must know, I was thinking about the past."

"Ah, not a good idea, lass. You're breakin' your own rules." He smiled, and my heart turned over.

"Cut it with the blarney, Trouvare. You're more Italian than Irish and you know it." But I couldn't help smiling back. "And do you even *know* the rules?"

He nodded. "I do indeed." He held up one finger. "Rule Number One: no touching. Rule Number Two: no reminiscing."

"So you have learned your lessons." *If only I'd learned mine.* "Tim," I said, "I don't want to be mad at you, and I don't want you mad at me. What happened at the restaurant—"

"Was no one's fault." He rested his hand over mine briefly. "Look, my manly pride was hurt, okay?"

"I kind of figured that one out already."

He squeezed my hand once and then put his back on the wheel. "And we'll always be friends, Vic, no matter what."

"You bet," I said. "Friends for always." And this time, my heart didn't turn over—it sank like a stone.

The Belmont Country Club sat high behind the seawall that overlooked Belmont's steep, narrow beach. The massive Victorian structure had once been a resort hotel for nineteenth-century New York financiers; along its walls were pictures of Astors and Vanderbilts sipping champagne in its dining room and taking turns around the ballroom. The magnificent ballroom featured a gallery of real Tiffany windows and hand-carved Grecian columns. Hopeful brides-to-be spent years on waiting lists (often before they were engaged) to be able to say that their weddings were held at the historic Belmont Club. And every one of these brides has something else in common: daddies with deep pockets. As we pulled into the long drive, I craned my neck to take in the architectural details, the gables and towers and the widow's walk that circled the central tower.

"Wow," I said. "This place is amazing."

"Costs a fortune to have a wedding here," Tim said.

"With waiting lists a mile long. I guess Dr. Chickie had an in, since he's the club's treasurer."

Tim shrugged. "All I know is the place has two Michelin-star chefs. I'm playin' with the big boys today."

"You nervous?" I should have asked whether he was embarrassed, considering that Tim's role was to throw some raw meatballs into chicken stock and to mix up a batch of cookie icing.

"Nah." He pulled into a small lot behind the club, in

an area obviously meant for deliveries. He turned to me and winked. "I can hold my own."

I was doubtful, but I only smiled at him as we got out of the car. He grabbed the cooler with the butter and sugar in it, and this time opened the door for me as I emerged with the precious container of cookies. I blinked as we stepped into the long, cavernous kitchen of the country club, outfitted in floor-to-ceiling stainless steel, from its state-of-the-art appliances to its gleaming countertops.

"Whoa," I said, "you could fit four Casa Lido kitchens in this place."

Tim smirked. "I've seen bigger. You forget, Vic, I worked at Chateau Fromage."

For three whole months. Ah, Tim, I thought. *Is there even room in this kitchen for your ego?* "Well, this might not be your beloved House of Cheese, but it's pretty impressive."

"May I help you?" a deep voice barked from the other end of the kitchen. I turned, nearly dropping the cookies. A stocky figure emerged from the shadows, and it was hard to tell at first whether the person was male or female. Like Tim, he/she wore a bandanna, but his/her kitchen clothes were black instead of white. Once again, the voice boomed from the dim corner. "What are you doing in my kitchen?"

Okay, I thought, *female, but a toughie. In her late fifties, maybe?* As she got closer, I noticed her heavy makeup: painted-on brows that gave her a look of perpetual surprise, dark eye shadow, false eyelashes, and a shade of lipstick that suggested she'd been eating orange ice pops. The line of foundation along her chin was much darker than the skin on her neck. Though a red scarf covered most of her head, a scraggly salt-and-pepper ponytail poked out from behind it. All that makeup seemed at odds with her broad shoulders and mannish chef's coat. Instead of the usual kitchen clogs, she wore heavy black shoes on her feet. "I asked you a question," she snarled, and I took a step back, still clutching the cookies to my chest.

Tim stuck out his hand. "We're here from the Casa Lido, Chef. I'm Tim Trouvare." He grinned in his most charming Italian-Irish manner, as though she should recognize his famous name. But Tim's hand hung unshaken in the air.

"I don't care who you are," she said, fixing me with a bright blue glare, "you don't belong in my kitchen. And what the hell's the Casa Lido anyway?"

"Um, it's a restaurant in Oceanside Park." I set the bin down on the counter, but didn't make Tim's mistake of offering my hand. "I'm Victoria Rienzi, one of the owners." Okay, I wasn't really, but this woman was clearly the impatient type; I wasn't about to launch into my life story and tell her why I was working at the restaurant. "We're here to serve the soup course. Our guys should be arriving with the van any minute."

"Ah yes." A slow smile spread across her face and she rubbed her hands together. "The famous Wedding Soup. Etienne is all ready for you."

"Etienne?" I asked.

"Etienne Boulé," Tim said out of the side of his mouth. "Michelin, remember?"

"Oh, right," I whispered. The scary chef's demeanor had softened, but there was a glint in her blue eyes. *She can't wait,* I thought. *She knows Mr. Michelin Star Chef Etienne hates the idea of an interloper in his kitchen, and she wants to see the fireworks.*

At that moment, she stuck out her hand. "I'm Kate Bridges, the pastry chef." I braced myself for a tight grip, but her grasp was surprisingly weak for such a strong-looking woman. She jerked a thumb toward the back of the kitchen. "I was working on the cake when you came in."

So she was the pastry chef. And like all chefs, she was proprietary about her kitchen. My eyes strayed to the container of cookies on the counter. *What will she do when she realizes there will be a tray of cookies competing with her masterpiece of a cake and her perfect Italian pastries?*

"Oh, we'd love to see it," I said, less than truthfully.

Her expression darkened, and she crossed her thick arms. "Nobody sees it until it's ready to be cut."

"We understand, Chef," Tim said quickly, and shot me a look. "Listen, can you point me to a place I can set up my *mise en place*?"

She gave a snort of laughter. "Now, that's up to Chef Boulé, isn't it? I'm sure he'll be *glad* to find you a spot for your *meez.*" She glanced at the container on the counter and then pointed. "What's that?"

I looked at Tim. Tim looked at me. But neither one of us spoke.

Kate narrowed her eyes, her fake brows wriggling

like thin black snakes. "You two aren't very good at answering questions, are you?"

I took a breath. "Those are my grandmother's famous ricotta cookies. The bride requested that there be a tray of them on the dessert table this evening."

"Oh, the bride, 'requested,' did she?" Kate asked, and took a step closer. My eyes were riveted to her false eyelashes and two bright spots of blush on her cheeks. She looked like a scary clown, and I stiffened. "Well," she continued, "if the bride wants these homemade jobs so bad, she doesn't need my pastries. Maybe she doesn't need my cake, either!"

Just then the kitchen door swung open, and I was relieved for the interruption—until I got a good look at her. A tall redhead walked toward us, bare-legged in a green sheath and gold metallic sandals. Though her complexion was pale, much lighter than my own, she had a look the magazines call sun-kissed, with a light spray of freckles across her nose and pink cheeks. And the minute her eyes met Tim's, it was over.

His hand strayed to his bandanna, and I knew he regretted that his dark curls weren't tumbling charmingly over his forehead. I watched him start to roll the sleeves of his chef's coat—*the better to show off your forearms, eh, Tim?* If he'd had plumage, he'd be puffing out his chest and dropping feathers all over the room. But whatever he was doing, it was working. The young woman addressed her words to Kate, but her eyes never left Tim's face.

"Now, Chef, our bride knows that your pastries are

unparalleled. But she has a sentimental attachment to these particular cookies. Might we not make just a bit of room on the dessert table?" She flashed a smile, revealing two rows of white teeth worthy of Dr. Chickie's best work. Kate seemed unmoved, but Tim was about to melt into a puddle on the floor.

Kate grunted, shook her head, and stamped off to her corner of the kitchen without a word. The redhead, still smiling, held out her hand. To me, amazingly enough. "I'm Lacey Harrison, Roberta's wedding planner. You're Victoria, aren't you?"

I couldn't help smiling back. "Yes, nice to meet you. We're—"

"From the Casa Lido, here for the soup service. I'm Tim," he interrupted, grabbing Lacey's hand and shooting her the same Black Irish grin to which Kate had been impervious. But not so Lacey Harrison. She cast her eyes down shyly, revealing thick eyelashes—her own, I noted. Her cheeks glowed pink, her lips curved in a sweet smile, and she made no move to remove her hand from Tim's. In my wrinkled blouse and serviceable skirt, I felt dumpy, frumpy, and old, though I was probably only about five years older than the enchanting Lacey. As I stood watching them, a wave of emotion washed over me, leaving regret and a tinge of sadness behind. If I'd entertained any hopes of getting back together with Tim, they'd just been dashed against the rocks.

"Very nice to meet you," Lacey said, finally slipping her hand from his. "Both of you." She turned to me, still smiling shyly. "I'm such a fan of your books. It's so cool to actually meet you."

Great, I thought. *I can't even have the satisfaction of hating her.* "Thanks," I said. I glanced at the kitchen clock. It was time to end this lovefest and get down to business. "Lacey, our guys will be here with the soup ingredients any minute. How are we doing for time?"

"Well, the church service was scheduled for three; it's a full Mass so they should be about halfway through it now. They'll be taking pictures for a bit afterward, and our cocktail hour begins at five thirty sharp. But I should warn you," she said, glancing at Tim, "that Chef Etienne and his staff will be here any moment to start preparing. The bulk of it was done yesterday, but with two hundred guests, there's still an awful lot to do."

Tim winked at her. "But I know you'll have it all under control."

Interesting. When I'm the one who has it all under control, it's somehow threatening, but when Lacey does, it's cute as a button. Lacey shook her head, her gold highlights glinting under the bright lights of the kitchen. "That's Elizabeth's job. Elizabeth Merriman—she's the president of the club and the events manager. And let me warn you again: She's a stickler. She's really big on the reputation of this place." She lowered her voice. "We call her the Iron Lady. You know, like Margaret Thatcher. Only she's worse."

From the back of the kitchen came a sound that was something between a growl and a curse, and Lacey grinned. "Kate hates Elizabeth. They really butt heads. But Kate's such an amazing pastry chef that Elizabeth puts up with her."

Tim cocked his head in Kate's direction. "Think

she'll give me a few lessons? I'm trying to branch out a bit in my work, maybe add *dessert chef* to my résumé." He lowered his voice, as though he were confiding something special. "In fact, I'm doing a little pastry work this evening."

I clenched my jaw to keep my mouth from dropping open. He was making the freaking icing, and had done nothing but complain about it since Nonna assigned it to him. As our current sous chef, Tim was interested in being a chef de cuisine, period, and lived every day in the hopes our chef, Massimo, would retire or move on so he could step in. I shook my head at him, but he was paying no attention to me—something I would have to get used to now that Lacey was in the picture.

"Uh, I don't know about that," Lacey said. "Chef Kate is kind of volatile. And, anyway, the kitchen arrangements would be overseen by Elizabeth. Once the reception is under way, I'll be leaving."

I could hear the regret in her voice; so did Tim, apparently, because he stepped closer to her. Inclining his head, he spoke softly. "That's too bad. But maybe I could see you another time?"

Her cheeks grew pink again. "Maybe," she said, and then nodded to me. "It was nice to meet you, Victoria."

"You too," I said, and we both watched her go. I turned to Tim. "Since when do you have aspirations to be a dessert chef?"

"Maybe you don't know me as well as you think, Vic. I'm a man of surprises."

"Right," I said. "How 'bout you surprise me by getting that icing ready?"

He shook his head. "Too early. And, anyway, I'm not making it. You are."

"Oh no you don't. My grandmother will kill me if she thinks I made the icing for her precious cookies. And I've never made it."

The scorn on Tim's face was withering. He held up his fingers. "It's three ingredients, Vic. There are industrial mixers here. Even you can't screw it up."

"Then the soup is all on you, mister. I'll oversee the portions, but don't expect me to be dropping meatballs into hot pots of stock."

"You might not have a choice, Vic. We'll need every hand here tonight and—"

Tim's back was to the kitchen door, so he didn't see the Belmont Club's master chef enter the kitchen until it was too late. But I did. I don't know what I was expecting Chef Etienne Boulé to look like. Rotund, certainly. And maybe somewhere between Batali and Lagasse on the attractiveness scale. But I wasn't prepared for the tall, elegant, silver-haired Frenchman who stood glowering down at us. And for the second time that day, I wished I'd worn a little black dress instead of a big white blouse.

Tim turned and slapped his hand to his chest. "Chef, *pardonnez-moi*, I didn't see you."

Chef Etienne's face remained impassive. "Obviously. I take it you are from—"

"The Casa Lido restaurant." I held out my hand and tried to smile Lacey style. "I'm Victoria Rienzi."

Though he didn't kiss my hand, he did treat me to a bit of French. "*Enchanté, mademoiselle,*" he said, and I stifled the urge to giggle. Tim frowned again and stepped in front of me, grabbing Chef Etienne's hand. "Chef, it's an honor. I'm Tim Trouvare, sous chef at the Casa Lido."

"That remains to be seen," Etienne said. He looked around at the miles of empty counter space. "I suppose I will have to find a place for you and your staff to work."

"Yes, if you please," Tim said, and I half expected him to drop to his knees with the request.

Chef Etienne crossed his arms and lifted his chin. "It cannot be done until my staff arrives. They have precedence, you understand? And how many do you bring, besides the *mademoiselle*?" He inclined his head in my direction, and I took note of his heavy-lidded dark eyes and full mouth. Despite the silver hair, he couldn't have been much over forty. He frowned slightly, and I realized he caught me staring.

Before Tim could respond, I heard rapid-fire Spanish outside the kitchen doors, followed by some vociferous French. The voices grew louder, and though I couldn't make out a word, it was clear there was a giant clash of cultures going on outside those doors. And other things, as well, judging by the clang and clatter of metal carts. Both kitchen doors opened at once, with our line cook, Nando Perez, manning one cart, and a short, dark man who appeared to be his French doppelgänger pushing the other. There wasn't room for both carts, and neither guy would give way. Nando shouted in Spanish to Tim, while his twin spouted off in French to Chef Etienne.

"Remind your man that he is a guest in this kitchen,"

Etienne said through his teeth. "Antoine, *entrez, maintenant*!

"I am sorry, Miss Victor," Nando said, still out of breath from his efforts. "But this one would not let me through."

At that, Antoine scowled and made a hand gesture that is universally understood in all languages, causing Nando to let rip again in Spanish. Judging from his motions in my direction, he was loudly reminding Antoine that there was a lady present. In response, Antoine took my hand in his sweaty paw and pumped it up and down, all the while pleading his case in French.

Tim then pulled Nando to the side; Etienne did the same with Antoine, who only reluctantly released my hand. By this time, all four men were talking at once in three different languages. Just then, the doors swung open again to reveal the Casa Lido's chef de cuisine, Massimo Fabri. Decked out in an Italian suit, he carried his chef's coat over his arm. Looking around the kitchen as though he smelled something decomposing, he wrinkled his formidable nose and made his daily pronouncement.

"I cannot work under these conditions," he said, tossing back his long hair. "I will not have this, you understand."

Chef Etienne turned to face him. "*You* will not have this? And who are you, pray tell?"

"Who am I?" he roared, and then launched into angry Italian, adding yet another language to the discordant verbal symphony playing all around us. I headed to the back to find Kate, but halted at the sound of the kitchen door opening behind me.

"What is this commotion? I thought I'd hired professionals, not children. I will not have this in my club, do you understand me?"

I swung around at the sound of her voice and came face-to-face with the Iron Lady herself—Elizabeth Merriman.

Chapter Three

*E*lizabeth Merriman never raised her voice. She didn't have to. Every word rang with authority and power, stopping us in our tracks. She was tall and broad-shouldered, and her iron gray hair formed tight curls around her head in a style that was popular fifty years ago. She had strong features, with high cheekbones and a long nose. Her gaze moved over us like a searchlight, but her blue eyes were clouded, and I wondered if she had cataracts.

Etienne, who had the least fear of her, stepped forward. "Please, pardon us, madame," he said. "There was a small altercation, but I believe"—he stopped and frowned at Nando and Antoine—"that it has been settled." He turned to Tim and Massi. "Has it not, chefs?"

"Yes, chef," Tim said hastily. Massi merely crossed and arms and sniffed in an injured manner.

"It had better be," Elizabeth said. She gripped a pearl-handled cane and pointed it at Tim and me. "And you people—I assume you're from that restaurant in Oceanside, correct?" My eyes were drawn to the large emerald ring she wore, as well as to her thick, reddened knuckles. *Arthritis,* I thought. *That ring will never come off.* "Well?" she asked sharply.

But before I could answer, Kate's voice came from the dim recesses of the long kitchen. "Don't hold your breath for an answer from those two, Elizabeth."

Squinting, Elizabeth Merriman frowned in the direction of Kate's voice. "Lurking back there, are you, Ms. Bridges? So you're an eavesdropper as well as a troublemaker, I see."

But it was clear she couldn't *see* much at all; she wasn't leaning on that cane because she was arthritic. She was using it to help her get around. When Kate's only answer was a sneering laugh, Elizabeth turned her attention back to us. "Is one of you going to answer my question, or have you all been struck dumb?"

"Yes, ma'am," Tim said. "I mean, no, we're not dumb." He shot her a blinding smile. "Well, we can talk anyway. We're here from the Casa Lido." With a respectful gesture to Massi, he said, "Our chef de cuisine, Massimo Fabri. And this is Victoria Rienzi, one of the owners, and that's our line cook, Nando Perez."

She nodded to Massi, and barely glancing Nando's way, Elizabeth Merriman's cloudy eyes landed on me. "So you're a Rienzi, eh?" Peering at my dark blond hair and hazel eyes, she gave me a skeptical squint. Except for my olive skin, I probably didn't look much like her idea of an Italian.

I nodded, but she said nothing further. If she'd heard of us, it had to be through the restaurant. It's not like anyone in my family hung out with WASP-y country-club presidents. "We're here because—"

"I know why you're here, young woman. The food we serve here isn't quite to the liking of the Natale family. Apparently, they prefer a more *rustic* cuisine." She gestured with her cane to Nando's cart, on which sat the tightly wrapped stockpots and trays of meatballs. "Wedding Soup, indeed. Call it what it is: a peasant dish."

I cringed at what I knew was coming. Chef Massi's face reddened. Scowling furiously, he held out his hands, fingers and thumbs pinched in a universal Italian gesture. "You dare call my food *rustico*?" he shouted, rolling his R's so hard that my ears rang. "Then I will take my leave of you." With that, he lifted his chin and stalked out the kitchen doors.

"Well," Elizabeth Merriman said, "there's a classic Italian temper, if I've ever seen one."

Tim heard my soft gasp and gave my arm a warning squeeze. Chef Etienne glanced in my direction, lifting one brow French-ily, as if to say, *She calls it as she sees it, mademoiselle.*

"Ah, well, it doesn't matter much," Elizabeth said. "Peasant food or no, after this evening, Dr. Charles Natale will no longer be a member of this club anyway." She rested one hand on the countertop, shifting her stare to Nando, who stood frozen with one hand still on the food cart. "Clear that cart at once, boy. That meat shouldn't be sitting out like that."

Except for a small tightening of his mouth, Nando

gave no response to the insult. But I was furious. So we serve peasant food. Our longtime line cook, a thirty-year-old man, gets called a boy. And now, thanks to Elizabeth Merriman, we were short a pair of hands in the kitchen. I shook off Tim's hand, took a breath, and opened my mouth to speak. Chef Etienne moved his head only a fraction, but it was enough to make me close my mouth.

"Madame," he said to Elizabeth, "this will be quite a busy night for you, no? Do you not trust me to run my kitchen the way I see fit?" He took her elbow and steered her toward the door. "I know that our . . . *guests* understand who is in charge. *C'est vrai*, madame?"

Elizabeth cocked her head, looking sideways at the chef. "*C'est vrai*, Etienne. So long as you understand who is in charge of the Belmont Country Club."

As the cocktail hour came to a close, Tim and Nando swung into action. Working in the small space allotted them by Chef Etienne, they set the stock simmering; I stood behind with the escarole, trying not to look at the two hundred soup dishes lined up on the counter.

"How will we get this done without Massi, Tim?"

"Don't worry, Vic. I got it covered."

"Chef," Etienne called out. "You must move more quickly. We will need every one of those burners for the second course."

"Yes, Chef," Tim called back, his arm moving like a machine from the tray of meatballs to the steaming pots. I winced each time he was splashed by the hot soup, but he didn't seem to notice.

"Miss Victor," Nando called, and I moved in, throwing handfuls of greens into the pot while he stirred. The kitchen was ungodly hot, and sweat trickled down the back of my neck. Chef Etienne had insisted I wear a chef's coat and a hairnet. The net was as itchy as it was ugly, and my feet hurt from standing. But I tossed those greens like a bride throws her bouquet. *You wanted to learn, Vic,* I told myself, swiping an arm across my forehead.

Once the escarole was cooked through, we'd have to start plating. The servers began filing in, and as the door opened, I could hear Elizabeth Merriman barking orders at them. At the same time, Chef Etienne moved among his own staff, directing them in French, Spanish, and English, and periodically reminding Tim to hurry it up. As Nando and Tim began plating, I counted meatballs and followed with a clean cloth to wipe the edges of the plates. I exhaled only when the last server took the final tray of soup bowls out the door.

I went to the sink and splashed my face, only to have Tim plop a dirty stockpot inside it. "There's more coming," he said shortly. "And clear 'em out fast—they need the sinks."

"Of course they do," I said through my teeth. I was up to my elbows in suds, at the pinnacle of sweaty unattractiveness, when Lacey Harrison came into the kitchen bearing a tray.

"Hey, guys," she said. "I have some food from the cocktail hour here." She beamed at Tim. "I thought you might be hungry."

He flashed the famous Trouvare grin and grabbed some canapés. "Thanks. Can you stay a minute?"

She shook her head. "I shouldn't even be in here. Just didn't want you to starve."

She turned to go, and Tim put a hand on her arm. "Hey, Lacey, do you have a card or something?"

"I do, actually." With that, she reached into the pocket of her green sheath and handed Tim a business card. "It's got my cell and e-mail," she said, her face growing pinker by the minute.

"Great." Tim tucked it into the breast pocket of his coat and patted it. "Close to my heart," he said.

He did not just say that, I thought, and scrubbed the stockpot with unnecessary vigor. *Did you expect him to keep trying, Vic? After you made it clear you weren't interested in getting back together?*

"Bye, Victoria," Lacey said. "Looking forward to the new book!"

"Thanks," I muttered, wishing I'd ripped the hairnet from my head when I'd had the chance.

"Hey, Vic," Tim called. "Nando will help me finish in here and then I'll do the icing." He came over to me and rested a heavy hand on my shoulder. "You need a break. You did great, by the way."

"Your mood's certainly improved." I lifted his hand from my shoulder and unbuttoned the heavy coat.

"Here's what you do," he said, and handed me his charge card. "Go get yourself a drink and something to eat in the club bar. It's full of that historic crap you love."

"You just can't keep that Cheshire cat grin from

your face, can you?" I plucked the card from his fingers. "But I think I'll take you up on your offer." I slid the card into the top of my blouse and gave my chest a little pat. "So it's close to my heart," I told him.

My first stop was the ladies' room, where I washed my face and reapplied my eye makeup. I already had a bit of a tan, and all that soup steam had given me a natural blush. But my hair, stringy from the heat of the kitchen, was pretty hopeless. I dug a clip from the bottom of my purse and twisted it into a weak approximation of an updo. Not one my mother would approve of, but from the neck up, at least, I was presentable.

Though I was curious about the bar, I was absolutely dying to see the ballroom, and I'd promised Mom I'd say hello to Dr. Chickie and come back with all the details of the reception. (My parents had gone to the church, but neither could be away from the restaurant on a Saturday night.) I actually gasped upon entering the ballroom, my eyes immediately drawn to the Tiffany windows. The late-day sun shone through the rich colors of trees, flowers, and birds that gloriously ornamented the panes. Chandeliers glittered from the ceiling, and large sprays of fresh lilies decorated each table, no doubt designed to echo the Tiffany flowers etched in glass.

Well, Vic, if you ever do the deed, this is certainly the place to have a party. At a certain point in my life, I was convinced I would get married, just like every other dutiful Italian daughter. But after things went so wrong for Tim and me, marriage grew more and more distant on my personal horizon. At almost thirty-four, I didn't see it happening for me, though it would be nice to have a man in my life. I would probably live out my days alone in Manhattan. I'd visit Jersey in the summer, write my books, and be a professional aunt to Danny's kids. Hey, it was good enough for Jane Austen.

Glancing down at my wrinkled white blouse and spotted black skirt, I realized the servers in this room were better dressed than I was. But I wanted a closer look at those windows, and, yes, I was halfway curious about what kind of bride Roberta Natale made. The bride's table was at the opposite end of the room, and I squinted. Could that tiny person in the white dress possibly be Roberta? If so, she'd dropped some pounds. It didn't take long for me to spot Dr. Chickie, however, as his shiny bald head was visible at fifty yards. Mrs. Chickie, also known as Brenda, was an overpowering vision in teal blue as she hung on her husband's arm.

"Victoria!" Dr. Chickie caught my eye and waved his arm. Brenda frowned and yanked his arm down, but she gave me a quick nod and smile. I made sure to smile back widely, as I always did when I ran into my old orthodontist, just to let him know that his work wasn't for naught.

"Hi, Dr. Chickie," I said, dropping a dutiful kiss on his cheek, and then another on Brenda's. Children raised in Italian families must kiss *everyone*, no matter how old, young, hairy, or stinky they might be. At least the Natales smelled nice.

"Victoria, the soup was luscious, just luscious,"

Brenda croaked. Years of smoking had lent Brenda's voice a froggy quality, and her wide, full-lipped smile only intensified the amphibian effect.

"I'm glad you liked it, Mrs. Natale," I said.

She swept her arm across the room. "And how bee-you-tee-full is this place?" Her gaze stopped at one side of the room, where a bunch of the groomsmen were making loud toasts with their beers. Brenda shook her head and sighed. "A Scots-Irish my daughter has to marry."

"He's got a nice family, hon," her husband said. "They're just a little different from us, that's all."

"Well," Brenda said, "Maureen—that's his mother—is a lovely woman. She's dealt with a lot." She leaned closer to me. "She lost her husband not long ago. Cancer," she said in a raspy whisper. Then she shook her head again. "And Dennis had that trouble a couple of years ago . . ." Her voice trailed off at a look from her husband.

"Dennis Doyle is a nice boy," he insisted.

And a big one, I thought, catching sight of the hulking, fair-haired guy at the head table. He was feeding the tiny Roberta bites of food, while she giggled and pushed his hand away. *God preserve me from lovebirds*. Suddenly conscious of my clothes, I looked for a way to politely escape, but Dr. Chickie grabbed my arm.

"Come say hi to Roberta. You won't recognize her. She dropped a ton," he said in a confiding voice.

In my periphery I could see the tall figure of Elizabeth Merriman, now dressed in a beaded gown. She was speaking to a tall man in dark glasses, their heads close together. She'd never see me from that corner, but I didn't want to take a chance. "I'd love to," I said, "but I'm really not dressed for a wedding. I just wanted a peek at the ballroom. I should really get back." But before I could take a step, there was Elizabeth, now frowning furiously in my direction. Leading with her cane, she headed straight for me.

"Young woman," Elizabeth Merriman rapped out, "what do you think you're doing out here among the guests?"

Though Dr. Chickie flinched, he gallantly stepped in. "Now, Elizabeth. Victoria is the daughter of an old friend. I was just bringing her over to say hello to Roberta."

"She belongs in the kitchen!" Elizabeth tapped her cane on the floor for emphasis. "Not out here in my ballroom. She can say hello to Roberta some other time." She squinted at Dr. Chickie, either because she couldn't see him or wanted to intimidate him. "You're lucky *you're* here, Charles." She gestured with her cane, narrowly missing my ankles. I stepped closer to Brenda, who was clinging to Dr. Chickie's arm like a barnacle. "It's only through my good auspices that you're even on the premises, and don't you forget it." She cocked her head to one side, attempting to focus her cloudy eyes on the Natales.

Dr. Chickie tugged on his collar, as though it had grown too tight. Brenda was gripping his arm so hard her knuckles were white. And suddenly, my curiosity was on high alert. What was going on here? And then I remembered something Elizabeth had said back in the kitchen: that after tonight, Dr. Natale would no longer be a member of the Belmont Club.

"Now, Elizabeth," Dr. Chickie said quietly, his voice shaking, "this is not the time or place for this discussion."

She leaned both hands on her cane and her mouth cracked in a tight smile. "You're right about that, Charles. Because this discussion will be taking place in court, won't it?" Still propped against her cane, she swung around to me. "You, girl, get back to that kitchen." With that, she turned her back on us and made her slow way back through the guests.

"Listen, guys," I said. "I should get out of here. I'll try to catch Roberta another time. Would you mind pointing me to the bar?" But as neither of them was paying attention to me, I slipped out the way I had come, Elizabeth Merriman's words echoing in my head: *This discussion will be taking place in court.*

Chapter Four

*B*y the time I found the bar, I was sorely in need of a drink, and the smells of the food in that kitchen had whetted my appetite. As Tim had promised, the bar was full of that "historic crap" I love. Out on the floor, leather chairs with brass rivets sat on either side of small oak tables, and high-backed chairs with matching leather seats lined the bar. I sat down in one with a sigh, and a middle-aged woman behind the antique walnut bar pushed a bowl of nuts in front of me.

"What'll you have, hon?" she asked.

"Any wine you pour that's dry, white, and cold," I said, taking an unladylike handful of almonds. "Oh, and do you have a bar menu?"

"Sure thing." She slid a leather-covered portfolio across the bar, then provided me with a generous pouring of chardonnay.

I took a sip and closed my eyes. "Ah, nectar of the gods." I opened the menu, fully intending to get a salad until the siren call of carbs caught me. "Could I have the goat-cheese pizza, please?"

"Good choice," the bartender said. She reached for

the menu, revealing a small horse tattoo on her wrist. "I take it you're not a wedding guest?"

I shook my head and held out the wrinkled lapels of my blouse. "Can't you tell? No, I'm here with two other chefs from our restaurant, the Casa Lido. We catered the soup course."

"Oh, that means you had to deal with Iron Lady. My sympathies." She stuck out her hand. "I'm Sally, by the way."

"Victoria. And now I understand that," I said, pointing to her wrist. "It's a mustang, yes?"

She winked at me, making a giddyup motion with her wrists. "Ride, Sally, ride," she sang. Then she ran a hand through her cropped, flame-colored hair and grinned. "At least I did in my younger days. Let me put that pie order in for you," she said, and disappeared through a door behind the bar.

"Separate kitchen, I assume," I said when she returned.

Sally nodded. "Yup. Separate staff, too. We're not super fancy over here."

I smiled at the image of Chef Etienne turning out bar pies. "I imagine the kitchen staff at the bar has to be easier to work with."

"Oh yeah." Sally wiped down my section of the bar and refilled the nuts. "I mean, Chef Etienne's okay— kinda hot, too, in a Frenchy sort of way. But he gets a bug up his nose about something and forget it. He does know how to handle Elizabeth, though; I'll say that for him. Not like that crazy Kate. Sheesh."

"You mean the pastry chef, right? Kate Bridges?"

"There's only one Crazy Kate. Been here a month and managed to piss everybody off, especially Elizabeth." Sally leaned in close, lowering her voice. "I just think there's something off about her, ya know? I mean, what's with all that makeup? Sure don't improve her looks any. And it seems like she deliberately antagonizes Elizabeth."

Maybe it was the writer in me, but right now my curiosity was sharper than my appetite. While Sally worked, I struggled with my conscience. If Elizabeth knew the club's employees were inclined to gossip with strangers, she'd throw a fit, and probably throw Sally out the door, but I couldn't help myself. I had to know what was going on here. I gave it another few minutes and a few more sips of wine before I spoke. "I would think it's pretty easy to antagonize Elizabeth Merriman," I said. "It's clear she has her own way of doing things at the club, and woe to you if you get in her way."

But before Sally could answer me, the door swung open and a waiter emerged with my pizza. As I contemplated the warm goat cheese, sautéed spinach, and caramelized onions sitting on a fragrant wood-fired crust, the urge to stuff my mouth fought with the urge to open it and ask more questions. Luckily, the pizza was too hot to eat, and Sally seemed inclined to talk. She pointed to the chardonnay and I nodded, hoping a second glass wouldn't impair my ability to ice Nonna's cookies.

"So, you all set?" Sally asked, rubbing her hands together.

"Yes, thanks. As long as I don't run into Iron Lady again."

Sally grinned. "Hey, stay far enough away and she won't even see ya."

"I don't know," I said. "I think all her other senses are heightened. She sniffed me out in the ballroom just now."

"Well, that's the truth. Nothin' gets by her." She jerked her head in the direction of the ballroom. "That's how she found out Father of the Bride out there was cooking the books."

Cooking the books? I dropped my head and cut into the pie, my mind racing. Elizabeth's comment about court now took on a sharp clarity, as did the Natales' fear. As treasurer of the club, had Dr. Chickie dipped his hand into the till? A wedding at the Belmont wasn't cheap. And Dr. Chickie was part of my dad's circle of high rollers we called the Rat Pack. Had his gambling pushed him into embezzlement? *This is not your problem, Vic,* I told myself. And because I still had a long night ahead of me, I fortified myself with a bite of pizza and a slug of wine.

Just then, a tall man with dark hair and sunglasses walked into the bar, followed by a slighter, shorter man. The taller man appeared to be the guy I'd seen in the ballroom with Elizabeth. Up close, I noticed his military haircut, cropped even shorter than my brother Danny's regulation police cut. The man's erect bearing and straight spine added to the impression of a military man. By comparison, the smaller man trailing behind him was rumpled and sported a thick head of wild gray hair. His slumped shoulders suggested submission, possibly resignation. He was also much older, by at least ten or fifteen years. The two sat at a table behind me, and the tall one motioned to Sally, who merely nodded.

She pulled a beer and a soda from the cooler and brought it to their table, along with a bowl of nuts. When she came back, she leaned in close again and whispered, "Do you know who the dude in the dark glasses is?"

"No," I said, resisting the urge to turn around.

Sally raised a knowing eyebrow. "The Iron Lady's boy toy. Jack Toscano."

I froze with a piece of pizza halfway to my mouth. "You're kidding me. He's my dad's age, easy."

"So what? He still almost twenty years younger than her." She shrugged. "Speaking by comparison, he's a boy all right. He's with her all the time. Takes her to plays, drives her around town—you name it." She lowered her voice again. "Grapevine says she bought him that condo he's got over on the bay side of town."

"I saw them in the ballroom together, but I never guessed that. She's full of surprises." I inched my chin to the right until I could capture a glimpse of Jack Toscano from the corner of my eye. He was a good-looking man in a rugged, old-movie kind of way, and though he had more lines on his face than my dad, was probably sixtyish. His face had that leathery look that said he'd spent lots of time in the sun. "Is he from down here?" I asked.

"Nah. Just showed up about six months back. But Merriman has him helping her manage the club."

I gave up any pretense of minding my own business and leaned over the bar. "So, who's the little guy with him?"

"Don't know his name, but I recognize him. Can't miss that Albert Einstein hair." Sally took a paring knife and set out some lemons and limes. "I don't think he's a member; I've only ever seen him with Jack, and he always drinks a diet soda." She motioned with the knife. "Bet you my last tip in the jar he's a twelve-stepper." She grinned. "Not that they allow us to have anything as tacky as a tip jar in this fancy out-fit."

Mustang Sally was a wealth of information. (My fictional detective, Bernardo Vitali, would call her a keen observer of the human condition.) But I needed to get back to the kitchen; if anything went wrong with those cookies, Nonna would have my hide. I reached inside my blouse for Tim's credit card, hoping it wasn't too sweaty. But Sally waved me away.

"It's on the house. You're part of the staff tonight; it's the least we can do, considering you have to deal with Elizabeth."

"Thanks, Sally." I dug in my purse and pulled out a crumpled ten. "For the nonexistent jar," I said. *And for the information,* I thought. *But I wish you'd told me more about what Dr. Chickie had been up to.*

On my way to the kitchen I was arrested by a series of whining groans, a cacophony so loud and dissonant I wanted to clap my hands over my ears. As I approached the ballroom, I spied the source of the noise—not a bunch of cats in heat, but six guys in kilts tuning up their bagpipes. The sound clashed wildly with the wedding band's version of *The Godfather* theme blaring from inside the doors. From my vantage point, I could see the cultural split in the room, with all the short, dark people on one side and the large, fair people on the other. *My mother will love this one*, I thought, *and Nonna will make gloomy predictions for the bride who marries outside her tribe.*

The kitchen was nearly empty when I got back. A few of Etienne's crew, including Antoine (who greeted me with a wolf whistle) were cleaning up. Tim was scarfing down a plate of pasta. In the back, the wedding cake sat on linen-covered table, and I could see Kate filling pastries, scowling and muttering as she worked.

"Is she doing that alone?" I asked.

"I offered," Tim said. "But she wasn't having it. Gave me a loud lecture about how nobody touches her pastries." He grimaced. "Like I'd want to touch anything of hers."

"Hey, that's just mean." I glanced over at Kate, who had recently reapplied her orange lipstick.

"C'mon, Vic," he said. "She looks like one of the Insane Clown Posse."

"I don't know. I kinda feel sorry for her."

"Hey, chick from the Casa Lido!" Kate bellowed. "You gonna get those cookies iced anytime tonight?"

Tim grinned and pointed to a large aluminum bowl set on ice. "The icing's ready, but it'll need a couple of minutes to come to room temp. Don't worry about her—we got plenty of time."

I took the bowl out of the ice and set the cookies out on a counter Tim had lined with parchment paper. "Tim, can you find me a small spatula? I don't want to ask her."

Tim brought back two and uncapped the container of silver balls. "C'mon," he said. "I'll help you. I sent Nando home and I'd like to get us out of here."

"Oh, before I forget." I took the credit card from my blouse and handed it to him. "I didn't use it, but thanks."

"Didn't you eat?"

"I did indeed. A friend brought me dinner." I neglected to mention that the friend was female, however, and shot him a look I hoped was mysterious.

"Good for you," he said cheerfully. He scraped the spatula across the surface of the icing. "It should be soft enough soon."

Once the icing was ready, Tim and I knocked off the job quickly. I started decorating them and sent Tim out of the kitchen for a break. Chef Etienne's crew had already cleared out; I was so intent on placing the silver balls in the same triangular pattern for each cookie, I didn't notice someone else was in the kitchen until I heard raised voices. Kate and the Iron Lady were going at it hammer and tongs.

How had Elizabeth come in without my seeing her? Was there a back entrance somewhere? And what was she even doing in here? I couldn't hear much of the argument, except for Elizabeth's final words: "Out! Do you hear me? Out, and I mean it."

She turned away from Kate and barreled straight toward me. *She doesn't see me yet*, I thought, and backed out of her path into a dim corner near the sink. She tapped her cane along the floor, stopping suddenly near the door, lifting her head like a dog with a scent. "Is someone there?"

I flattened myself against the wall. Some instinct told me not to reveal either myself or that I'd overheard their fight. The tapping started again, followed by the whoosh of the kitchen door. I stepped out of my hiding place, only to face Chef Kate Bridges, her hands on her hips, her clown face fierce.

"That old bitch," she growled. "Somebody oughta put her lights out."

And before the night was over, somebody did.

Chapter Five

We sat at the family table in the back of the restaurant, the *Asbury Park Press* spread out in front of us. Despite a morning espresso, I was still groggy from my late night at the wedding reception, and couldn't quite believe the words in the headline. But my dad helpfully read them aloud.

"'Body of Belmont Club President Found on Beach.' What a terrible thing," he said, shaking his head. "And to think you were there last night, hon."

My mother peered over my dad's shoulder. "Poor woman. And I know this sounds terrible, but I hope it happened long after all the guests were gone." She stood up abruptly. "I should give Brenda a call. Excuse me a minute, hon."

"Dad, could I see that?" I turned the paper so I could read it:

In what appeared to be the result of a fall, Elizabeth Merriman, philanthropist, Belmont Country Club president, and former owner of Merriman Industries, was found dead on the beach below the club early this morning.

Ocean County Prosecutor Regina Sutton would not comment except to say that an investigation was already under way . . .

The article went on to describe Merriman's accomplishments and indicated that she had no known surviving relatives. I let out a long breath; my mind was certainly clear now. If Merriman fell, it had to be due to her eyesight. I wondered if that cane was anywhere near the body. And I couldn't help the other questions that crept into my brain like thieves. *How did she fall, and from what?* The answer, of course, depended on where the body was found. I tried to see the building in my mind's eye. *Could she have gone out an open window? The widow's walk was a possibility, but why would she be out there in the dark with an event going on downstairs? And if she'd fallen from that tower balcony, was it likely the body would end up on the beach? The seawall was also a contender, but would a fall from that height kill her? Was she pushed? If so, how did the murderer get her out there? Who had a motive?*

At that one, my head snapped up, and I met my dad's startled eyes. "You okay, baby?"

"I'm fine, Dad," I lied.

He covered my hand with his. "You're not worried, are you, Vic? I mean, this was an accident." He lowered his voice and looked around, probably to make sure Nonna wasn't within earshot. "It's not like what happened in May."

I felt a rush of affection as I looked into his still-handsome face. He had the same hazel eyes as mine and Danny's, but he didn't have our healthy skepticism. His trusting nature and unfailing optimism, while endearing, had led him to bet long odds—at the track, in the casino, and in life. "Let's hope not, Dad," I said.

"You just listen to your old man." He winked at me, pushed his straw fedora to the back of his head, and turned his attention back to the paper. But the only thing I could concentrate on was the fact that I'd been there. That I'd taken part in a significant conversation with the Natales and the deceased. That I'd overheard an argument and listened to a whole lot of gossip, all of which might have some bearing on this case. The county prosecutor, Regina Sutton, would be taking statements from anybody who came into contact with Merriman. *Well, Vic, you escaped Sutton before, but not this time.* No, this time I would have to face the tiger in her den and tell the truth of what I'd seen and heard— that Merriman had threatened Dr. Chickie with a court action, giving him a whopping motive for murder.

I stood up from the table. "I'm gonna get started on the setups, Dad."

I headed down the narrow hallway toward the pantry and kitchen, and looked up to see my brother coming through the kitchen doors. He was in street clothes, but his look meant business. "I came in through the back," he said quietly.

"I already know why you're here, Danny."

He peeked out into the dining room, where my dad was still studying the *Press*, then stepped back into the hallway where he wouldn't be seen. "You heard the news, I take it?"

"We just saw the paper. But there's something else." I hesitated, knowing full well my brother's reaction to my next words. "I was there last night."

I was well acquainted with my brother's "you are kidding me" face. It's the same one I'd get when he landed on my Boardwalk hotels in Monopoly, or when I said I hated fishing, or when he caught me meddling in a murder investigation. "What the hell, Victoria!"

"Ouch. You never use my full name. Believe me; I'm not happy about it, either. But Tim and Nando and I were there to cater the soup service. And I was out in the ballroom for a few minutes and—"

"And what?"

"I, uh, heard Elizabeth Merriman sort of threaten Dr. Chickie. She mentioned something about a court action. And a bartender at the club told me that Merriman caught him cooking the books."

He ran his hand down his face and sighed. "So that's out there." He glanced out toward the dining room. "What do Mom and Pop know?"

"Just what they read in the paper this morning. And they know I was there, but not what I heard. But Mom's probably talking to Brenda right now, so she'll probably get more of the story."

He rested his hand on my shoulder. "You know you're gonna have to give a statement, right?"

"Yes, Detective. I know the drill. Unfortunately, I think I'm what you guys call a material witness." Danny's face told me he was doing some cop calculations, adding up a dead body, a motive, and opportunity. "This doesn't look good for Natale."

"C'mon, Danny, this is Dr. Chickie we're talking about. Do you really see him pushing an old lady to her death?"

"*If* that's how she died, Vic. We don't know that yet. It could be an accident. But you'd be surprised at what people do when they're desperate." He shook his head. "Look, they've got him on the embezzlement. He could even be looking at time."

"Don't they usually make some kind of deal? Like, if he pays the money back?"

He shrugged. "Maybe. But this is a lotta money we're talking about."

"How much?"

Danny crossed his arms. "You know I can't tell you that. In fact—"

"You shouldn't even be telling me this; I get it." But I kept going, my words coming faster and faster. "Danny, the newspaper article isn't clear on where the body was found. Unless she went out a window on the ocean side of the building, I don't think it's likely she'd end up on the beach. And those windows just aren't big enough. If she'd gone off the tower, I think she would have hit the main roof first, and there's no telling where she'd land." I grimaced at the image of the old woman's body going off the tower and bouncing off the roof. Even Elizabeth Merriman didn't deserve an end like that. "And wouldn't someone have seen her fall out of or off the building? But the seawall is surrounded by dunes and brush. It's overgrown; it would be harder to see someone out there. But I wonder if a fall from that height would kill somebody, but then again, she was elderly and—"

He held up his hand. "I can't comment on any of that," he said firmly. "But I can tell you something that's common knowledge: That seawall is eighteen feet high. That's almost two stories, sis."

"And a two-story fall is high enough to kill a nearly blind old woman." My brother's face was impassive, and I figured I'd learned as much as I was going to. I looked down the hallway. "Listen, we should let them know you're here, or they'll think we're up to something."

Danny shot me a grin. "We're always up to something."

"Hey, speaking of being up to something, how's my beautiful sister-in-law?"

At the mention of Sofia, Danny's tough-cop expression softened. "Sassy as ever." But he smiled as he said it.

"Look, you can tell me if this is too personal, but are you guys back together?"

"*Mezzo mezzo*," he said, illustrating with his palm.

"How can you be halfway back together? Are you back home or not?"

Danny let out a sigh. "My wife and I are *dating*. If you can believe it."

"I don't get it."

"Here's the thing, sis. For a while there, things got a little . . . intense. And Sofia thinks we should step it down a little—you know, take it slow."

After our recent run-in with some dangerous types, Sofia landed squarely back in Danny's arms, much to my grandmother's delight and my mother's chagrin. I needed to have a chat with my SIL (short for "sister-in-law") stat.

"Listen, Dan, you should go say hello. Mom's gonna be off the phone any minute and then you'll be picked up on the Mommy Radar anyway." I linked my arm through his and led him down the hall.

Danny pointed to my father, whose head was still bent over the paper, pencil in hand. "He's doing the puzzles. He don't even know I'm here."

But the minute we entered the dining room, my dad leapt to his feet. "Hey, is that my wayward son?" He embraced Danny in a classic man hug, which involved a lot of backslapping but little actual touching.

"Did I hear Daniel?" My mother came in from the street and clicked her way across the dining-room floor. Like I said, radar. "Hi, darling," she said breathlessly. "I'm so glad you're here. I just got off the phone with Brenda." She gripped Danny's arm. "Chickie's in trouble; they're afraid he's going to be arrested."

The question *for murder?* formed in my brain and threatened to travel straight to my mouth. Luckily, Mom kept going, shaking Danny's arm for emphasis. "He's accused of stealing money from the club. And suddenly the woman who's accusing him is dead. Daniel, we have to help them!"

My brother gently removed Mom's clutching hand from his arm. "I'm not a lawyer, Mom. I'm not sure what I can do."

When my dad finally got a word in, he did it in classic Frank Rienzi fashion. "Guys, it's a mistake," he said, opening both palms as if to say *there's nothing here, see?* "I've known Chickie my whole life. He's a stand-up guy."

Not according to Elizabeth Merriman, Dad. I glanced at my mother's worried expression and my brother's bland one. I think they both knew more than they were saying. "But, Frank," my mom said, "You know that Chickie—"

"What, hon?"

"Never mind, sweetie." She dropped a kiss on my dad's cheek. "I need to see about that reservation book." She looked at my brother. "Daniel, will you at least talk to the Natales?"

"If you think it will help, Mom." Danny said. "Listen, I'm gonna head over to the marina while I can. I'm on duty tonight." At the door, he looked back at me. "Keep me in the loop."

"You got it."

After he left, I made a beeline to my mother's small office in the back of the restaurant. She was at her desk and appeared to be studying the reservation book. But I knew better.

"What were you about to say to Daddy?"

"My goodness, Victoria!" My mother pressed a hand to her ample chest. "Don't sneak up on a person. Don't you have work to do in the kitchen?"

"Yes. Now, what about the question I asked you?" I leaned against her desk, my arms crossed. I wasn't going anywhere, and she knew it.

She sighed. "Close the door, please." She pushed back from the desk and looked up at me. "What I started to say to your father was that Chickie has a gambling problem." She gave a small shake of her auburn curls. "But I thought the better of it."

Though I had a pretty good idea of the answer, I asked anyway. "Why?"

But Mom's radar was still set on high. "You know very well why, Victoria."

I took her hand. "It's because Daddy has a gambling problem, too."

"But he doesn't see it that way. He thinks that what he does, what Chickie does, what their whole Rat Pack does, for that matter, is just fun. A way to let off steam. A way that grown men can play." Her eyes took on a pleading look. "And he's been better, honey. You know he has."

"His bets have been smaller, you mean. Yes, he's been better. But it's always there for us, that little, nagging worry. That one of these days he'll backslide and bet the restaurant away in a poker game."

"Oh, honey, don't even say it." She squeezed my hand and then slipped it from mine. "And we're talking about Chickie now, not your father."

There but for the grace of God, Mom. "So, you're saying it's possible that Dr. C. really did steal money from the club." I didn't add that my brother had already confirmed it.

"It's certainly possible. They've spoiled Roberta terribly, and all she talked about was a wedding at the Belmont Club. He waited years to become a member and fought to be on their board." My mother's normally sweet face tightened. "Did you know that the Belmont Club only started letting in Italian-Americans about ten years ago?"

My eyes widened. "Stop it. It's the twenty-first century!"

"Some practices are entrenched." She shook her head. "I know because we tried to get in ourselves when you and Daniel were small."

"Well, what did they do—just tell you 'No, we don't accept Italians'?"

She smiled. "Oh, nothing so obvious as that. No, they simply waited us out. Said the list was very long, et cetera." She shrugged. "After a while it became less important, so we withdrew our application."

I nodded. "As they knew you would. I guess by the time Dr. Chickie applied, things had changed a bit."

"A bit, yes."

"Well, I can see why someone would want a wedding there. That ballroom is stunning." From there, the conversation turned to Tiffany windows, bagpipe players, and sparring chefs. I entertained my mother with as many details as I could dredge up, just to take that strained look from her face.

But I left out the most salient details of the night— Elizabeth's threat to Dr. Chickie and her fight with Chef Kate. It was highly likely that I'd have to give a formal statement, and my instincts told me to keep my mouth shut about what I'd seen and heard until then.

"By the way, Mom," I said. "It's after ten. Shouldn't

Nonna be back from church by now?" St. Rose's was around the corner, and Nonna usually walked to the restaurant after Mass. I crossed myself as I thought about my own spotty attendance at church, and hoped Nonna wouldn't mention it.

"She should be here any minute, hon."

And she was. As soon as I stepped out of my mother's office, Nonna greeted me with a hail of questions. (It was better than a cross-examination about why I wasn't in church, but still exhausting.) Did I count out the meatballs for each plate? Was the escarole cooked properly? Was the soup hot enough when it went out? And the cookies—were they decorated to her specifications? Most importantly, were they finished by the guests?

After my four yeses and an "I don't know," Nonna still looked at me with suspicion. "I sent you there to do a job, Victoria."

"And I did it. Honestly, Nonna. Everything turned out fine." *Except for that dead body on the beach.* I searched my grandmother's face for any indication she'd heard that piece of news, and I wasn't going to be the one to tell her. My dad got there first anyway.

"Ma, did you hear?" He walked up to us, waving the paper like a flag on the Fourth of July. "You know Elizabeth Merriman? The club president? She's dead."

My grandmother stood stock-still, her only movement a quick shift of her eyes behind her glasses. "Did you say she's dead? Elisabetta?"

"Yes, Nonna," I said. "They found her body on the beach early this morning."

She pressed her palms together, perhaps in prayer. "Then may God rest her soul," she said, and turned to go into the kitchen.

It wasn't until later that evening, in the middle of taking orders, carrying trays, and clearing tables that it struck me: My grandmother had referred to Elizabeth Merriman as Elisabetta—a name that was as Italian as Nonna herself.

Chapter Six

*I*sabella trudged along the cobblestone street, her hand curled around the few coins she possessed. Enough to buy bread, at least, *she thought, the word coming to her in English—not* pane, *but "bread"* . . .

Okay, so Isabella's learning English. I stared at the screen through gritty morning eyes. In the two months I'd been back in Jersey, I'd managed to get a start on my historical novel. And though I'd brought my main character Isabella to America, I wasn't really sure what do with her next. I cranked open my bedroom window and breathed in the sweet sea air. The cottage I'd rented from Sofia was at the end of a beach block far from the noise of the boardwalk, a perfect place to work. The ocean glittered a silvery blue in the morning sun, and if I concentrated, I could hear the crash of the waves. While I loved my city view back in Manhattan, there was something about the ocean—its timelessness and predictability—that soothed me.

But the ocean wasn't providing much inspiration this morning. And it didn't help that I kept expecting County Prosecutor Sutton's phone call. I'd already had one run-in with Regina Sutton because of my involvement in a murder investigation, and here I was likely to be in the middle of another one. But besides my statement, how many others would need to be taken? I tried to do some quick calculations: two hundred wedding guests, plus the staff and anyone who might have been in the bar, equaled days of questioning. But that also depended on the time of death. Once that was established, it wouldn't be difficult to narrow that pool of witnesses to whoever was in or around that building when Elizabeth Merriman met her death.

I paced the small bedroom, turning the same question over in my mind: *Did she fall or was she pushed?* I strained to remember my first sight of the old hotel and its proximity to that seawall. I settled back at my desk, minimized my document, and with apologies to Isabella, accessed the Web site for the Belmont Beach Country Club.

The building had been a seaside hotel, the Windswept, from the late nineteenth century until about 1950, when it was sold and converted to the Belmont Beach Country Club, keeping its patch of private beach for club members. But that beach was steep and narrow, protected by a seawall built to buttress the dunes; the only way to get down there was via a creaky stairway. A historic photo of the club showed a wooden pathway with railings that led from the side of the building to the wooden platform and the steps down to the beach. Had Elizabeth Merriman traveled that walkway on Saturday night, ending up at the platform two stories above the beach? *Now, if this were in my book,* I thought, *my detective, Bernardo Vitali, would find Elizabeth's cane or that emerald ring up there as a convenient piece of evidence.* But as I've learned the hard way, life doesn't unfold like a neatly plotted book.

Well, I would only learn so much staring at a screen. The best thing to do would be to get over there and take a look at the property again, and it was at this moment that the voice of my conscience interrupted me, sounding a whole lot like my brother Danny. *You're not going anywhere,* it said, *except to Sutton's office to make a statement. Stay out of this.*

I wanted to stay out of it, I really did. But the question of how she ended up on that beach wouldn't let me go. I looked back at the picture of the old Windswept, as though it held the answer. *Did she fall? Was she pushed?* And a third possibility slowly dawned: *Had Elizabeth Merriman jumped to her death?*

Come summer, the Casa Lido is open seven days a week, and I was scheduled for the lunch shift, so later that morning I hopped on the old Schwinn bike that came with my cottage rental and cycled through the busy town. Though weekdays were a bit quieter, Oceanside Park was still packed with vacationers on a Monday morning.

I went around to the back of the restaurant, where Nonna's garden was in full bloom with flowers, herbs, and tomatoes. Because of my experience in May— finding a dead body among the tomatoes—being in the garden still gave me a bit of a creeping chill, even on a hot summer morning. I took a quick look and went in through the back door that led straight into the kitchen, where Nando was already getting started on prep.

"*Hola*, Nando. The sauces smell great."

"Thank you, Miss Victor. Today's *especial* is beef ragu." Nando gave the sauce a stir and adjusted the heat.

I inhaled the scent of simmering meat and tomatoes; behind that was a hint of basil. "Oh my God," I said, "I could eat that right out of the pot."

Nando gave me a toothy grin. "You do that and your *abuela* will—" He stopped and drew his palm across his neck in a cutting motion.

"Don't I know it." I tied on my apron, rolled up my sleeves, and started scrubbing my hands. "Is she coming in for the lunch shift?"

He shook his head, his long braid swinging with the motion. "Probably for dinner only. Also, your papa call to say he and your mama will be coming later."

"And Chef Massimo is off today," I said, "and Tim should be on his way soon."

"But Calvin is here," Nando said, furiously chopping herbs.

"So Cal's back?" I tried to keep my tone neutral, even while my stomach did a flip-flop. The scruffily attractive Calvin Lockhart, originally from New Orleans, was restoring our carved-wood bar. We'd struck up a flirtation back in May, and things were going nicely until I sort of implied he was a murderer, causing a bit of chill to form between us. About ten days ago, he'd taken off on an apparent vacation. Considering he worked only a few hours a week on the bar, I couldn't understand why he suddenly needed a break. But there were lots of things about this Southern charmer I didn't understand—there was definitely more to him than met the eye.

But what met my eye when I walked out into the dining room was an altogether pleasant sight: Behind the bar was Cal on a stepladder, sandpaper in hand, his lean but well-muscled form in a pose that emphasized a number of his masculine gifts. I tilted my head for a better look.

"Mornin', Victoria," he said without turning around.

"How'd you know I was here?"

"Got radar where you're concerned, *cher*." He used the New Orleans endearment that from just about anybody else would have been offensive.

"You and my mother." I pointed. "Hey, have you actually cracked a smile there, Mr. Lockhart?"

He turned, leaning back against the ladder with his arms crossed. His sun-streaked brown hair had grown a little shaggy again, and he was back to wearing his Saints cap, backward, as always. The better to see those sleepy green eyes.

"I supposed you could call it a smile," he said, exaggerating his drawl so that "smile" became "smahl." He patted his flat tummy. "Might just be a touch of indigestion, though. What y'all call ah-gi-tuh."

"Funny." I stepped closer to the bar. "But I would think with a half-Italian mama, your pronunciation would be a bit better."

"You would, wouldn't ya?"

I held out my hand. "So, are we friends again, Cal?"

He came down from the ladder and grasped my hand in his broad palm. "We were never *not* friends. You just got my Southern temper up, is all."

"I know." I smiled, unaccountably relieved to be on good terms with him again. "You can let go of my hand now."

But before doing so, he raised it to his lips and dropped a warm kiss on my knuckles, leaving me with a case of the tingles. He winked and climbed back up the ladder. "No rest for the wicked," he said, and went back to his sanding.

Wicked is right, I thought, judging by the various sensations produced by that little kiss on my hand. What might a real kiss feel like? I was still in a dream-like state as I set up the coffee station, wiping down the espresso machine with loving strokes.

"Girl, what are you smiling about?" Lori Jamison, our head waitress and my oldest friend stood with her hands on her hips, a knowing look on her face.

"Oh, hey, Lori. I'm not smiling about anything." I emptied an espresso packet into the basket of the machine.

"Right." She tucked a clean pad into the pocket of her apron. "Could it be that what you're *not* smiling about is back from vacation? And looking mighty fine out there in his tight T-shirt?"

"Lori Jamison, you rascal, you. A married lady like yourself."

"A married lady who still has eyes in her head. And speaking of fine eyes, where's Chef Tim this morning?"

"Probably in the kitchen." At the thought of Tim,

my floaty feeling turned distinctly earthbound. I wondered if he'd called Lacey yet. If I knew Tim, they probably had a date already.

"Oh, Vic, by the way," Lori said. "I heard what happened out at the Belmont Club." She shook her head. "That poor old lady."

"She wasn't so poor. And to tell you the truth, she wasn't so nice, either."

Lori's eyes grew round in her freckled face. "You don't think—"

I held up my hand. "I don't know. According to the papers, she died from a fall."

"And you were there." She looked around the empty dining room. "Like last time," she whispered.

"This is *not* like last time," I whispered back, even though we were alone and Cal was too far away to hear us.

"You're a regular Jessica Fletcher. Murder follows you wherever you go."

"Cut it out, Lori," I said. But *was* this death another murder? Maybe it was suicide. I shook my head. There was nothing about Elizabeth Merriman that suggested she was despondent. She struck me as a tough old bird, an Iron Lady who would hold on to life with both hands. Unless . . . could something have driven her to it? Or more likely, some*one*.

I was so lost in thought that I didn't hear the front doors opening. Nor did I see Lori trying to send semaphore signals with her eyebrows. But I did hear a rich contralto behind me, one that froze me into position like a Roman marble statue.

"Ms. Rienzi—now, isn't this lucky? I take a chance on coming here to speak with you, and, lo and behold, here you are."

I turned to face County Prosecutor Regina Sutton, decked out in designer sunglasses and a canary yellow suit that flattered the warm brown of her skin and her ample curves. She was surely not the only woman to hold such a position in our state, but she had to be the most fabulous, from her cropped blond Afro to her metallic copper manicure and snakeskin pumps.

I held out my hand, hoping it wasn't shaking too much. "Ms. Sutton. Nice to see you again."

"Somehow I doubt that." She took off her sunglasses, revealing her unusual amber eyes. "But I'm certain you know why I'm here."

I swallowed, my mouth suddenly dry, and Lori handed me a glass of water. "Be in the kitchen if you need me," she said out of the side of her mouth.

With a quick nod to Regina Sutton, she disappeared down the hallway. I took a gulp of water and nodded. "It's about what happened at the Belmont Club. Are you here to take my statement?"

She smiled almost sympathetically. "I don't conduct county business in Italian restaurants. Unlike some of my colleagues," she said dryly, and I smiled in spite of myself. *So she's not completely humorless*, I thought. *That's gotta be a good sign.* "I'm just here to let you know you'll be coming in."

"You came all the way over here just to tell me that?"

Her smile tightened. "Face-to-face is so much more effective—don't you think? I mean, one might ignore a phone message or text, or even pretend she hadn't received it. This way, I see you, you see me, and you see that: I. Mean. Business." She held out her card. "Your appointment is on the back. My office is in Ocean Township. Don't be late, Ms. Rienzi," she said, and sashayed out the door.

Chapter Seven

1 stared down at the card with its raised gold seal and Regina "I Mean Business" Sutton's name in black letters. On the back was my appointment. Well, it wasn't a surprise; I knew I'd be called in to give a statement. But so would a number of other people, and I had more than a week before I had to show up. *More than a week to solve it, Vic?* I asked myself. Then I sat down at a nearby table to think.

The last time I'd seen Elizabeth was in the kitchen around nine, when I'd overheard the argument between her and Kate Bridges. The wedding reception had been scheduled to end at eleven. If Merriman had gone over that seawall before eleven o'clock, wouldn't someone have noticed? And if her death was not an accident, would a murderer have taken such a chance with the club filled with guests? No, I was betting—in the fine Frank Rienzi tradition—that Elizabeth Merriman died sometime after that reception had ended. But that still left a number of suspects and possible witnesses who would have been at the club. *At least I can't be accused of murdering her,* I thought.

Who still would have been in that building after the wedding reception? The whole clean-up staff and probably anyone left in the bar. But that didn't preclude any of the wedding guests, who might have waited and then gone back to find her, including Dr. Chickie. It was likely that Merriman had been lured to her death—otherwise, how did she get out on that platform? And that suggested someone she knew. If Sally's gossip was accurate, it seemed there was at least one person with whom she'd *willingly* walk to the beach after eleven at night, and that was Jack Toscano.

"Victoria, you've got nothing to do that you sit and daydream?" Nonna's voice sliced through my reverie.

I jumped to my feet. "Just taking a quick break, Nonna."

She frowned. "A break? Your day just started. Are the vegetables prepped?" Without waiting for an answer, she pointed to the kitchen.

I was about to head back when my parents came through the door. "No, Frank," my mother was saying. "I will not have her mixed up in this again."

My dad appealed to me. "Honey, your mother says I shouldn't ask you to help Chickie. I mean, you were so smart about it last time, figuring how the guy died and all."

Right, Dad. I messed with a police investigation, got Danny in trouble on the job, put Sofia in danger, and nearly got myself killed. Oh, and made a permanent enemy of Prosecutor Sutton. I was brilliant, all right. "Daddy, I—" I began, but my mom cut in front of me.

"Absolutely not, Victoria," she said. "I will have no argument on this."

Then Nonna had her say, uttering words she'd probably not spoken in forty years. "Your mother is right. This is not your business."

"But, Mama," my dad said, "this doesn't look good for Chickie. And if anybody can figure this out, Vic can, and—"

My mother stamped her high-heeled foot, her curls bouncing. "I will not have her involved, Frank!"

"*Basta!*" I shouted. "Enough, okay?" I held up Sutton's card. "I am involved. Whether we like it or not."

Mom took the card from my fingers, turning it over in her hand. "You have an appointment with the prosecutor's office?"

"Well, it's not for a manicure, Mom."

"But why you? There had to be dozens of people in that club."

"More. And Sutton's office might have to talk to all of them." But I didn't add that I had crucial information with a direct bearing on the case. Did Sutton already know about the conversation I'd heard involving the Natales and Elizabeth Merriman?

"Honey, I'm speaking to you," my mother said, shaking my arm. "Do we need to call Johnny?"

Another of my dad's cronies, Johnny Tremarco, was an attorney who specialized in the defense of some colorful characters around town. "Mom, I'm not a suspect. I don't need a lawyer. Listen, all of you. I will go to her office at the appointed time. I will answer her questions honestly and I will sign the statement. And, hopefully, that will be the end of it." *If I can stop thinking about things like cause and time of death, motive, opportunity, and alibis.*

"It had better be the end of it, Victoria." The edge in Nonna's voice was harsher than usual. "You are not to go digging around and asking questions, you understand?"

"Last time you *insisted* I go around asking questions."

"This is different. That woman's death has nothing to do with us." Her beady eyes swept over us. "Now don't we all have work to do?"

Shoving the card in my pants pocket, I hurried down the hallway to the kitchen. And as much as I wanted to concentrate on scraping carrots and rinsing lettuce, I couldn't stop thinking about my grandmother's words. Today she had referred to her as "that woman," but yesterday she'd called her Elisabetta. Granted, my grandmother had a propensity for Italianizing names; Cal was "Calvino," for example. But there was a familiarity about how she used Elizabeth Merriman's name. And she didn't want me asking any questions—that was for darn sure. But why?

When my shift was over at the restaurant, I called my sister-in-law, Sofia, to meet for dinner. "Sure," she said, "anywhere but at the Casa Lido. I don't want to run into your mother."

As my mom tended to blame Sofia for the problems between her and Danny, things had been a bit strained between Sofia and her mother-in-law. It didn't help that Nonna adored Sofia, and wanted nothing more than for her and Danny to get back together again. As Sofia had once remarked, "You need a freakin' score card with that family of yours."

We were meeting at the Shell Café, one of the few places in town that was BYO. I showed up early, a bottle of Cabernet in hand. When Sofia arrived, she made quite an entrance in her tropical-print maxi dress. The bright colors set off her dark skin and hair, and revealed her slender but curvy form. We chatted about work—Sofia owned a dance school—until our food came: a grilled salmon salad for Sofia and the roast chicken special for me.

"So, I can't believe you haven't burned up the phone lines calling me, SIL," I said.

"Why?" Sofia pushed the salad around on her plate and ate a small bite of salmon.

I grinned across the table at her. "Because I know you've heard about Elizabeth Merriman, and I told you Tim and I were working that reception. I fully expected you to grill me." I happily tucked into my roast chicken and mashed potatoes.

"I did see it in the paper. I guess my mind's been on a bunch of other things." She looked up from her food, and I thought her eyes seemed a little tired. "So fill me in."

"Oh my gosh, where to begin?" I started with Kate Bridges, and the battle of the chefs in the kitchen, and then moved on to my conversation with the Natales and the fight between the Iron Lady and Chef Kate. I could see Sofia getting interested in spite of herself. During our "adventure" in May, she had nagged and prodded until I agreed to investigate. The two of us had quite a partnership, despite how it almost ended.

"So, we're fairly sure she went over that seawall." She put down her fork and took a sip of water. "You think she was pushed?"

"Maybe. Or she could have fallen. But I don't think she jumped. She's just not the suicidal type. Her nickname was the Iron Lady." I pointed to her still-full wineglass. "Are you gonna drink that? Because I hate to see a good Cab go to waste."

She pushed the glass my way. "It's all yours." Then she smiled faintly, a flicker of mischief in her eyes. "I can only imagine Princess Roberta Natale finding out somebody gets bumped off at her wedding reception."

"I forgot that you know Roberta," I said. "You graduated high school together, right?"

She nodded. "And I liked her better when she had a few pounds on her. But I do feel bad about what happened at her wedding."

"But it could have been afterward, Sofe. Elizabeth was still alive at nine o'clock. For all we know, Roberta didn't even find out until it hit the papers."

"True." She thought for a moment. "I guess the big thing is when she was killed."

"Right. And I sure hope Dr. Chickie can account for his time that night." I downed what was left in my own glass of wine and then moved on to Sofia's. "Hey, did Dr. Chickie do your teeth, too?"

"Nope. I never needed braces."

Looking at my sister-in-law's delicate bone structure, straight nose, and perfect mouth, it seemed a silly question. "Of course you didn't. And neither did Danny. The two of you will produce children with beautifully straight teeth and save a bundle on orthodontia."

Sofia, staring down at her salad plate, didn't respond.

"I'm sorry—should I not have mentioned Danny? Aren't things better with you guys?"

"They are, I guess. He's even coming around to the idea of me applying to the police academy."

I reached across the table and squeezed her arm. "That's great."

"It is. I mean, we've come a long way." She frowned. "It's just that there are some issues of timing right now."

I waited for her to go on, but she just picked at her salad. This was the quietest I'd ever seen my normally voluble sister-in-law. "Is everything okay, Sofe?" I asked.

"Yes. We're still working some things out." She grinned at me, and for a moment was her old self. "You know what that's like, right, Vic? How *are* the Macho Twins these days?"

"Well, they're both speaking to me. Cal's flirting with me again."

"Glad to hear it. And what about Tim?"

I sighed. "Tim swore me his eternal friendship. And is likely dating a redheaded wedding planner named Lacey."

"Ah." She shook her head. "Those gingers will get you every time," she said, wrinkling her nose. "Did you say her name is Lacey?"

"She's actually very nice, despite her name and hair color. We met her at the reception." I looked down at my unfinished meal, slowly losing my own appetite. I shrugged. "Look, when I came back, I made it clear there was no hope for him and me. I guess he got the message."

"But you still wear the necklace he had made for you."

I touched the silver choker with its small pendant of green sea glass. "I like this necklace."

Sofia's dark eyes were serious. "What do you really want, Vic?"

"Well, I want to finish this novel I'm writing and publish it under my own name. I want to learn to cook like Nonna. And I want to get some beach time this summer." I shook my head. "But when it comes to my romantic life, I don't have a clue."

"Speaking of clues, Vic, where do we start?" The old enthusiasm was back in Sofia's voice. *Here we go again*, I thought.

"Look, I'll admit I'm curious about what happened to Elizabeth Merriman. And I'd like to help Dr. Chickie." I lowered my voice. "According to Danny, an embezzlement charge is pending, which gives him a motive, but—"

"But what?" Sofia was leaning on her elbows, her eyes wide.

"Regina Sutton came to see me at the restaurant this morning, just to give me this." I held out the card. "I have to go down there and give a statement."

"That doesn't mean you can't do some research," she said, waving her hand in dismissal.

"Doing research nearly got us killed."

She grinned. "So we know better this time." She

pointed her fork at me. "And don't tell me you haven't been going over it in that mystery-writer brain of yours. You're driving yourself crazy over how that woman ended up on the beach."

"You're right about that one."

"Okay, so if she *was* pushed, who are the suspects?"

"Anybody's guess, Sofe. But not one person I spoke to that night had a good thing to say about the Iron Lady. Any one of them might have 'helped' her off that platform." I scooped up the rest of my mashed potatoes, as my appetite was returning. "But she was threatening Dr. Chickie and had a loud argument with Chef Kate. Plus, there's a boyfriend."

"I thought you said she was pushing eighty!"

"She's not allowed to have a boyfriend because she's old? Not only that"—I leaned in closer for emphasis and to get a good look at Sofia's face for this part— "he's almost twenty years younger than she was."

"Get out." She shook her head. "On second thought, good for her. Wait a minute," she said, narrowing her eyes. "Didn't you say she was rich? I wonder if she left him anything."

"According to Mustang Sally, the club bartender, she'd paid for his bayside condo."

"Maybe he was in a hurry for the rest of it." She leaned forward, her eyes interested. "So, who else we got?"

"Not sure. It could be any one of a number of people who were at that wedding—guests, club staff. Or even somebody who wandered in off the street." I had another thought. "She had a giant emerald ring on her finger. Maybe it was a robbery gone bad."

"But that doesn't explain what she'd be doing out on that seawall." She shook her head. "We're flying blind without the time of death."

"True. And I don't imagine Regina Sutton will be sharing that information with me."

"Danny might." Sofia looked down at her plate and speared a bit of lettuce, but didn't put it in her mouth.

"I don't know about that. He came to see me in the restaurant after the news broke, and he couldn't tell me much. Don't forget, it didn't happen on his patch."

"He's got friends on the Belmont force."

"True. But I think Danny will be careful about what he says and doesn't say. He has to be." I winked at her. "Maybe you can charm it out of him."

She shook her head. "He was not happy I got involved in that last one. Come to think of it, why are *you* so hot to get involved? You told me never again."

I sighed. "I know I did. But I'm a witness. And there's Dr. Chickie to consider. My dad's after me to try to help."

"And your mom wants you to stay out of it." At the mention of my mother, her eyes looked sad again.

"Mom will come around, Sofie."

"I hope so. I wish she were happier that we're trying to work things out."

"She will be, once things are more settled. C'mon, she's a protective Italian mama. You've got one of those. And someday you'll be one yourself."

"Right." She pushed her plate away and took another sip of water.

"So, what do you think?" I asked. "Dessert?"

"I don't think so, Vic."

I pointed to her nearly full plate. "You hardly ate anything."

"I know. I think it's the heat."

I looked at her slender arms. "I mean, you're not trying to lose weight or anything, are you? You teach dance all day. You must burn a million calories."

She raised one of her beautifully arched brows. "In case you've forgotten, I don't have to *try* to lose weight."

"Show-off." I patted her arm. "Okay, I'll be virtuous and I won't have any, either."

"Right. And then you'll stop at the boardwalk for *zeppole*."

"Oooh, there's an idea. Maybe food will take my mind off this case."

"I doubt it. In fact, when I go home, I'm taking out the red folder."

The infamous red folder had held all our notes and information for our first—and I had hoped last—investigation. "Didn't the newspaper say she owned Merriman Industries? I think that's a good place for me to start, don't you?"

"Given your formidable research skills, yes. I think my focus should be the club."

"Does this mean we're on the case?" Sofia held out her hand.

"Against my better judgment, but yes." I took her hand and shook it. "God help us," I added.

We paid the check and said our good nights, and I headed out of town toward my cottage, determined I would not eat another thing. But as the smells of boardwalk food drifted my way, I walked up the nearest ramp. I'd landed close to the rides pier, with the carousel house at one end and the Ferris wheel at the other. Though not a rides person, I'd taken a spin on that wheel with Cal not so long ago. The lights of the rides streaked the darkness in lines of neon color, illuminating the faces of those strolling the pier. I had missed this in New York; this was home, my history. Even the summer crowds didn't bother me. I walked past the game stands and the arcade, halfway tempted to stop in for a quick game of Skee-Ball. But the lure of fried dough won out.

I bought a half-dozen *zeppole* and walked down the ramp to the street, shaking the bag to properly coat the little Italian doughnuts with several layers of powdered sugar. *I will not open this bag,* I thought. *Not till I get home.* At which point I would make myself a cup of decaf, put two (maybe three) fried treats in a napkin, and sit out on my deck to eat them. But my happy thoughts darkened considerably as I approached my cottage and saw that I had visitors. Standing in front of my door like two mismatched sentries was none other than the newly married happy couple, Dennis and Roberta Doyle.

"We've been waiting for you. You weren't at the restaurant," Roberta said accusingly. "So your dad told us where you live."

Thank you, Frank. I gripped my bag of *zeppole.* In less

than three minutes, these babies would be too cold to eat. I sighed. "Shouldn't you guys be on your honeymoon?"

Roberta, whose dark hair was styled in a complicated upsweep that mimicked her wedding look, narrowed her eyes at me. "We don't have a honeymoon, thanks to that old bitch getting killed."

"Yeah, that was really thoughtless of her. Look, I'm sorry about what happened at your wedding. But why are you here?"

"Your dad told my dad that the county prosecutor came to see you. I wanna know what you plan to tell her."

Frank strikes again. "I plan to tell her the truth, Roberta."

She pointed a French-manicured fingernail at me. "You mean you're gonna tell her about what Elizabeth said to my dad and get him arrested for murder."

"Whoa," I said, holding up my palm. "You're getting way ahead of things here."

She put her tiny fists on her hips. "Am I really? Everybody in town knows he took money from the club, and then Elizabeth ends up dead. On the night of my wedding!" she wailed.

"Okay, I know it doesn't look good for him." I thought about trying to comfort her, but realized she was in no mood for it.

"It sure doesn't." Dennis, who until this moment had been silent, chimed in. "The guy's got a motive."

"Shut up, Dennis," Roberta snapped. "You're not helping." She pointed at me again; I wondered if her

mother had ever taught her that it's rude. "And neither are you. You don't care if this whole town knows
somebody died after my wedding reception or that
people think my father did it!"

Well, I did care about *one* of those things. "Roberta,
people who know your father will know he's not ca-
pable of such a thing, and— Hang on, did you say *after*
your reception?"

Her face grew wary. "I don't know when she died,
but I do know that old bag was still alive when we left
the reception."

"Yup." Big Dennis nodded in agreement, giving me
a hopeful smile. I smiled back, thinking he was too
nice for the bratty Roberta. "We left at eleven thirty,"
he said. "And she was still in her office. I could see her
through the window when we got in the car."

Still alive at eleven thirty. Now we're getting somewhere.
"Was anybody else around?"

"How should I know?" She frowned deeply. "All I
know is my wedding was ruined and my father might
end up in jail."

"Like I said, I'm sorry, but—"

"But nothing. C'mon, Dennis. Let's get out of here.
We're not gonna get anywhere with her." She grabbed
her husband's arm and pulled him down the stone
path to the street, looking like a Yorkie tugging on a
compliant Labrador.

I let myself into the front door of the cottage to drop
off my things (leave the purse, take the *zeppole*), and
cupping the bag in two hands to keep it warm, I
headed out to my tiny deck. I took a deep breath of the

night air and closed my eyes to listen to the crash of the surf. So Elizabeth Merriman was still alive at a time when most of the guests would have already cleared out. Who would still be around? And among them, who would want Merriman dead?

I decided I would think more clearly with a *zeppola* in my stomach. I opened the bag and was greeted with the sweet smell of deep-fried goodness. I took a bite— the first of the season—and, despite a mouthful of fried dough, smiled. *Worth coming home for,* I thought. After I'd polished off two more, I still hadn't figured out how many people had access to Elizabeth Merriman or who they might be. But I was closing in on her time of death. And by the time I ate my fifth *zeppola,* a nice case of *agita,* as well.

Chapter Eight

As I emerged from my heavy, *zeppole*-induced sleep, I was conscious of bright slashes of morning sun piercing the slats of my window blinds. And "Glory Days" was playing somewhere in the vicinity of my ear. I squinted at my Bruce Springsteen 2008 tour poster. Bruce was leaning against an amp, looking wise and world-weary. He wasn't singing to me, but apparently my phone was.

"Hell-o, Victoria!" The bell-like tones of Nina La-Guardia's television voice rang in my delicate ears. *Not again*, I thought in a panic. *Please not again*. Though not the sharpest knife in the journalism drawer, Nina was a local television news anchor. I'd managed to keep her at bay the last time I got sucked into a murder investigation, but I wasn't sure I had the energy to do so a second time.

"You *must* know why I'm calling," she said gleefully.

"Oh, I can guess," I muttered. I rubbed my eyes and raked a hand through my bed-head of hair. "Must you always call so early in the morning?"

"Journalism never sleeps." I winced as she gave a tinkly laugh. "I've been up for *hours*. So, when do we conduct our interview?"

I groaned. "Nina, I already gave you an exclusive."

"That was *weeks* ago. Old news, darling. This is a *new* story. A juicy one. And there *you* are, right in the middle of it. *Again!*"

Nina's italics were making my head hurt. I lowered my voice, hoping that she'd follow suit. "I am not in the middle of it. I was at the wedding reception, along with about two hundred fifty other people. Why don't you go wake them up?"

"My, aren't we grumpy this morning? No, sweetheart, there's no need for me get in touch with people who don't have any relevant information for me." She paused. "Or who weren't on the premises when Elizabeth Merriman was killed."

I sat straight up in bed, my head suddenly clear. "And you know when that was?"

"Oh, so now I've got your attention. Yes, I happen to have that information in my possession. Are we doing a little investigating, dear?"

I answered her question with one of my own. "How do I know your information's accurate?"

"I have a number of reliable sources, Victoria. And if you're willing to talk to me about what transpired at that wedding reception, I might just share what I know."

Hmm. Do I take this deal? I met Bruce's eyes across the room. His expression seemed to say, *Go with it, darlin'. You can handle her.* I gave him a wink. "You got it, Boss."

"What's that, Victoria?"

"I said okay. You tell me the time of death and I give you a statement. But I have it on good authority that she was still alive at eleven thirty. So unless you have something different to offer me . . ." I crossed my fingers and waited.

Nina's voice dropped to a whisper. Finally. "It's likely she died sometime between twelve and one, with cause of death severe head trauma."

She seemed talkative, so I pressed my advantage. And grabbed the pencil and pad I kept near the bed. "She went off the seawall, right?" I asked her.

"That's the scenario the police and Sutton are working from."

No surprise there, I thought. "Was she seen with anybody? Have they picked up any of the suspects for questioning yet?" But my questions were met with silence. "Nina? Hey, are you there?"

"I'm here," she sang out. "But I'm done talking until you schedule a time to talk to me. Today. Or tomorrow, at the very latest."

"Well, that's a bit of a problem, Nina. You see, I have an appointment with Regina Sutton's office to provide a statement. And I'm sure she won't want me talking to the press until afterward."

"What?" she shrieked. "You think you're smart, don't you Victoria?" Nina's melodic tones had grown shrill. "She won't want you talking to the press at *all*, and you know it, you b—"

I cut off the call before I could discover what Nina had called me, though I had a pretty good idea. I also had a good idea of where to start now—to find out who was still in that building at midnight.

That morning in the restaurant kitchen, I found Tim in a place he normally avoided like the plague: the vegetable station. But there he was, happily tearing lettuce. And singing a Sinatra song while he did it. This behavior could mean only one thing, and that thing had long legs and red hair.

I set the tray down on the butcher block worktable. "Morning, Tim."

"Morning, sunshine," he called over his shoulder, and resumed his off-key version of "Summer Wind."

"Could you bring the volume down there, Chef?"

He turned and shot me a sideways grin. "You don't like Sinatra?"

"Please. In my house, there was a Chairman of the Board long before there was a Boss. I love Sinatra. Which is why I'd like you to shut up."

Strangely, Tim did not take offense at this comment, and, in fact, stopped singing. His smile just grew broader.

"Someone is awfully chipper this morning," I said.

Instead of answering, he handed me a box of plastic wrap. "Wanna cover that fruit, babe?"

"I have not been your babe for years." *But I bet you've got somebody else lined up for that position, Trouvare.*

"And a shame it 'tis, lass," he said with an exaggerated sigh.

Was it a shame? Or a blessing? Watching—okay, admiring—his tall, lean figure at the sink, I had to stifle a sigh of my own. I'd missed Tim in the time I'd been gone. And when I first came back home, it looked as though we might get close again. But he'd hurt me badly all those years ago, and the incident at the restaurant in May served as a vivid reminder of that time. "I suppose it is a shame," I said quietly.

Tim turned from the sink, his gray eyes serious. "Vic, you made it clear there was no chance for us," he said. "And I'm trying to respect that."

"And move on, no doubt." I smiled to let him know I was fine. *(Am I fine?)* "Given your unusually sunny mood this morning—singing, prepping vegetables without a complaint, not yelling at me to get out of your way—I'm assuming that you've been in touch with the lovely Lacey."

"Yes, I have. I'm seeing her tonight."

"Oh." There was a big difference between thinking about Tim dating Lacey and knowing it for sure. "Well, good for you." And then, without my permission, the words left my mouth: "She's a little young—don't you think?"

This time he turned completely around to face me, resting his back against the sink with crossed arms. Not a good sign. "Not that it's any of your business, but she's twenty-eight."

And you're thirty-six. "That makes her a veritable grown-up. I hope you'll have a good time," I said, trying hard to mean it.

"Thank you," he said, inclining his head as though he were a king pardoning a wayward subject. "I'm sure I will."

I stood with my hand on the kitchen door. "So, anyway, if you don't need me in here, I'll go help Lori in the dining room."

"Thanks, Vic, but you can go. I don't need you." And I left the kitchen with his words echoing in my ears.

Because we were busy, the lunch service flew by. Once I had time to catch my breath, I took a seat at the back table, poured myself a coffee, and forced my thoughts away from Tim and in a more promising direction— Elizabeth Merriman's time of death. If Nina's information was accurate, the crucial window of time was likely between midnight and one o'clock Sunday morning. I took out my crumpled list from this morning:

- How far is beach path from platform? How to access it from building?
- Who or what got her out there?
- Is suicide a possibility?
- How high is railing on platform? Had it been tampered with?
- WHO WAS IN BUILDING BETWEEN 12 AND 1??????

This was only a start. There were dozens of other questions. Who had motive? *Dr. Chickie, for sure. Maybe Kate Bridges, as well.* Who stood to gain by her death? *Possibly Jack Toscano.* The article about her death indicated she had no known relatives, but it was early days yet. Who knew who might come out of the woodwork with a claim on Merriman's will? For that matter, who else might have a grudge against her? I shook my head. The field was wide open on that one.

"There she is!" Hearing my father's voice behind me, I shoved the list back into my apron pocket. But when I turned around, I saw that my dad wasn't alone. "Look who's here, honey," my dad said. Standing next to him, bleary-eyed and unshaven, was my former orthodontist.

"Uh, hi, Dr. Chickie," I said. "Are you here for lunch? The kitchen's closed, but I'm sure we can get you something." I stood up in the flimsy hope that he'd come in for the Casa Lido's famous pasta special and not for the services of its resident sleuth.

Dr. Chickie shook his bald head sorrowfully. "I'm not here to eat, Victoria."

Of course you're not. "Listen," I said, "I think I know why you're here—"

"Honey, hear him out." My dad gently pushed me back down in my chair, took a seat, and motioned for Dr. Chickie to do the same.

"Thank you, Frank," Chickie said. "Victoria, I know that you have to give Sutton a statement. And I know that you have to tell her the truth."

I let out a breath; I was sure he was here to ask me to lie to the county prosecutor. "I'm glad you understand that. Roberta came to see me with Dennis last night. I think she's a little upset with me."

Chickie waved his hand. "She's always upset. She had a perfectly nice wedding. Nothing happened till afterward."

Well, don't stop now, Dr. C. He folded his hands and looked straight into my eyes. "She was alive when we left the reception. And I had nothing to do with that woman's death. But that is all I can say at this time."

"He's working with Johnny Tremarco," my dad said in a confiding voice.

I noticed he didn't say a word about embezzlement, but Tremarco had probably counseled silence on that topic. "Dr. C., you have a lawyer. Why are you coming to me?"

The orthodontist leaned closer. "Everybody knows how you figured things out last time."

"This is not like last time." Seriously, did I have to get a T-shirt made?

But he just kept going. "You're a smart girl. If you can find out who did this, maybe we can uh, minimize some of the damage."

"Honey," my dad said, "please say you'll help."

"Daddy, Mom will kill both of us. If Nonna doesn't get to us first." Who was I kidding? In my pocket was a list I'd started. Sofia was already at her computer. I couldn't stay out of this case and I knew it. I just didn't want my family to know it.

My dad gave me the kind of nod that said Frankie had a sure bet. "You leave them to me."

Right. I'd seen how my father had handled the women in his life. I looked from his confident face to Dr. Chickie's desperate one. "Okay, both of you listen to me. I will look into some things, talk to a few people. But I can't do anything that could get me in hot water with Sutton. You understand that; right, Dr. C.?"

He nodded, and patted my hand. "I understand, Victoria. I know there are some things I have to face. I'm willing to accept the consequences for the things I've done. But not for the things I haven't."

I watched my dad walk him out, his arm around Dr. Chickie's shoulder. What to make of the little orthodontist? A gambler? No doubt. An embezzler? Probably. But a murderer? I didn't think so.

Chapter Nine

I shouldn't be doing this, I thought as I turned the key in the elderly blue Honda I'd bought when I'd moved back here. *Sutton might find out. Danny might find out. Or, worse, Nonna might find out.* But I kept seeing Dr. Chickie's haunted eyes, and I couldn't tamp down the sparks of my own curiosity. As I traveled down Ocean Avenue toward Belmont Beach, I pondered how best to get into that club to find out what I needed. It was after four, so the bar would likely be open. I had to hope that Mustang Sally was on duty and as talkative as ever.

When I reached the club, I parked at the far end of the lot in one of the two guest spots that were open. The parking lot was on the beach side, so I had a clear approach to the walkway. But so had the Belmont police, as bright yellow caution tape laced the railing along the walkway like a grim bridal decoration. I looked around me, and the grounds seemed quiet. Behind the building was a small picnic area where one or two members were having drinks. Otherwise, there appeared to be few people—and no police cars—around.

From where I stood I could see that the walkway to the beach was lined with a mix of natural vegetation and flowers that grow in sandy soil. The path was a good distance from the club, and the beach grass was high enough to obscure anyone walking there, especially at night. I crept along the side of the path, my heart thrumming in my chest. Sneaking around in places I shouldn't be was the part of detecting that I hated (and Sofia thrived on). In the distance was the ocean; in front of me the platform and a steep drop to the beach below. I kept my eyes on the horizon as I approached the platform, trying with little success to look as though I belonged on a crime scene. The railing around the platform would have been waist high for my sixty-five inches; Merriman was taller. But there was no gate across the stairway and the steps looked narrow. She probably fell forward, straight over the stairway. I dropped to my knees next to the left side of the platform and flattened myself against the sandy ground. I scooched as close as I could, trying to ignore the caution tape that told me in bold black letters and exclamation points (POLICE LINE—DO NOT CROSS!) that what I was doing was highly irregular and probably illegal.

I reached out and ran my hand across the platform, feeling grit, sand, and splinters, one of which embedded itself into my palm. Saying a forbidden word under my breath and wondering why I was trying to save Dr. C.'s felonious behind, I rested my chin on the edge of the platform and squinted in the late-day sun. At the edge of my periphery, something glinted in the crevice between two of the wooden boards. I stretched my fingertips as far as I could, and using my nails in a way that would appall my mother, dug the tiny object from the crack. It rolled and skittered across the platform; I slapped my hand over it, wincing as the splinter dug deeper into my palm. Pinching it between my thumb and forefinger, I brought it to my face and blinked. Prickles rose up and down my arms when I saw what it was: a tiny pink bugle bead, exactly like the ones on the dress Elizabeth Merriman was wearing on Saturday night.

Still holding the bead between my fingers, I slid sideways and creaked to a standing position. I slipped the bead into the zippered section of my wallet, brushed the sand from my jeans and, heart pounding, made a dash back to the parking lot. Taking slow breaths, I walked the long way around from the lot toward the circular drive at the front of the building, shaking my sore palm. I would have to deal with the splinter later.

I walked up the stone steps and entered through the front doors of the club, hoping there wouldn't be anyone checking for membership cards. But I was lucky, and passed through the foyer alone, stopping to peer into the ballroom, where a couple of male staffers were setting up tables. Had Dr. Chickie risked everything—his reputation, his freedom, his practice—just so Princess Roberta could have a wedding reception in this room? Even those glorious windows and glittering chandeliers weren't worth that. *The things we do for love*, I thought, and headed down the hallway for the bar.

I blinked in the bar's dim light, hoping for a glimpse

of Sally's bright hair. I jumped when her head popped up.

"Well, look who's here!" Sally came out from behind the bar to greet me. This was better than I could have hoped for—who knew she'd be this happy to see me? She shook her finger at me and grinned. "I know who you are, lady. You're not a caterer. You're that mystery writer."

"Guilty," I said, raising my right hand and dropping it quickly in case she tried to shake it. "You met me as Victoria, but I write as Vick Reed." Before I could come up with a reason for being there, Sally supplied one herself.

"And I know why you're here. It's to do research, isn't it? Because of what happened to the Iron Lady?" Her eyes were bright with excitement, and who was I to disappoint her?

I put my finger to my lips. "Shh. Can we keep it on the down low, please, Sally?"

"Oh, you bet. C'mon, sit down." She stepped behind the bar. "Can I get you something?"

"Just an iced tea, thanks."

She poured the tea, dropped in a lemon slice, and slid it across the bar. "So, this is for a new book, right?"

"I guess you could say that," I said. I leaned closer and lowered my voice. "I don't suppose you have any idea who might have still been here after that wedding reception ended?"

Relishing her role as informant, Sally looked around the empty bar to make sure there were no prying eyes or ears and then nodded. "There's the clean-up staff."

I took out a pad and pen. "How many?"

She lifted a skinny shoulder. "Not sure. Maybe a dozen. But I don't see any of them killing Merriman. Why would they?"

"That's the question, isn't it? What about wedding guests?" I asked, quickly scrawling some notes—not easy with my stinging hand.

She shook her head. "They clear out quick after an event, especially a wedding."

"What about the families of the bride and groom?"

"Not exactly sure on that one. I do know that Dr. Natale was still here, though."

I stopped writing and looked up from my pad. "What time did you see him?"

"Maybe quarter to twelve. I know because we closed the bar early that night."

So Dr. Chickie *was* on the premises, despite what he himself had said about leaving at eleven thirty. Did Dr. C. double back that night? There was also Dennis Doyle's assertion that they'd left fifteen minutes previous, which neatly lined up with Dr. C.'s story. Was Dennis lying to protect his new in-laws? I made a note to check into Doyle's background, hoping I could read it later. That splinter was doing a job on my writing hand. "Who else, Sally?" I asked.

"Jack Toscano was also here, and so was the dude with the crazy hair. They were in the bar till I closed at eleven thirty."

Now, that was interesting. Toscano was still around, as was the man with the Einstein hairdo. "Hey, Sally,"

I asked, "I don't suppose you have the name for the white-haired guy?"

She shook her head. "Nope. I can try to find out for you if you want."

"Don't worry about it; it doesn't matter." Of course it did matter, but I was supposed to be researching a mystery, not conducting my personal investigation. "How about the kitchen staff? Were Chef Etienne or any of his guys still here?"

"Don't think so, but I wouldn't swear to it. I do know this, though: Crazy Chef Kate went marching past this bar around eleven thirty, cursing up a storm. We all heard her. And then she left, right out through the front doors."

"How do you know?"

She laughed. " 'Cuz I followed her ass. I was gonna let her know to keep her voice down, but she was too fast for me and got out before I could stop her."

"That doesn't mean she couldn't have come back," I said, more to myself than Sally.

"But think about it, Victoria—she's pretty darn recognizable. With that bright red scarf and all that makeup. If she came back, she took a heck of a risk."

"Well, somebody took a risk." *Was* it Kate Bridges? That night in the kitchen she'd said of Merriman that somebody should "put her lights out." Then she made a noisy exit a half hour before Merriman was killed. If she'd killed her, why be so obvious? Unless it was all an elaborate ploy. But Kate struck me more as the hot-tempered type who'd act impulsively rather than someone who would coldly calculate a murder. I took a deep slug of my tea and wrapped my throbbing hand around the cold glass. Then I took my questions in a new direction. "Sally, how well do you know this building?"

"Pretty well. I've tended bar here for almost ten years."

"Okay, so what's the closest door to get to the walkway to the beach?"

She leaned close enough for me to see her glittery green eye shadow. "You think she went over that seawall, don't you? Hell, she must have—the cops have it roped off. So, you gonna kill off your next victim that way?"

I thought about the bead sitting deep within the confines of my wallet. A piece of evidence that the police and Sutton's team had missed, and one I certainly should not have in my possession. I swallowed nervously, prompting Sally to refill my tea. "Let's just say that's a possibility, okay?"

She shot me a wink. "I get it. So, back to your question. There's a side door off the kitchen—that one's the closest. But not one that the members use. If you go back out here to the main hallway and continue to your right, you'll see two doors at the end of the hall— the one on the left leads outside. The other one takes you up the stairs."

I grinned at her. "To the mysterious tower?" I asked in my best horror-movie voice.

She waved her hand. "It's all boarded up. But you know what? In your book, I think your character should get pushed off the tower instead. Much more interesting."

If and when I get back to my mysteries, I might do just that, I thought. *In the meantime, I have to focus on real life.* That's when another thought occurred to me—one so obvious, I should have lost my private-eye license, if only I'd had one. I leaned forward on the bar. "Sally, Merriman didn't drive, did she? I would think with eyes that bad—"

"Nah," Sally interrupted. "Toscano drove her everywhere. Or she took cabs. She was big on taking cabs."

I wrote *Toscano drive/cabs* on my pad, then a colon followed by these words: *How was she planning to get home that night?*

Sally turned my pad around to face her, tapped my notes with her fingernail, and pushed the pad back. "Now, that's the sixty-four-dollar question, ain't it?" she said.

I followed Sally's directions and reached the two doors, just as she'd described. Holding the door open in case it locked behind me, I noted that it was about twenty-five yards to the beach path, and the grass was overgrown. Elizabeth Merriman would have needed a strong arm to help her through the grass and onto the wooden walkway. *It had to be somebody she trusted*, I told myself. *Like Toscano.* Glancing upward, I saw a light fixture—perhaps a sensor light? A sensor light would have illuminated this whole area, allowing anyone walking past or even out on the road a pretty good view of a woman pitching over that stairway. I made a note to find out whether members used the beach at night. I stepped back inside, pulling the door closed as quietly as I could. When I turned to leave, my hand still on the doorknob, I nearly collided with a tall redhead.

"Victoria?" Lacey Harrison stepped back to get a look at me. At least today I wasn't wearing a hairnet, but my jeans, T-shirt, and sandals were no match for her linen trousers and crisp white blouse.

"Oh, hi, Lacey," I said, as though skulking around hallways in a place I didn't belong was a totally natural thing to do.

"What are you doing here?" A frown creased her pretty brow—confusion? Or suspicion?

From my last little adventure, I'd learned that when lying, it is always best to stay as close to the truth as possible. "Okay, I know this sounds really morbid, but I was curious about the beach path. Too many years of writing mysteries, I guess." *Lame, Vic. Truly lame.* I snatched my hand back from the doorknob. But if I expected disapproval from Lacey, I was mistaken.

"The police think Mrs. Merriman fell from the seawall, don't they?" she whispered.

"I guess. I mean, I don't know," I said in a normal tone that echoed loudly down the hall.

"But it's cordoned off," Lacey said, glancing toward the door. "It must be significant." She looked back at me. "I got a phone call from the county prosecutor's office. I have to make a statement," she said nervously.

"Me too. Just tell the truth and don't worry about it too much." I paused, but Lacey clearly wasn't going anywhere. "Well," I said, "I should leave." I pointed back at the door. "And would you mind not saying anything about this?"

"Sure. But you know the club is private. It could be awkward if the manager saw you."

"I'm on my way. And if I run into anybody, I'll just say I got lost. Bye, Lacey."

"Bye, Victoria," she called out. "I'm sure I'll be seeing you around."

God, I hope not, I thought. It was bad enough to imagine Tim and Lacey together; I sure didn't want to watch the romance play out in front of me. But as I kept reminding Tim, he and I were over a long time ago.

Giving myself a firm reminder not to get distracted—and not to get caught here—I hesitated. The side door was closer to the parking lot, but the front door was for public use, probably a better choice if I got caught on the premises, so I scampered down that hallway and darted out the main doors. But I had only about three seconds to savor my clean getaway.

"May I help you?" Jack Toscano, hands on hips, stood at the bottom of the stone steps that led into the building.

"Oh," I said, "I was actually on my way out."

"I see that." He smiled in a forced way. "Were you interested in having an event here? Or adding your name to the membership list?"

Again, I tried to straddle that border between truth and lies. "No, thank you. My friend Sally tends bar here, and I was just stopping in to say hello."

He tilted his head, his dark glasses disconcerting. "You look familiar."

Was he a reader of mysteries? Or did he recognize me from Saturday night? *Go for the truth, Vic.* "Actually, I was here the other night to cater the soup course of the wedding."

"Ah, that's right. You were in the bar." He reached out his hand. "I'm Jack Toscano, the club manager."

Well, that was quick, Jack. Did you promote yourself already? Without thinking, I offered him my right hand, which he gripped enthusiastically. "Ow," I gasped. "Sorry. I'm Victoria Rienzi," I said, and attempted to pull my hand from his.

Instead he turned up my palm and winced. "No, *I'm* sorry. That's quite a nasty splinter you've got there, isn't it? Have you cleaned it?"

"I'm, um, heading home to do that, in fact."

He nodded. "Good." He dropped my hand, but his face loomed close to mine. My heart, which had begun pounding again when I ran into Lacey, started in double-time as I took in his dark glasses and tight expression. He pointed at my head and I flinched. "Sorry," he said again, but didn't smile. "But I was just about to tell you that you have some dried grass in your hair."

"Oh." I shook my head and watched a couple of blades flutter to my feet. *Good job there, Vic,* I thought, and realized something else: *This is a guy who notices things.*

Toscano suddenly smiled, which struck me as more frightening than his scary face. "It's a pleasure to meet you, Ms. Rienzi," he said. "And I'm sorry if I seemed suspicious just now. We've been fending off reporters."

You and me both. "Of course. I'm sorry about what happened to Mrs. Merriman. What a terrible thing."

"It certainly was. She was an admirable lady, and to die in such a horrific accident . . ." He shook his head in an expression of sorrow. "It's a real loss to me." The dark glasses made it hard to tell if he was sincere. But he'd clearly been watching me behind those glasses, because he tapped the side of the black frames. "You'll have to excuse these. I've had some recent surgery and my eyes are very light sensitive."

"I understand." There was an awkward pause, and I realized there would be no more information forthcoming. "It was nice to meet you." I glanced back at the building. "And if I ever do want to have an event here, I know whom to call."

He nodded. "You do that. Have a good day, now." Though still smiling, Toscano crossed his arms in an *I'm not going anywhere* pose, and remained that way until I reached the parking lot.

On the ride back, I marshaled my thoughts to share with Sofia later on. Sally had provided crucial information about Kate and Dr. C. And Lacey had to give a statement, which was not so strange. But she hadn't mentioned why *she* was headed to the second floor. And Jack Toscano had called Merriman's death an accident. Did he know something? Or was it just wishful thinking?

By five I was sitting in our unofficial base of operations—Sofia's office at the back of her dance studio. The infamous red folder already held a sheaf of printed pages.

"When did you have time to do this?" I asked her, leafing through the pages.

"I cut back a bit on some of my classes and combined some. It's a little slower in summer, anyway, so I had some down time."

"That's good. And I guess you haven't had time for the beach, either."

"Why do you say that?"

"Because by July, you're usually darker than I am. But not this year." I held my forearm next to hers.

"I told you, the heat's been getting to me. And if you're done comparing tans, we've got work to do." She opened the folder and took out several pages of notes, including some handwritten ones.

"There's a lot here, already," I said. "How deep did you have to dig for this stuff?"

"Well, I found a lot of it on the Internet. But it also helps that Merriman Industries employed a ton of people in our area, including my uncle John."

"Really? Good luck for us. What did he do there?"

"He used to work on one of their construction crews," she said, "and he knows a lot about their operation. So here's what I got: Elizabeth goes to work for Robert Merriman in the fifties; by 1960, she's married to him. He's, like, fifteen years older than she is, and they have no kids. He had started Merriman Industries from a single construction firm in the fifties; by the eighties, there are a bunch of businesses—construction, heating and insulation, asbestos removal, and some other stuff, too. In any case, he builds up one lucrative conglomerate. He dies in 1990."

"And leaves everything to her, I take it."

Sofia nodded. "And she takes over as CEO. And apparently alienates everybody, from her board of directors to the guys on the various jobs. She was a micromanager."

"I can see that." I thought about Elizabeth's role at the Belmont Club; besides being president, she had appointed herself events manager as well. She was the kind of woman who needed to have her hand in everything. I could imagine her in a hard hat, visiting construction sites and making the crews miserable. "Was there anybody in particular who had a beef with her?"

"There's probably a list a mile long, but my uncle gave me two pieces of information that I think could be important. First, when Elizabeth takes over, she immediately butts heads with her late husband's right-hand guy."

"Do we have a name?"

"Yup. William Fox. My uncle says he and Robert Merriman were friends, too, and Merriman relied on him for everything. He had a key position in that company—executive assistant to Merriman himself—and, for some reason, Elizabeth found him a threat. She pushed him out."

"Did she fire him?"

"I think even the Iron Lady wouldn't do that," Sofia said. "He took an early retirement, at her strong suggestion, apparently. At the time of Robert Merriman's death, Fox was only in his fifties, and not ready to retire."

"What happened to him?"

"He didn't take it well. He started drinking. Big time. Then his wife leaves him, he ends up on the outs with his kids. I mean, it all goes south for him."

"Is he still alive?"

Sofia nodded. "Yes. In fact, my uncle thinks he's still in the area."

"Well, that's good." I wrote *William Fox* in my notebook. "He's got a motive anyway," I said. "I wonder if he was anywhere near the Belmont Club last Saturday."

"But I've got more." Sofia leaned across the desk, her eyes lit with enthusiasm. It was good to see her feeling better. "And here's where it gets really interesting. According to Uncle John, when it came to running the companies, she started cutting corners. She got greedy and took shortcuts, even with safety issues. So their injury rates go up, along with workmen's-comp claims. Then some workers bring a mesothelioma suit against Merriman Industries."

"From the asbestos removal?" I knew that handling asbestos was dangerous, and that there were strict protocols in its removal and disposal. "It's carcinogenic, right?"

She nodded and held up three fingers. "Three men brought suits against the company." She pushed a sheet of paper my way and I read the three names: Lorenzo DePonti. Darnell Jones. Michael McBride.

"So it's just these three. I'm surprised there aren't more guys who brought suits against them," I said.

She shrugged. "They were exposed to the stuff for the longest period of time. And they were able to prove that working with asbestos was directly responsible for making them sick."

I looked at the names again. "They're all dead, I take it."

"Oh yeah. I don't have exact dates, but I think by the mid-nineties they're all dead."

"And their families would have inherited that money."

"Still," Sofia said, "that doesn't mean somebody connected with one of those families wouldn't have carried a grudge."

"But after all this time?" I shook my head. "Why wait almost twenty years to get back at her? And the same would apply to William Fox, right?"

"I don't know," she said. "Maybe opportunity? Maybe somebody at that wedding was related to one of the men or William Fox, saw Elizabeth and took a chance." She paused and looked at me. "You don't think it's a plausible, do you?"

"I wouldn't rule anything out, but that time lapse is problematic. What else do you have?"

"Well, after the asbestos settlement, she sells off the different businesses, but because it's the nineties, she makes money, despite the big payout to the families. By 'ninety-eight, she's a lady of leisure. Buys a fancy condo on the beach in Belmont, joins the country club, does charity work. By 2002, she's president of the club and wields a lot of power in Belmont Beach."

"Does she run for public office or anything?"

Sofia shook her head. "She was more a behind-the-scenes type, throwing her power and money around that way."

I nodded. "That was certainly her MO around the club."

"Speaking of the club, it's your turn, Vic. What did you get there today?"

"So glad you asked, SIL." I took my wallet from my purse and carefully extracted the glass bead. I set it on the desk between us. "Look what I found out on the platform over the seawall. It was cordoned off, by the way; I had to sneak under."

Sofia, unfazed by my crossing a police line, rolled the bead between her fingers. "It looks like it's from a dress."

I nodded. "Merriman's dress. It was stuck in a crack between the wooden boards. Which is how I got this." I held up my reddened palm.

"Pretty." She took my hand. "Do you want me to operate?"

"I'll do it, thanks." Then I filled her in on all that I'd learned from Sally, as well as from my encounters with Lacey and Toscano. "But Toscano saw the splinter," I said, "And noticed that I had grass in my hair."

Sofia stopped writing and pointed her pencil at me. "Watch out for him. And be careful next time."

"I'm hoping there won't *be* a next time. Finding the bead proves she was out there, so we know for sure now how she died."

My sister-in-law shook her head. "Not to burst your bubble there, Vic, but I would have thought yellow police tape made that one obvious." She handed the bead back to me. "Sutton probably has a baggie full of these."

"Thanks loads. But I'm not sure it's as cut-and-dried as you think. I also saw a sensor light over that door that leads to the walkway. Those things are bright. Would a murderer take that kind of chance?"

"He—or she—could have loosened the bulb."

"You'd need a ladder; it's set pretty high. Putting the light aside for now, the question for me is how she got out there in the first place. One," I said, holding up my pointer finger, "she decides to take a midnight stroll to look out at the ocean. Two, she goes out there to commit suicide. Three, she goes out there with someone she trusts. Four, she's coerced in some way."

"Hmm," Sofia said. "For the sake of argument, let's assume we can discount one and two and look at this from another angle. Who stands to gain by her death, Vic? What's that Latin phrase you told me?"

"*Cui bono*. Now, there's a question. This was a very rich woman. According to the newspaper article, she has no surviving relatives. Where would all that money go?"

Sofia frowned. "Her charities? The club?"

"Maybe. But just because she didn't have any relatives doesn't mean she doesn't have a beneficiary. I'd love to find out if Toscano was named in her will."

"Didn't the bartender say he'd only been around about six months?"

"Yup. But if they were lovers? Women do awfully stupid things when it comes to men."

Sofia looked back to her screen. "No argument from me there. I guess if you're a lonely old lady and a guy shows you attention—"

"Six months might be long enough to name him in your will."

Sofia jotted a few more notes and then turned back to me. "So, what *was* going on between Elizabeth Merriman and Toscano?"

"That's something we need to find out. Because if he's got a motive, Jack Toscano is the front-runner in the Belmont Club Murder Stakes."

Chapter Ten

On Thursday, the *Press* ran an article indicating that Elizabeth Merriman's body had been released and that a wake for was planned for Saturday. The cause of death was severe head trauma, just as Nina LaGuardia had said. I hoped that meant her sources were accurate about other things as well, such as the time she died. I sat in my bedroom, mulling over this news, as well as what Sofia had learned. During Elizabeth's time as CEO of Merriman Industries, she had clearly made enemies. But would any of them have waited two decades to take their revenge? Was Sofia right? Was it merely a case of someone having an opportunity the night of the wedding?

As my mind worked, the cursor on my computer screen blinked at me reproachfully. My manuscript was open, but I hadn't added a word. I wasn't expected at the restaurant for a while yet, and I should have been writing, not detecting.

"Sorry, Isabella," I said to my novel's protagonist, "but you'll have to wander the streets of nineteenth-century New York a little while longer."

I closed the document and opened a Google search page. Sofia had already tried to track down the obituaries of the three men who had died due to asbestos exposure, but with no luck. Getting that information would require a trip to the library and a long slog with a microfiche machine. Was it worth that time? And even if I could track down their family members, what would I be likely to learn? Two decades had passed. While I couldn't rule this piece out, neither could I afford to spend lots of time on it. William Fox, on the other hand, was still alive. My own curiosity and a sense of urgency spurred me on; I had to find out for myself.

I started a people search, cursing the commonness of his name. There were way too many people in New Jersey with some version of the name William Fox. I printed the list and grabbed a marker, crossing off any William Fox who was younger than seventy and older than eighty. That still left about a dozen candidates. Of those, four lived in the shore area. At least I was narrowing them down. We had only Uncle John's word that Fox had stayed in this area, but those in a thirty-mile radius seemed the place to start. I highlighted the names and numbered them in order of proximity:

1. *William Fox, Jr., Asbury Park*
2. *William Fox, Dover Township*
3. *William R. Fox, Barnegat*
4. *Will Fox, Cape May*

What I needed was a picture. If I knew what William Fox looked like, I might remember seeing him on

Saturday. But a Google image searched turned up several guys who were too young to be the Fox I was looking for. (However, two of them *were* looking for dates. Too bad they weren't my type.)

What were my options? Call each one on a pretext and ask if he'd worked for Merriman Industries twenty years ago? Drive all over New Jersey on stakeouts in hopes of getting a peek at him? In my last foray into sleuthing, I'd used my position as a writer to talk to people connected to the case, but that was a hand I didn't want to overplay. I made a note to ask Sofia to talk to her uncle again, but stopped suddenly, my pen still in the air. *Hang on*, I thought. According to Uncle John, Fox had become an alcoholic after he was forced out of Merriman Industries. Was he still drinking? Because if not, it's likely he attended AA meetings.

Okay, so they were two big ifs, but it was worth a look. It took me all of thirty seconds to learn that there was only one place in our area that held regular meetings—and there was one scheduled for tonight. I texted Sofia: *You up for another road trip, SIL?*

That afternoon at the restaurant we had a full dining room for lunch, and since I was on alone, I didn't have a moment to even think about William Fox or any of our other suspects. By the time the rush was over, I'd barely had a chance to rest my feet before Chef Massimo arrived. I found myself on peach duty, prepping the fragrant Jersey fruits for Nonna's peach *torta*, the Italian version of peach pie, and tonight's dessert special. While the smell of the fresh fruit was intoxicating, I'd have to get every last bit of peel and slice them perfectly, or I'd hear about it from my grandmother. But it wasn't the worst job at the Casa Lido, and at least I got to enjoy the garden on a sunny shore day. As I was bringing in the tray of fruit, our head chef was arriving.

"*Ciao*, Massi," I said, greeting him with a kiss on each cheek, Italian style.

"*Ciao, cara*," he said. "Was our luncheon busy?" Massimo buttoned his chef's coat, pushed his long hair behind his ears, and sat his toque on his head.

"*Sì, maestro*. Tim has the sauces going, and the fruit is prepped for the peach *torta*."

He nodded toward the tray. "So I see. *Bene*. Nando will make the pastry when he comes in."

I sighed. "He gets the fun part."

"Good prep work is vital, *cara*." He patted my cheek. "And you wanted to learn, did you not?"

"As everyone is fond of reminding me." I followed Massimo into the kitchen, partially to observe his work, but also to ask him a few questions about his colleagues at the Belmont Club.

"Hey, Massi?" I asked. "Do you know Chef Boulé? I mean, before you saw him on Saturday?"

Chef Massimo stuck his Roman nose in the air and gave a small sniff. "By reputation only. He is *il maestro* when it comes to the French cuisine, I will give him that."

"But not Italian, I take it."

Our master chef gave me a look that would wilt escarole. "I would say that is obvious, Victoria, no?"

"What about Kate Bridges, Massi? Do you know her? Do you know her work?"

Massimo went to the sink, rolled up the sleeves of his coat, and started scrubbing up like a surgeon. "Again, we had not met personally. But she is known to be a skilled *pâtissière*," he said, using the formal French term for pastry chef. "And she is not young; she has come through the ranks slowly but steadily. Ambitious, that one."

That's not surprising, I thought. Kate Bridges was tough, supremely confident of her abilities. I wondered about her garish makeup: didn't she worry that her appearance might put people off? Or, worse, that she wouldn't be taken seriously as a chef? "Has she always looked like that?" I asked.

He grimaced. "You mean like the clown from *la commedia dell'arte*? I do not know. But many stories and rumors float about regarding Signorina Bridges—that she has been fired from half her jobs, that she is independently wealthy, that she studied in Paris with Fabrice Le Bourdat, that she is a self-taught genius—it is hard to tell which are true."

Now, this was interesting. Did rumors swirl around Kate Bridges because of her outsized personality and tendency to alienate others? Or did she cultivate them herself to keep people guessing about her? "So she's not an easy person to know."

"No." Massi looked up from the sink. "Still, I admire her, despite the attitude and the orange face. She works at her craft because she loves it; she is good at it and does not care what others think."

"That's for sure," I said. *And judging by her behavior to*

Elizabeth Merriman, she sure doesn't care whom she offends, either.

He dried his hands on a clean towel and tucked it into a back pocket. Once he started tasting the sauces, I knew that would be the end of any conversation that didn't involve tonight's menu. I stayed long enough to taste the spicy arrabbiata sauce and to submit to a quiz from Chef Massi about the flavors. Then I insulted him by mistaking his use of red chiles for the dried variety, and ended up banished to the dining room. And who was sitting there quite cozily but Tim and his new lady love, Lacey Harrison.

Tim hadn't yet changed into his kitchen clothes, and, I had to admit, he looked a treat in a blue button-down shirt and snug-fitting jeans. Without his bandanna, his newly cropped curls only set off his gray eyes. *Do not release that sigh, Victoria,* I told myself, and lifted my chin in an attempt to convey indifference. Not that it mattered, as neither one of them was paying attention to me. Lacey was seated like a queen at the center table; Tim was leaning over her and whispering something into her golden red hair. She giggled, and I cleared my throat. Or perhaps gagged.

"Oh, hey, Victoria!" Lacey waved to me. "Tim's cooking for me—isn't that cool?"

"You bet," I said, and glanced at my watch. "But lunch is over, Tim."

"I know what time it is, Vic. I'm making Lacey a special meal."

"Yeah, but aren't you supposed to be helping Massi with dinner prep?"

As if on cue, Chef Massimo appeared in the dining room bearing a plate of bruschetta.

"Welcome, *signorina*," he said, setting the plate down on the table with a flourish. "A little taste for you of what is to come. It is like toast with a fresh tomato mixture on top—a little onion, some basil. Is verrrry nice."

Okay, who needs *bruschetta* explained to them? I raised an eyebrow at Massi, but he was too busy admiring the lovely Lacey. "Oh, thank you, Chef Fabri," she said. "It looks delicious."

Massi nodded regally and started back to the kitchen, but paused to inform me to learn the specials for dinner. "And when you taste them, Victoria, be sure to appreciate the full complexity of my flavors."

"Uh, chef," I said, "I'm not on for dinner tonight, so—"

"So you think you do not need to learn the specials, is that it?" Massi brought his palms together, not in prayer but in an Italian gesture that can mean anything from *please* to *I can't believe you're so* stupido. I was pretty sure which one he was going for. "If you wish to learn the cuisine, Victoria, you must apply yourself to the task." Lifting his chin, he walked back to the kitchen.

"Yes, chef," I said to his retreating back. *And thanks for reminding me that I am an underling in front of Tim and the babe.* Though since I was once again wearing server clothes—black slacks, white blouse—my role was quite obvious. *Might as well play it to the hilt, Vic.*

"May I get you anything to drink, Lacey?" I asked, in a tone so cheery that Tim shot me a look.

"Just some water, thanks. Gosh, these smell good,"

she said, picking up her knife and fork. She then proceeded to cut her bruschetta into dainty quarters.

I shook my head at such foolishness, and Tim frowned at me. "I'll just go get that water," I said, deciding to treat her to a San Pellegrino, our imported Italian brand. On my way back to the table, I noticed Cal coming in the front door, and I cheered up immediately.

"Hey, Cal." I lifted the water bottle in greeting.

"Afternoon, Victoria," he said. "Your dad here yet, by any chance? I got something I need to ask him about that stain for the bar."

"Nope. But Tim is." I gestured to the center table, where Tim was still whispering sweet nothings into Lacey's ear. "And so is his new squeeze."

Cal's eyebrows rose under the brim of his Saints cap. "Now, ain't that interesting?"

Not too interesting, I hope. "C'mon," I said, "I'll introduce you."

I set the water down in front of Lacey and made the introductions. Cal's response was only one word, but it made my heart sing: He lifted the brim of his cap, smiled, and said, "Ma'am."

She smiled prettily back at him, but even that was even too much for Tim, who hovered around her like a protective knight-errant. He scowled at Cal, who grinned even wider and clapped Tim on the shoulder. "Where ya at, brother?"

It was hard to contain my amusement as I watched Cal toy with Tim. The two had set themselves up as rivals for my affection a couple months back and, despite Tim's new relationship, his antipathy for Cal was still evident. Was it shallow of me to enjoy the moment?

Tim lifted Cal's hand from his shoulder and proceeded to ignore him. Instead, he gave Lacey's hand a quick squeeze and promised her, in a suggestive tone, "the meal of her life." Lacey responded with a playful swat on the arm, while I strained my ocular muscles to keep my eyeballs from rolling back in my head. Tim breezed past me with a "Later, Vic," as he returned to the kitchen.

"If you'll excuse me, Lacey," I said, and turned to follow him.

"You can't stay away from me, can you, Vic?" In the kitchen, Tim was buttoning his chef's coat, a particularly smarmy look on his face.

"You're irresistible, Tim. What can I say?"

"Children," Chef Massimo warned, "play nicely. There is a dinner service to prepare, and there is no time for this nonsense."

Oh, but there's time to make Lacey a special meal. But that was a thought to keep to myself if I wanted to learn anything about Italian cooking. As usual, I was consigned to the vegetable station, prepping the sweet little Sicilian eggplants now in season. If I were lucky, I might even get to grill them out in the July heat. But as ordered, I watched and listened as Tim and Massimo prepared the veal special for tasting, with an extra serving for the special guest in the dining room. After I dutifully tasted the sauce and submitted to questioning by both guys, I readied a plate for Cal.

"Where're you going with that?" Tim called over his shoulder.

"Just bringing Cal a taste," I said as I pushed through the kitchen door. Behind me, Tim had a few choice words to say about that, including a few of the four-letter variety.

"Yours is coming," I said to Lacey as I hurried past her. *And I'm sure Tim will stand over you, cutting your veal into delicate pieces and waiting for you to swoon over his cooking.* But these thoughts weren't worthy of me and probably unfair to Lacey. Grateful for Cal's presence, I headed to the bar, wearing a smile that wasn't forced.

"Here you go," I said. "A sample of tonight's veal special and your favorite San Pellegrino water."

"Well, thanks, Victoria." He uncapped the bottle and took a long swig.

"I figure it's the least I can do," I said, taking a moment to appreciate his well-muscled arms.

"For what?"

"For calling that sweet young thing 'ma'am.' It made my day."

"If that's what makes your day, *cher*, you needa get out more."

"True that, as my sister-in-law, Sofia, would say. You're late today, by the way."

"I know. Got another project I'm working on at the moment." But he didn't elaborate. "This smells great." Cal took a healthy bite of the veal and nodded in approval. "So, how long's the Iron Chef been dating Miss Lacey?"

"Like, two days. He just met her."

"Well," Cal said, shaking his head, "no accountin' for taste, is there?"

"Nope." I glanced back at the dining room, where Tim and Lacey were sitting, their heads close together.

Cal jerked a thumb in their direction. "That bother ya any?"

"Nah," I lied. "Tim and I were done a long time ago."

"So you've told me." Cal finished the veal and nodded again. "The guy can cook—that's for sure. But I can't hardly say a word to the man without he gets in my face."

"You know you mess with his head."

He grinned. "Yeah, but he lets me."

"I know. Tim's got some growing up to do." I pulled out a stool and took a seat at the bar.

"Took the words outta my mouth." He leaned both arms on the bar, staring me down with those distracting green eyes. "So, are you gonna wait for that to happen? Or move on?"

I dropped my eyes and folded a bar napkin into tiny pleats. "I wish I had an answer," I finally said.

He pulled the napkin from my hand. "You're a smart, beautiful woman. There's no end of men out there who'd appreciate you." One side of his mouth curved in a half grin. "Me included."

"Is that so?" I said, meeting his eyes again and feeling a flush of warmth at the compliment.

"That's so. Now, no doubt but we got off to kind of a rocky start back in May. What with you playing Nancy Drew and all."

"Hardly Nancy Drew," I said. "Maybe a much younger Miss Marple."

He flashed me a grin, the effect of which disconcerted me. "In any case," he asked, "what do you say to trying again?"

Cal had asked me on a date before, one which ended up an uneasy mix of socializing and interrogating. I hadn't been completely fair to him then. But I liked him. He was different from the guys I'd dated back in New York—an interesting, seasoned man. And damned attractive. A burst of feminine laughter came from the dining room, but I kept my attention on Cal. "I'd like that," I said.

"Good, then. No time like the present. How 'bout having dinner with me tonight?"

Tonight? Tonight I had plans with Sofia to stake out an AA meeting in the hopes of identifying William Fox. Tonight I was hoping to get one step closer to figuring out who killed Elizabeth Merriman. I couldn't go tonight, and I couldn't tell him why.

"Oh, Cal, I'm sorry. I can't tonight." I dropped my eyes so I wouldn't have to look at him.

"Are you on dinner shift?" he asked.

"No, I'm not. But I am tied up tonight. Can we make it another time?"

His smile faded. "Sure," he said. "Maybe some other time." And he turned back to his work without another word.

Chapter Eleven

"**T**his better be worth it," I muttered. In a far corner of the parking lot of St. Theresa's Church in Bayview Township, Sofia and I sat in her car, watching people enter through a side door. We were in stakeout clothes—at least our idea of such: dark clothes, hair in a ponytail tucked into a ball cap, and sunglasses.

"Hey, coming here was your idea." Sofia adjusted her glasses and settled her cap firmly over her hair. "You upset because you sacrificed a date with Mr. Down on the Bayou? He gave up kinda easy—don't you think? Is his ego that delicate?"

"I don't know, Sofe. I guess after last time—"

"You mean when you implied he was a murderer?"

"Don't remind me." I looked in her rearview mirror for anyone coming in from the sidewalk.

"Do you recognize anybody?" Sofia asked.

"Not yet. It's getting too dark anyway," I complained.

"I think we should go in."

"No way! If you think I'm going in there—" I jumped at the sound of a light rap on Sofia's window.

Sofia already had the window down and had whipped off her sunglasses. Standing outside the car was a sweet-faced nun bearing a smile that could only be described as angelic.

"Are you here for the meeting, girls?" she asked.

"Uh . . ." I began, but, as always, Sofia jumped in.

"We are, sister. Thank you," she said.

"Well, you're in the right place. They're held in the church basement, right through that door. I'm Sister Elizabeth. Of course, I'm not part of the organization, but I like to provide support to those who are struggling."

"Thank you, sister, but—" I said.

Sofia interrupted, dropping her voice to a confidential tone. "My friend here is trying to decide whether or not to go in."

I shot Sofia a murderous glance, but Sister Elizabeth gave me such a sympathetic look that I nearly launched into an Act of Contrition right there. "I know it's hard, my child," she said. "But the Lord will see you through. And so will I." Then she opened the driver's side door, which Sofia had so helpfully unlocked. She held out her hand to us. "Come, girls. I'll walk you both inside." Then she pointed to my hat and glasses. "But you'll have to take those off."

"Sure," I said, slowly removing the ball cap.

Sister Elizabeth smiled brightly. "The glasses, too, dear."

Once the glasses were off, I felt as naked as the day I was born. As I trailed behind Sofia and Sister Elizabeth, I wondered how I'd be able to explain my presence at an AA meeting if I were recognized. The old *I'm doing research for a book* story was growing mighty thin.

We took the last two seats in the last row, and I scanned the room quickly. I didn't recognize anybody, and I had to hope like mad no one recognized me.

"So?" Sofia asked. "Any wedding guests or staff from the Belmont here?"

"No," I said. "So you can just stop asking me."

"Oooh, someone's grumpy." She shifted in her folding chair, which squeaked loudly; I fought the urge to hide under my own.

"I can't believe you talked me into this," I said out of the side of my mouth.

"You're the one who came up with the idea of the AA meeting."

A middle-aged man in front of us turned around and smiled. "Recognizing the problem is the first step." He stuck out his hand, and I shook it weakly. "I'm Rick," he said. "You won't be sorry you came. Can I get either of you a coffee?"

I shook my head, and Sofia said, "No, thanks." But she rewarded him with a classic Sofia smile, and his cheeks actually got pink.

"You let me know if there's anything I can get you girls," he said, and turned back in his chair.

"Nice way *not* to call attention to yourself there, Sofe," I whispered. "And it might have been my idea to come here, but I didn't mean we should *attend* the meeting. I figured we'd sit outside and watch people go in."

"Better this way." She pointed to a podium at the front of the room. "When they go up there to talk, they give their names. Then we'll know for sure."

"Yes, but how many of these will we have to sit through? And what if somebody sees us?" I had a sudden image of Nina LaGuardia at the anchor desk at News Ten, detailing the story of the famous mystery writer spotted at an Alcoholics Anonymous meeting. I hunched down in the rickety chair.

"For God's sake, Vic, it's *anonymous*. Hence the name. The idea is that you protect the identities of the people in here." She shook her head. "So just chill out."

"Sure," I said, "and let's see how chill you'll be if the mommy or daddy of one of your dance students shows up—"

"Excuse me, ladies." A slender African-American woman in a maxi skirt stood at the end of our aisle. "I see that you're new, and I just wanted to welcome you," she said softly. "I'm Leticia, the group leader. I hope you'll consider sharing your stories with us today." She nodded, her feather earrings swaying. "I know it takes courage just to show up."

Oh, Leticia, you have no idea. Will I have to stand up there and give a fake name and tell a fake story in front of people who have overcome so much? The panic made its way up my spine, manifesting itself in beads of sweat on my forehead.

As though Sofia could read my mind, she gave my arm a less than gentle squeeze. Then her face took on an expression of modest shyness. "I think we'll just listen today, Leticia. Thank you."

"Whatever you feel comfortable with, ladies. If anyone asks you to speak, just say 'I pass.'" She handed Sofia a small card. "In the meantime, you may want to take a look at this." Leticia turned and moved gracefully through the room, greeting some with a handshake and others with a kiss.

"Why is everybody so damn helpful?" I hissed.

"Temper, temper," Sofia said. "Remember why we're here, SIL." She passed me the card.

"What is it?"

"It's the twelve steps. I figure you ought to learn them."

I snatched the card from her hand and stuck it in my jeans pocket. After an introductory prayer (to which I added a couple of my own: *Please, Lord, don't let this be a mistake. Please, Lord, don't let anyone see me*) the meeting got started. Leticia read from some AA literature, made a few announcements, and explained how the meetings worked. Then a basket was passed around for donations.

"This is like sitting through Mass," I whispered to Sofie, who shushed me and frowned. I put a five in the basket and looked around for a small man with crazy white hair. What if he wasn't here? We'd be losing valuable time. But my own worry faded in the face of those who stood up, identified themselves, and talked about their struggles. I was so lost in people's confessions that I almost didn't notice the person making his way up the main aisle.

A small man with stooped shoulders, a resigned air, and wild white hair like Albert Einstein took his place behind the podium. "My name is William," he said, as he looked out at the audience. "And I'm an alcoholic."

"Oh my God," I said, as I got into Sofia's car. "Sally was right. She called him a twelve-stepper. He was with Toscano that night in the club bar, and it wasn't the first time. Sally said she'd seen them there together before."

I braced myself against the dashboard as Sofia pulled out of the parking lot. I was always nervous when my sister-in-law drove the getaway car, but tonight she was moving at a relative crawl—only two miles over the speed limit, as opposed to ten.

"What connection could there be between Fox and Toscano?" she asked.

"As Sally would say, that's the sixty-four-dollar question. But let's back up here. Toscano comes to Belmont Beach about six months ago. How does he meet Elizabeth Merriman?"

"He joins the club?" Sofia said, turning off the GPS.

"Possibly. Or he's a former Merriman employee, too." I took out my pad. "Would you check with your uncle on that?"

Sofia nodded. "If he used to work for them that would explain how he knows Fox."

"That's assuming *this* William Fox is the same one who worked for Merriman. So far, we're going on a hunch here."

"True. For now let's assume he is, so we can think this through."

"Okay," I said. "You know, I hadn't thought about

Toscano as somebody from Elizabeth's past, only her present. But if Toscano didn't work for Merriman, how does he know Fox?"

"Maybe he's a twelve-stepper himself?"

"He was drinking a beer in the club bar." I shook my head. "You know, Sofe, as I watched them together, I got the sense that Fox was somehow submissive to Toscano."

"You mean like Jack's the big dog and William is the little one?"

"Exactly. My instinct tells me that Fox needs Toscano more than Toscano needs him. But for what?"

"Money?" Sofie asked. "Information?"

"Or an exchange of one for the other. You've got me thinking. What if Toscano set out to get into Elizabeth's good graces? What if he knew she was a wealthy widow and found out Fox used to work for her?" I pointed to a green sign on our right. "Don't miss the parkway entrance."

But for some reason, she sailed right past it. "I'm going a different way. Back to Toscano," she said. "You think that he found Fox and was paying him for information about Elizabeth?"

"It's a reasonable theory, isn't it?"

"I don't know. That's a lot to base on two guys having a drink in a bar."

"Maybe. But we have to start somewhere."

"And I know just where that is," Sofia said. "We're gonna confirm whether or not our William Fox is the same one who worked for Elizabeth's husband."

I held up my hand. "Oh no, you don't. If Sutton

finds out, I'm dead. Not to mention what my brother will do to us both for getting involved in this mess. I've already trespassed at the club, crossed a police line, and pocketed evidence. And I'm tired of lying to people, Sofe—" At which point my sister-in-law let out a giant yawn. "Oh, I'm sorry. Am I boring you?"

She grinned and shook her head. "Well, actually, you are, but I'm also tired. C'mon, Vic. What harm would it do to talk to William Fox?"

"He'd probably run right to Toscano with it. You said yourself that we need to watch out for him."

"I said that *you* need to watch out for him. He doesn't know who I am. But you have a point." Sofia made a sudden turn onto an unfamiliar road, her eyes fixed straight ahead while she spoke.

It wasn't until we passed a sign for Dover that I finally caught on. We were stopped at a light, giving me a clear view of the driver in front of us, and my stomach sank. "Sofia Theresa Delmonico Rienzi, are you following that car?"

Her thick-lashed brown eyes widened in a semblance of innocence. "What car?"

I pointed. "You know what car. The one in front of us with the little old man driving."

"What little old man?"

"Cut it out, Sofe. There's only one car and one old man; he's got crazy hair and he's stopped at the same light we are. Really, what do you plan to do? Track him to his house and ambush as him as he gets out of the car?"

"Hmmm." She raised an eyebrow. "Not a bad idea."

"It's a terrible idea! Turn around right now and get us back to the Garden State Parkway so we can go home."

"Look, now we know he's the Dover Township William Fox, right? I just want to see where he lives. Maybe look around a bit." She tugged on the brim of her cap. "After all, we're dressed for it."

"And I suppose you've forgotten what happened to us last time?"

"Oh, last time was no big deal," Sofia said, dismissing me with a lazy wave of her hand.

"No big deal? Do I have to remind you that we were almost killed?" I shivered at the memory of how my last "adventure" had ended. "I should never have gotten myself into this. I don't care if Dr. Chickie spends the next twenty years in Rahway Prison."

"Yes, you do. And you can't help yourself; you want to solve the puzzle." She leaned close to the steering wheel and squinted through the front window. "YRB-763. Write it down."

Though I was skeptical, I wrote down the number anyway. The light changed, and we both moved through the intersection, Sofia keeping a respectable distance behind Fox's car. "You really think Danny's going to run a check on his license for you?"

She grinned. "If I ask nicely enough. And I know lots of ways to ask nice."

At that moment, Fox put on his left signal, and Sofia increased her speed slightly. "This area's more residential," she said. "He's gotta live around here somewhere."

I shook my head. "This is crazy. It's a risk. What if he's a nut job?"

"He's one little old guy. I can take him myself if I have to." She hesitated. "Vic, I wouldn't be doing this if I thought there was any real danger. Especially now."

"What do you mean, 'especially now'?"

She hesitated before she spoke. "Just that Danny and I are really working on things, and I don't want to him mad at me."

We passed two residential blocks, but Fox's signal still blinked. "I don't want him mad at me, either—that's why I think we should turn around and go home."

"We will, as soon as we get a look at Fox's house. You can learn a lot about a person that way. That is, if he ever makes this turn."

When Fox finally turned, Sofia slowed down, putting an extra car length between our vehicles. He lived only a few houses in; we waited until he pulled into his driveway, and then drove past slowly. "Watch out the back window," Sofia said. "Let me know when he goes in. Do you think he noticed us?"

"It doesn't seem like it. He just went inside," I said. "And now the lights are going off."

"Great." Sofia made a k-turn and we cruised past the house to get a better look. "He's not exactly livin' large, is he?" she said.

"No." I looked at the sad little house with its missing roof shingles and broken sidewalk, the plastic flowers stuck in a window box. There were old newspapers, still in their plastic bags, littering his front walk. "The poor guy," I whispered. "If he's the same William Fox who worked for Merriman, he sure has come down in the world."

"Well, that's what we need to find out."

"Don't you think we've found out enough for tonight? Let's get out of here before anybody sees us."

But Sofia was already parking the car. Facing the intersection, I noted, no doubt for a clean getaway. "Just hang on a minute, okay?" she said. "There's nothing illegal about sitting in a car on a quiet street on a summer evening."

"Yes, but you won't leave it at that. In about thirty seconds you're going to suggest that we get out of the car on this lovely summer evening and snoop around this poor guy's house."

"You say that like it's a bad thing," she said, turning off the ignition.

"Guess what, Sofe? Trespassing *is* a bad thing!"

But as usual, Sofia wasn't listening. "Look," she said, "His garage door is open. And notice how far the garage is from the house."

"Not as far as we're gonna be when you start that car back up. Let's get out of here, please."

"All in good time, my pretty." She handed me my ball cap. "Put this on."

I groaned. "What could possibly be in that old man's garage that would help us with this case?"

"That's what we're here to find out. Would you mind getting the flashlight out of the glove box, please?"

At the mention of the flashlight, I had a terrible sense of déjà vu. The last time we'd, um, *explored*, using Sofia's flashlight, we'd ended up facing down an angry cop. "I will get the flashlight," I said, "but I'm not leaving this car until we come up with a reasonably plausible story for why we're here if we get caught." I set the flashlight on the seat and turned to my sister-in-law. "Well, Watson?"

"First, I'm not Watson. Second, I have a story all ready. Put your hat on and I'll tell you."

I sighed and put the ball cap back on, tucking my ponytail inside. "Okay, boss. Disguise in place."

She nodded. "Very good. So here's what we'll say if William Fox or any of his neighbors sees us on the property: We're lost."

"*We're lost*? That's it? And how do we explain the black ninja clothes and hats? The flashlight? Our presence in this old guy's garage at ten thirty at night?" I pointed to her dashboard, my voice rising. "And look, a state-of-the-art navigation system. I'm pretty sure *we're lost* isn't going to cut it!"

"Will you keep your voice down? Look, we can sit here all night and argue or we can learn something. I'm thinking William Fox is in a deep snooze by now. That garage is wide open; he parked in the driveway, so we can duck behind his car. We'll do it fast—in, out, and back in the car. Five minutes, tops." She held out her hand. "Are you in?"

"I'm in, but I'm not shaking on it," I said, slapping her hand away. I looked up and down the deserted street. There were few lights on around the neighboring houses, and no street lights. Maybe we could take a chance on a quick look in that garage.

"C'mon," she said. "And be quiet when you close the car door."

My stomach churned as we stepped out of the car. *I wish I hadn't sampled so much of that veal,* I thought. Sofia led the way, staying to the sidewalk until we came to the apron of Fox's driveway. The overhead garage door was stuck in place, and for a moment I indulged in frightening fantasies of us being trapped inside or, worse, getting whacked on the head with that door. Sofia, who knew me well, grabbed my arm. "It's okay," she whispered. "We'll go quick. I won't turn the light on till we're all the way inside."

Our sneakers crunched on the loose gravel, setting my heart pounding. We ducked behind his car and slipped inside the garage. I scurried behind Sofia, who trained her light inside. It was clear why Fox had parked in his driveway: there wasn't an inch of room in the garage. Stacks of newspapers and magazines covered two of the walls. Open cardboard boxes of tools, chipped dishes, and all manner of junk lined the cement floor. There were old bicycles, garden tools, and a rusted red wagon. Had it belonged to one of his children? The sight of it filled me with sadness and not a little remorse. We were intruding, not only on his property, but into his personal life.

"Holy crap," Sophia whispered, running the light around the walls and floor. "This place is a hoarder's paradise."

I grabbed her arm. "Clearly we're not going to learn anything here, Sofe. Let's just *go*."

"Not yet, Vic. Can't you hang on a minute?" She

aimed the light at the far wall, revealing several rect-angular objects. "C'mon, let's check these out."

As we got closer, the rectangles proved to be plaques, haphazardly tacked to the back wall. I squinted. Each one bore a logo with a stylized M. "They're from Merri-man," I whispered. "Awards of some kind."

"So, he's the right William Fox," Sofia said. She shifted the light. "This one is for twenty-five years of service."

"He must have started there as a young man," I said.

"Think about it, Vic," Sofia said. "You work at a place for all those years and suddenly somebody pushes you out. That's gotta be tough. Then your whole personal life falls apart. You'd be mighty pissed—maybe even angry enough to kill somebody."

"But why wait twenty years?" I whispered.

"What does it matter? He was *there* that night," she insisted.

"So were a whole lot of other people." I looked around nervously. "Turn off the light so we can get out of here, please."

She linked her arm through mine and grinned. "C'mon, scaredy-cat. Sofia will take care of you."

I ducked under the lowered garage door with a ham-mering heart and a disturbed conscience. We sprinted for Sofia's car. I had my door open, one foot already inside, when I heard his voice.

"Are you ladies looking for me?" William Fox asked.

Sofia and I turned slowly, simultaneously, just as though we'd choreographed the move. Fox stood on the sidewalk in his pajamas and bathrobe, his hair so wild I expected him to begin a lecture on relativity. I braced myself for the inquisition: *Who were we? What were we doing here? Did we know trespassing was a crime?* But instead, William Fox did a curious thing—he smiled.

"Please excuse my attire," he said. "I sometimes like a nice breath of air before I go to sleep."

And if he'd decided to take that breath about two minutes earlier, my sister-in-law and I might be occupying the back of a police car right now. But I was holding my breath too tightly to even exhale with relief.

"So," Fox said, "is there anything I can help you with?"

Gee, I don't know, William. Unless you'd like to confess to the murder of Elizabeth Merriman. "I—" I began to say, but Sofia pressed sharply on the toe of my sneaker with her dainty foot.

"We're so sorry to disturb you," Sofia said. "But we heard you speak at the meeting tonight. And—you'll forgive us if we don't introduce ourselves?"

At this, William Fox beamed. "Of course," he said, nodding. "Are you looking for a sponsor; is that it?"

"I'm not," Sofia said, beaming back brightly, "but my friend here is."

I turned to Sofia indignantly, my mouth open wide enough for Dr. Chickie to do some follow-up work. Still smiling, she said, "You don't have to be embarrassed. Mr.—er, William—understands."

"I certainly do," he said. "But I'm already sponsoring a candidate." He cocked his head and seemed to be studying my face. *Oh, please don't be a reader of mysteries*, I thought. My photo was on the back of all my books. But when he spoke, his voice was gentle. "You know," he said, "at the meeting, they did put out a call for those who need sponsors—"

"She's shy," Sofia interrupted.

"I understand," William Fox said. "But it would probably be best for your friend to attend another meeting."

"No!" I said, my voice panicky. "I mean, thank you, really, you've been very kind about us showing up unannounced"—I shot Sofia a look—"but I think I'd like to go about this my own way."

He nodded. "Well, we all have to find our way, don't we? And now I'll bid you ladies good night." He turned, lifted one hand, and shuffled back down the sidewalk.

My hand shook as I reached for the car door. The minute I pulled it shut, I turned to Sofia. "Are you crazy?" I exploded. "You just identified me as an alcoholic!"

"It's anonymous, Vic. Calm down." Sofia started the car and smoothly pulled away from the curb, her hands steady on the wheel.

"You're not even nervous," I said. "It's unnatural."

She shrugged. "I'd make a great cop. Wish your brother saw it that way." She glanced in the mirror. "Is that Fox still outside?"

"Who else with Albert Einstein hair would be standing outside in his bathrobe and pajamas?"

"Ooh, sarcasm. Watch it there, SIL."

"Sorry," I said with a sigh. "I just feel bad about doing this tonight. The meeting, snooping in his garage—all of it."

I dug the card from my pocket, my eye drawn to one of the twelve steps on the list: "We made a searching and fearless moral inventory of ourselves." Stung by the words, I wondered what I'd find in a moral inventory of my own. As I watched William Fox's figure grow smaller in the distance, I regretted ever getting involved with the mystery of Elizabeth Merriman's death.

Chapter Twelve

On Saturday, there was a small item in the paper about Merriman's wake and funeral. I toyed briefly with the idea of going, but since my "moral inventory" was coming up short these days, I changed my mind. I'd have no reason to go there except my own curiosity. How might Toscano act, for example? Would he sit up front as "family," meeting and greeting people who'd come to pay their respects? Or would some long-lost relative appear to fulfill that role? Would William Fox show up? Belmont Club employees? Dr. Chickie? In my books, Bernardo often attends the funerals of the victims, and usually learns something incriminating from one of the mourners. I thought about my worldly-wise detective in his linen suits and trademark Panama hat; lately I'd begun to wish he were real, as I could use all the help I could get.

I biked down to the restaurant along the boardwalk so I could lose myself in the sight and sounds of the ocean, because it often it helped me think. Elizabeth Merriman had been dead a week. I had a pretty good idea of when, how, and where she died. Dr. Chickie and William Fox each had motive and a history with the victim. Kate Bridges, while no fan of Elizabeth's, didn't appear to have a clear connection to her or an obvious motive. And Jack Toscano, who by all reports was close to the victim, may have gained by her death. All four were on the scene that evening. Had one of them killed her? Or was there someone else at the reception, a staffer or a guest still unknown to us, who took an opportunity to murder an old enemy? Because one thing was clear: Not one person surrounding this case had a good thing to say about Elizabeth Merriman. And that left the field wide open.

I brought my bike around to the back of the restaurant, as Nonna had indicated that my battered old Schwinn was an eyesore and I shouldn't leave it in front. I also wanted to see if Cal's truck was in the parking lot, but the only vehicles were Lori's minivan and Tim's motorcycle. So Tim was riding it again, most likely as a way to show off for Lacey. I came in through the kitchen, where Tim was working on lunch prep.

"Hey," he said, without looking up from his work.

I peeked over his shoulder to see him using a meat rub made with Nonna's dried herbs. "Short ribs, right?"

"Yup."

"Are you making them over orzo? With carrots? I love them that way."

"Right again." He turned and gave me a grin. "You're learning, Vic."

"I try," I said, but my cheeks were warm from the

compliment. "Maybe one of these days I can actually cook something."

"Maybe. But in the meantime, you mind heading to the pantry and getting me more dried thyme? You know what thyme looks like, right?"

"Of course I do," I lied. All the dried stuff in Nonna's pantry looked alike to me; in fact, back in May, I'd been convinced there was something more menacing than cooking herbs hanging from the rafters of that room. "Be right back," I called, taking my purse with me. (It had my phone in it.)

Once inside, I was struck by a series of images. Tim and I as teenagers, stealing a kiss in the corner. Tim and I as adults, spending a night in here that took us both by surprise. *No time for this, Vic.* I slipped my phone from my purse and searched "thyme." Once I had the image up, I studied the dried bunches of herbs and grabbed a handful of the likeliest candidate.

"Here it is," I said, setting it down next to Tim.

He turned to face me, his hands on his hips, but smiling. "You looked it up on your phone, didn't you?"

"I may have." Some treacherous impulse had me smiling back, so I forced myself to ask a question to which I didn't really want an answer. "So, how are things going with Lacey?"

"They're movin' along, thanks." He crushed the thyme between his fingers and added it to the blend.

Frankly, I didn't want to think about how far things might have moved since the day Lacey had shown up in the dining room, so a second change of subject was called for. "Has my grandmother been in yet?"

"Been and gone. Just long enough to lecture me on the perfect spice proportions for the rub, how deep a sear I should put on the ribs, and how long I should let the sauce reduce."

"Sorry I missed it," I said, putting on an apron. "Is Lori out front?"

"Yeah. I think she's working on tables, so you might want to get the coffee set up."

I sighed, wondering if filling the coffee basket was as close as I'd get to preparing a dish at the Casa Lido. "Hey, girl," I called.

"Hi, Vic," Lori said. She moved swiftly from table to table with place settings wrapped in linen. "You wanna do coffee?"

"I'm already on it." But I was still holding an unopened coffee packet when my attention was drawn to a white square of paper on the floor. Nonna would go crazy if she saw trash in the dining room. But on closer inspection, the paper wasn't trash.

It was a card rimmed in gold; on the front was an image of St. Francis with a line from his writings: *Grant that I may not seek to be consoled as to console.* This was a memorial card, the kind one might find at wakes; my grandmother collected these things like trading cards. Before I even turned it over, I knew whose name would be on the back. I tucked it into the pocket of my pants and hurriedly untied my apron.

"Cover for me, L. J., would you?" I called to Lori. "I have to run out for a minute."

"Sure, Vic. Everything okay?"

"I hope so," I muttered as I headed out the doors. I

grabbed my bike from the back and got moving. My parents' home on Seventh Street, the house where I'd grown up, was only a few blocks away. It was a classic seaside Victorian, but like so many of that era had been broken up into two large apartments. Nonna occupied the third floor, and my mom and dad lived in the first and second. I dropped my bike next to the front steps, not even stopping to admire the wraparound porch, where I'd spent many an afternoon curled up with Carolyn Keene and Agatha Christie. Instead I walked up the driveway and headed to the back stairway that led to my grandmother's apartment. Not for the first time, I wondered how much longer she could handle these stairs.

When she saw me at her door, she frowned, but that's how she normally greeted me. She was wearing summer slacks and a lightweight cardigan, both black. Her hair was styled and sprayed, and her lipstick was fresh. She was not dressed for a morning at home.

"What are you doing here?" she asked. "You're supposed to be at the restaurant."

"I came to ask you something." I followed her into the kitchen and took a seat. She tied on an apron, and without asking ("You only ask sick people") she dropped a plate of biscotti in front of me and ran water into the base of her espresso pot. Since resistance was futile, I took one of my favorites, a chocolate cookie with hazelnuts.

"So ask me." She kept her back to me, pressing ground espresso into the metal pot.

"Would you sit down, please?"

She set the pot over a low flame and sat down across from me, suspicion etched into every line of her face. "I'm sitting," she said.

I took the card from my pocket and held it out to her. "Nonna, what is this?"

She snatched it back from me and slipped it into her apron pocket. "It's mine."

"I know it's yours. It's from Elizabeth Merriman's wake." I gestured to her clothes. "And you're in your funeral clothes. What were you doing there?"

"What was I doing there?" She threw her hands up at the foolishness of such a question. "Paying my respects. That's what you do when someone dies."

"Right," I said. "When you know the deceased. And I heard you call her Elisabetta, so I think you must have known her. Did you, Nonna?"

Saved from answering by the boiling espresso pot, she rose quickly, took a potholder, and removed the pot from the stove. She poured us each a cup, went to the refrigerator, took out a quart of milk, and set the sugar bowl on the table, all with maddening slowness. When she finally sat, she shifted her eyes from me and she fumbled in her apron pocket, no doubt holding on to that card for dear life. "Please answer me," I said softly.

"Here's your answer: You should pay attention in the kitchen the way you pay attention to things that are not your business." She stirred sugar into her cup, took a sip, and nodded. Her coffee was always perfect.

I finished my cookie and drank my coffee slowly, hoping the silence would pressure her to talk. But of course, I was the one who caved. "If you know something important about Elizabeth Merriman, Nonna, I wish you'd tell me about it."

"Why should I tell you anything?"

I took a gamble. "Well, you can tell me or you can tell Prosecutor Sutton."

Though her look was skeptical, my nonna is not one to take chances. "All right," she said with resignation. "I guess it's time." She took the card from her pocket and set it down in front of her, pointing to Merriman's name. "Her real name was Elisabetta Caprio. We grew up in the old neighborhood together."

"She was Italian?" I remembered Merriman's words when we were introduced: *So you're a Rienzi.* She was connecting me to my family—and to Nonna.

My grandmother nodded, and when she spoke, her words were as bitter as the greens in her garden. "But she hid it. Like something she was ashamed of. She wanted to make herself into somebody else."

"I think she succeeded," I said. "I thought she was old money, maybe English or Dutch background. I mean, she used her married name, and her coloring is fair." I remembered her cloudy blue eyes.

Nonna nodded. "She was blond when she was young. But she was embarrassed of her parents. Their dark skin. Their accents."

"So she turned herself into the country-club lady," I said.

"She didn't start out that way," she said. "When I knew her, she was the only child in a strict Catholic family. Her father kept her under lock and key. But she was stubborn, headstrong."

"Not surprised," I said.

But my grandmother didn't appear to be listening to me. Her face was thoughtful, looking back to a past I knew little about. "And she wanted what she wanted," Nonna said.

"What *did* she want, Nonna?"

My grandmother's face cracked in what might have been a smile. "His name was Tommy Romano. He was in my year in school; Elisabetta was younger."

I couldn't resist the next question. "Did you have a crush on him, too?"

She frowned and waved me away like a bothersome sand fly. "No. I was already going with your grandfather."

Which would not necessarily preclude a crush on another boy. But I wisely kept that thought to myself. "Tell me about Tommy."

She took off her glasses, rubbed the bridge of her nose, and this time smiled for real. Just for a second, I had a glimpse of the younger Giulietta. "All the girls were crazy about him," she said. "He was tall, with curly black hair and blue eyes." She shook her head. "Those eyes were the most beautiful blue. My mama, your great-grandma Ida, used to say they were *come il cielo veneziano*—like the Venetian sky."

I rested my chin in my hands, watching Nonna's

face as she talked about Tommy, who sounded a bit like Tim in looks, though Tim's eyes were gray. "So, he was the neighborhood heartthrob?" I asked.

Nonna nodded. "Yes, but he only had eyes for Elisabetta. And she for him. She was sixteen; he was three years older, already out of high school. She would sneak out of her house to see him." She shook her head. "It was . . . sad."

"Sad? It sounds romantic." I put my hand on her arm. "What happened with the two of them?"

"Well, he left for the war in Korea, December of 1951." She paused in the story and looked briefly out the window.

"You remember what month he left?" I was having a hard time believing that Nonna's feelings for the dashing Tommy were purely platonic.

"I remember because the boardwalk was decorated for Christmas. We had holly and greens all over the restaurant." As she spoke, I was imagining the Casa Lido in the 1950s, with its dark wood paneling and exposed brick, thinking it probably looked much the same as it did today. "So, we said good-bye to Tommy. Then a month later I said good-bye to your grandpa." She stopped again, shook her head slowly. "Men and their wars," she said quietly.

"What happened after that, Nonna?" I was hanging onto each word, imagining it all, and wishing I had some paper to take notes for my own story about Isabella.

She turned the memorial card and looked at the image of St. Francis. "She came to see my mama. Your great-grandma was a kind of nurse, and even a mid-wife sometimes for people in the neighborhood who couldn't afford the doctor. Anyway, Elisabetta knew she was pregnant and came to her for help. I think she came to her hoping that my mama would give her something." She stopped speaking and looked down at the table.

"You mean to end the pregnancy," I prompted.

She nodded. "There were women in those days that would do that, before it was legal. But not my mama. Instead she counseled her to tell her parents. She offered to go with her, even. But Elisabetta refused, said that if my mother wouldn't help her, she would find someone who would." Nonna stood suddenly. "Would you like some water? Even with the coffee, I'm dry from talking."

And it was no wonder. In my entire life, I'd never had such a long—or personal—conversation with my prickly grandmother. "Yes, thanks," I said.

She brought us our water and sat down, still with that faraway look on her face. She took an absent sip and then turned the glass in her hand. "Two months later, we heard Tommy was killed. His mother and father and little sister were devastated. The whole town mourned him. And not long after that, the Romanos moved away."

"What about Elisabetta?" Funny how the iron-willed Elizabeth Merriman, even in death, commanded less sympathy than the frightened, pregnant girl who had so loved Tommy Romano. They were two different women and I couldn't reconcile them.

She lifted one thin shoulder. "People said she took it hard. For a long time I didn't see her. Until—"

"Until when, Nonna?"

She put her glasses back on and looked at me. "Until the night she tried to kill herself."

Chapter Thirteen

"She tried to kill herself?" *And if she tried it then, might she have tried it now?*

My grandmother nodded. "One night, not long after we got the news about Tommy, I was walking home from the restaurant, on the boardwalk side." She shook her head. "It was May, but still windy and chilly. And you know the rock jetty down by the fishermen's beach?"

My head moved in a mechanical nod. I knew what she was about to say. "You saw her standing out there, didn't you?"

"Yes." She took another sip of water. "At first I couldn't tell who it was, but I could see her blond hair. I ran out on to the beach and climbed the jetty. I could tell she was thinking about jumping."

My grandmother's words were like tiny lights illuminating my dark, cluttered brain. If Merriman had been murdered, did the killer know about her past? Was it poetic irony or coincidence that Merriman met her end, more than sixty years later, on a beach? I imagined the young Elizabeth poised to jump into the sea. How terrified—and how desperate—she must have been. "And you stopped her."

"I grabbed her by the arm. I told her what she was doing was a sin. Taking two lives." She stopped, shook her head, and stood up abruptly. She cleared our coffee cups and water glasses, pausing at the sink. I sat tensely, waiting for her to finish.

"By then Elisabetta was showing, but to most people she just looked like she had gained weight. But it wouldn't be long before everybody knew." She looked at me, her eyes sad and serious behind her glasses. "It was different in those days."

"I know. What did you do?"

"I talked her out of it and dragged her home with me. Mama called her parents, said she was staying with us for the night. And that's when your great-grandmother came up with a plan." Her voice hardened, and she moved her water glass to one side, studied the pattern in the tablecloth. This part of the story was clearly troubling to her. I took a chance and spoke.

"What was the plan, Nonna?"

My grandmother, who is not the dramatic type, released a sigh worthy of my mother. "Your great-grandma told Elisabetta's mother that our cousin in Atlantic City needed help running her boardinghouse for the summer season. This cousin was looking for reliable girls to clean the rooms."

"Was that true? Did you have a cousin with a boardinghouse in Atlantic City?"

"Yes, my mother's cousin Antoinette; she asked every summer for me to come. But they could never spare me at the restaurant."

"Until that summer."

"Yes." She smoothed out a spot on the tablecloth. "I didn't want to go, but it would work only if I went along. I would go to the boardinghouse, and Elisabetta would go to a charity home for pregnant girls. She would learn some skills there, and when the time came, have her baby."

"And Elisabetta's parents let her go? Even the father?"

"Like so many families in that neighborhood, Elisabetta's parents were poor. They saw a chance to have some money come in."

"But she wasn't working."

"No, she wasn't. But I was." She looked out the window again.

"Oh, Nonna—did your money go to *her* family? That's so unfair."

In a rare gesture of affection, she put her hand over mine. "Victoria, it was different then. It was, I guess, like a duty to help your *paesani*, those who came from your country. My family was doing well. We had the restaurant; her family had nothing. Those people would never have let her go to Atlantic City alone. It was the only way."

I tried to imagine myself at nineteen, away from home, away from my friends, working a whole summer for somebody else. "Still, Nonna, it was a lot to ask of a young girl."

She nodded. "It was, but my mama felt strongly

that this baby deserved a chance at life, and, for that matter, so did Elisabetta."

"You saved her life twice, you know." I felt a sudden surge of anger at Elizabeth Merriman. Had she understood what my grandmother had done for her? What my great-grandmother had done? Had she known what she owed my family? The life she ended up with—a life of privilege and power—was in no small measure due to the sacrifice of these two women. "So, you went there together," I said. "And she had her baby?"

She nodded. "That August. The charity home arranged for an adoption."

"She gave the baby up?" As I spoke, my anger at Elizabeth faded.

"Yes. But of course she didn't know where the baby ended up. It was all a secret in those days."

But it's not secret now, I thought. "What about Tommy's family? Did they know they had a grandchild?"

"I don't know. When Elisabetta got back on that bus with me to come home, she was dead silent. I tried to ask her questions, but she wouldn't answer me."

"Do you know if the baby was a boy or a girl? Did it have a name?"

Nonna shook her head. "She said only one thing about the child: that it had Tommy's beautiful blue eyes. And then she cried. But once she wiped her eyes, I never saw her cry again."

"Did you stay in touch?"

My grandmother snorted. "She avoided me like the

plague. Once she was working for her husband, she pretended she didn't know me."

"How awful."

"Not really, Victoria. I knew her secret. In her mind, that gave me power to hurt her." She pushed away from the table and brought her glass to the sink. "I've kept this secret for more than sixty years," she said. "And now she's dead, it's a relief to tell it."

"Thank you for trusting me with this."

"So now I've told you, and I hope it wasn't a mistake. I don't see how what happened all those years ago will make a difference or help Chickie Natale. As far as I'm concerned, that one caused his own problems." She fixed her eyes on mine. "Did someone kill Elisabetta?"

"I think so, Nonna. And I think that's what the police believe, too."

She nodded, crossed herself, and slipped the memorial card back into her apron pocket.

I left my grandmother with the promise that I would tell Elizabeth's story only if I had to. On the way back to the restaurant, my mind spun faster than the wheels of my bike. What my grandmother said was true—in the 1950s, Elizabeth would have no way of knowing who had adopted her child. But things had changed in the intervening years. I knew little about adoption laws (*note to self: put Sofia on this one*) but it was much easier now for adopted children to find their birth parents. Elisabetta's baby would be about sixty years old now. And if it could be proven that he or she was her natural child, that person would stand to inherit a fortune. And that raised a question so obvious it should have been framed in blinking neon lights: Was Jack Toscano Elizabeth Merriman's long lost son?

"Wow." Sofia let out a long breath on that one syllable. "That is some story."

We were sitting in Sofia's office at the back of the dance studio; we'd each finished our workdays and had our sore feet propped on either side of her desk.

A water bottle and an open container of yogurt sat in front of her. "She must have been terrified." Sofia said. "And desperate."

"Those were exactly the words that came to my mind. But I'm still shocked that Nonna ended up with that responsibility." I shook my head. "And it makes me furious at Merriman."

"But to have to give up her baby, Vic," she said softly. "How awful."

"I know. But young Elisabetta and the adult Elizabeth Merriman seem to be two distinct people."

Sofia pointed her yogurt spoon at me. "*You* see her that way, and that's a mistake. She's both the scared pregnant teenager and the miserable old lady. The question is: Which of them is the one this case turns on?"

"You're right, and I think once we figure that out, we'll have a better idea of who wanted her dead."

"But do you really think that Elizabeth Merriman's long-lost kid showed up and shoved her over that seawall to collect an inheritance?" She shook her head.

"I'm having trouble wrapping my mind around that one."

"C'mon, Sofe. You're usually the skeptic."

"I don't know, Vic. To kill your own mother for money?"

"Okay, do you read the paper? It happens all the time. It's horrible, but there it is. People might do anything where that much money's involved. Danny even said that about Dr. Chickie."

At the mention of my brother's name, a pained look appeared on Sofia's face. I held up my hand. "I'm not trying to introduce the subject of Danny. Really."

"I know." She looked sad for a moment, then straightened up in her chair and rapped on the folder. "Right now we have things other than my personal life to take care of." She grabbed a pencil and a legal pad. "First," she said, "we need to find out the name of that charity hospital. Was it *in* Atlantic City?"

"Nonna was a bit vague on that point. But what good would it do to find out about that hospital? It probably closed years ago, and will we be able get our hands on sixty-year-old medical records?"

"I was thinking there might be somebody who worked there who would remember Elizabeth."

"They'd be over ninety. At the very least," I said.

But Sofia was stubborn. "I still say it's a place to start." She thought for a moment. "I can't shake the feeling that this case has deep roots. Even if I could imagine Dr. Chickie as a murderer, which I can't, his involvement with Merriman is too recent. I think that the reason she was killed goes way back."

"I agree. How far back? Back to Elisabetta Caprio, pregnant with Tommy Romano's baby? Back to the widowed CEO who reinvents herself as a country-club matron? Or back six months, to the day Jack Toscano showed up in Belmont Beach?"

Sofia's head snapped up. "He's the right age, isn't he? What color are his eyes?"

"I've never seen them." My mouth opened ever so slowly as the light dawned. "The dark glasses. Oh my God, he said he'd had surgery, *eye* surgery. Merriman had bad eyes. Can you inherit eye conditions?"

Sofia was writing furiously. "I think so. Something else to look up." She stopped writing, but still gripped her pencil. "Hey, how old did you say the crazy pastry chef was?"

"Kate Bridges? I don't know exactly. She looked maybe late fifties or so. It was hard to tell with all the makeup." I flashed on Kate's painted face, remembered the dark brows and false eyelashes—and something else, as well. "Her eyes are blue, Sofe."

"Now we're getting somewhere."

"But having the same eye color can be coincidental, and it doesn't necessarily prove anything. The baby's eye color might have changed, and, unfortunately, we can't go around snipping people's hair or swabbing their spit for DNA tests."

"Too bad."

I grinned at Sofia. "I could just see you with a pair of scissors and ziplock bags, sneaking up behind our suspects."

She pointed her pencil at me. "Hey, don't give me

ideas." She stopped to take a small spoonful of yogurt and a sip of water, but it was an effort for her. She seemed thinner to me, and she still lacked her usual healthy color.

"You still feeling crappy?" I asked.

She nodded. "The heat's been messing with my appetite." She looked away from me, her glance falling on the red folder. "Oh my gosh. I almost forgot this." She pulled a sheet from the folder and handed it to me. "The story about Elizabeth knocked everything else out of my head. Do you recognize him?"

I was holding a mug shot of a long-haired bearded man of about thirty. It wasn't a particularly intelligent face; he was sporting a purple shiner on one eye and an expression of hurt surprise. He'd been arrested for assault in 2010. I handed the paper back. "It's none other than Dennis Doyle, the happy bridegroom. And it also explains something Brenda Natale said the night of the wedding—that Dennis had some trouble a couple of years ago."

"So, what do you think?" Sofia asked.

"Are you asking if it's important that he's got a record? I'm not sure. He struck me as a great big teddy bear. Roberta leads him around by the nose."

She tapped the mug shot. "But he was arrested for assault. That means he's got a history of violence."

"But I'd like to know if there was a conviction. What were the circumstances?" I made a note to ask Danny, but whether he would check on it for me was a crapshoot. "He's got a black eye in the mug shot, so maybe he was defending himself."

"Maybe. But we can't ignore the simple fact that a guy with an assault record was on the scene of a murder."

"True. And he *did* make a point to tell me that he and his in-laws left that reception at eleven thirty. He claimed that Elizabeth was still in her office when they pulled out of the parking lot. But Sally the bartender said she saw Dr. Chickie at eleven forty-five."

"Now, that's interesting. Did he lie? Or was he confused about the time?" She looked at the mug shot again. "Dennis has blue eyes, Vic."

"Too young to be her son."

Sofia threw me a *do you really think I'm that stupid?* look. "I was thinking grandson, Vic. What if he tracked her down and knew she was rich?"

"But that would mean that one of Dennis's parents is the missing child."

"Exactly," Sofia said. "I wonder if one of them was adopted."

Then I remembered something. "I don't know about that, but Brenda did mention that the dad is dead. I'm not sure if that's significant or not."

"Hmm. It might be," Sofia said. "Let's say the Doyle father *is* Elizabeth's kid. Maybe he never tried to find his birth mother. Or he knew about her but didn't want to see her. But Dennis is curious, and once his dad passes, he does a little investigating himself. Don't you see, Vic? Losing his father might have prompted him to find out more about his history."

"Possibly. But this is all based on assumptions: The Doyle father is the missing child. Dennis Doyle is violent enough to kill an old lady. He has a wedding reception in the very club his biological grandmother presides over. He sees an opportunity to get rich and leads his own grandmother down the beach path to her death. Then he gives himself an alibi for eleven thirty."

"But this could all be true!" Sofia insisted.

"Maybe."

"Okay, how do you explain the blue eyes? I don't know a whole lot about genetics, but I do know that blue eyes aren't as common as brown. Yet we've got a blue-eyed victim, and at least two people—Kate Bridges and Doyle—both with blue eyes and both on the scene. If Toscano's eyes are blue, he makes a third."

I shook my head. "It's still all supposition. And wild guesses."

Sofia slapped her palm down on the desk. "And that's how we'll eventually get to the truth—by taking crazy guesses. Can we really ignore Dennis Doyle's arrest or the color of his eyes?"

"No. But we need more information."

"Exactly. So you'll talk to Dennis?"

It's not like I hadn't seen this coming. "Oh, sure, Sofe. And I know just what I'll ask him. 'Hey, Dennis, can you fill me in on that assault arrest? Is one of your parents adopted? Oh, and did you shove Elizabeth Merriman off a two-story platform?' That'll be a fruitful interview."

"So maybe you won't talk to Dennis. But what about Mrs. Natale? You can go there with the excuse you're helping Dr. Chickie."

"By accusing her son-in-law of murder? How is that helping?"

She patted my hand. "I trust you to be subtle."

"Well, I guess it couldn't hurt to talk to her. She might be disposed to talk about Dennis's family. And his 'trouble,'" I said. I also might learn about the relationship between Dennis and his new father-in-law. Was it possible that he could have killed Elizabeth to protect Dr. Chickie? Without a father himself, he might have grown close to his father-in-law. Or maybe his motives weren't so pure. Maybe he didn't like the idea of his name being linked to that of an accused embezzler, and decided to eliminate the accuser.

But before I could tell Sofia, she stood up abruptly, her face deathly pale. She swallowed hard and held up a finger. "Excuse me. Be right back," she said, and hurried out of her office toward the bathroom. I gave her a minute and then followed. Outside the door, I heard retching sounds. Feeling sneaky and dishonest, I pressed my ear to it, heard the toilet flush, water running in the sink, then a soft sound that might have been crying. My own stomach lurched in sympathy.

"Sofie, you okay?" I finally called, but she didn't answer. *The hell with privacy*, I thought, and pushed open the door. She was brushing her teeth gingerly, as though she didn't want to gag. She rinsed her mouth and looked over at me. "Are you okay?" I asked again.

She nodded, but she was still pale. She straightened up, gripping the sides of the sink. "Just in case you're wondering, I don't have an eating disorder."

"I know that." I put my hand on her shoulder. "You look like crap. And you're not the type. Are you sick?"

Sofia turned her face to me; there were circles under her eyes and her face was drawn. But there was a ghost of a grin on her face. "You're a little slow on the uptake there, detective."

"Oh my God!" My hand flew to my mouth. "You're not—"

Sofia pushed a strand of hair off her sweaty forehead, looked me straight in the eye, and nodded slowly. "I am."

Chapter Fourteen

$\mathcal{A}$t the news, a rush of feeling spread through my entire body. My cheeks got warm; my hands and feet tingled. A baby—there was going to be a baby, and I would be an aunt. But behind the joy was a whisper of loss: *You wish it were you*, it said, and then faded to silence.

I went straight to her, wrapping my arms around her thin frame. "I'm so glad," I said, my throat tight. I stepped back and wiped my eyes. "Some solver of mysteries I am. I thought you had a stomach bug."

She wet her face again, dried it with a towel, and shook her head. "Not me. I think I knew from the moment of conception."

"How far are you?"

"About seven weeks."

I counted backward and grinned. "So you and Danny did get close after our little adventure in May." I grabbed both her hands. "Oh my God, what did Danny say? Is he over the moon? I'm so happy for you guys, I can't stand it! Good Lord, can you imagine Nicolina and Frank as grandparents?" The longer I babbled, the stonier Sofia's face grew. I dropped her hands, thinking I was squeezing them too hard. "Sofie? Are you okay? I mean, Danny's happy about the baby, right?"

"Danny doesn't know about the baby, Vic. My parents know. And now you, but that's all." She took one of my hands back and gripped it. "And you can't tell him. You have to promise me."

"Of course. It's not my place to tell him, but—"

"But what?"

"He's your husband."

"We're separated. We're still trying to work things out. And this—" She pressed her hand to her abdomen. "This complicates things."

"For God's sake, Sofe, it's not a complication, it's a baby." I studied her face. "Are you happy about it?"

She blinked, her dark eyes brimming with tears. "I'm thrilled about the baby," she whispered. "But I'm worried. Danny and I aren't even living together right now."

"He'd be back in a heartbeat, and you know it."

"I know. But I want us to reconcile for the right reasons." She grabbed a tissue and dabbed her eyes. "He was just coming around to the idea of me applying for the police academy. Once he knows I'm pregnant, all bets will be off."

I took both her hands. "I know this is important to you, but you have to shift your focus to the baby, at least for right now. The police academy is not going anywhere. You can always apply when the baby's older."

"Oh, really? How supportive do you think your brother will be once the baby comes? There is no way he'd go along with both of us on the job with a child in the picture. He'd never take that risk. And I don't see Mr. Macho Man giving up *his* job. Do you?"

"No, I don't. But he loves you, and he wants you to be happy. I'm sure the two of you can work out a compromise—"

"It's easy for you to say, Vic," Sofia snapped. "You're single. You're a writer with a cool New York apartment and you can come and go as you please. So you're tired of writing mysteries, and boom"—she snapped her fingers—"you're back in Oceanside, working on a history of the family. Everybody in town wants your autograph, *and* you have two guys chasing after you!" She plopped down on the closed lid of the toilet, still sniffling.

I grinned, even though she was in no mood to smile back. "You make it sound so glamorous." I knelt in front of her, taking her hands in mine. "For one thing, no one has asked for my autograph except Gale the librarian. And, yes, I have a cool apartment, but it gets a little lonely sometimes. And as for the guys, Tim's busy with the lovely Lacey, and I think Cal's given up on me." I pulled her gently to her feet. "You, on the other hand, have a man who's crazy about you; more than that, he's committed to you. And he'll make an amazing father."

She nodded, the tears spilling down her face. In all the years I'd known my sister-in-law, I'd rarely seen her cry. "I know he will. I just feel like I can't tell him yet."

"Correct me if I'm wrong, SIL, but for you to be in this interesting condition, Danny had to have been there. Didn't he know there was, shall we say, a malfunction?"

She sniffled and shook her head. "The 'malfunction' was on my end. And I only realized it afterward, and didn't think to mention it to him."

"Well, I think you're gonna have to mention it to him soon." I handed her a fresh tissue and tugged at her hand. "Now can we get out of this bathroom, please?"

"Yes," she said, and blew her nose with a loud honk. "I spend way too much time in here as it is."

Back in her office, Sofia wanted to get back to the case, but I put the red folder aside. "We'll talk about this stuff later. How are you feeling?"

"Better." She sipped her water slowly. "The doctor says this can go on for a while, though." She took a packet of crackers from her desk and nibbled at one, taking careful bites.

"You're not even two months along, right?" I asked.

"Right. That's also why I don't want to tell Danny just yet." She rested her hand on her nonexistent belly. "It's too early."

"Is that the only reason?"

"No." She let out a sigh. "While it's still a secret, I feel like I have some control of the situation."

"Control? Are you kidding? Your mother knows. Do you really think that Lucia Delmonico will allow you any say in this?" Sofia's mother was a fifty-year-old version of my sister-in-law—sharp-witted, feisty, and strikingly attractive. And someone you didn't want to cross.

"I had to tell her, Vic. I was so sick and I was scared. But she's driving me crazy, calling me, texting me. Not only that, she's threatening to move back to Oceanside!" Sofia shook her head. "And you know how well she and Nicolina get along."

I winced as I imagined the two mothers-in-law occupying the same state, let alone the same town. My mom tended to blame Sofia for the couple's troubles; Lucia was certain Danny was at fault. And once that baby came, all maternal hell would break loose with those two crazy women fighting over their grandchild. No wonder Sofia wanted to keep the news to herself for a while.

"What does your dad say?" I asked.

"Not much." She smiled. "You know my dad."

"Yes, I do." I'd never heard Dave Delmonico string more than three words together in any conversation. My mom always said that Lucia and Sofie did enough talking for all of them.

"Listen, Sofe," I said, "I understand this must be hard for you. But everything else aside, Danny is the baby's father. He has a right to know." I took her hand. "I will keep my promise to you, but once you pass the two-month mark, will you tell Danny?"

"Okay." Her tone was resigned. "But you know that once I tell him, he's gonna be giving me a really hard time about this." She pointed to the red folder.

"I didn't even think of that. He wouldn't be too happy to know that my future niece or nephew had already accompanied us on our adventure the other night." I grinned. "You know those baby books where you keep track of their first haircut, their first word, etc.? Yours will have a page for first stakeout."

She swatted my arm. "It's not funny, Vic! I like our investigations."

"You say that like they're a weekly occurrence. I'm hoping this is the last one."

"That's what you said in May."

"True," I said with a sigh. "Anyway, I'll e-mail you my notes tonight. I have a few more ideas about Dennis Doyle." I stood up and walked over to her chair. "Stay right where you are," I said, giving her a hug. "Go home and take care of yourself. And try to eat something."

I stopped at the door of her office. "I'm so happy about this, SIL."

"Me too," she said, and I could tell that she meant it.

I headed down the hall toward the front of Sofia's studio, the murder all but forgotten. Instead my head was full of plans to a buy full set of Nancy Drew books and a baby-sized Bruce Springsteen T-shirt. So lost in thought as I headed out the door, I nearly collided with a tall, handsome cop—my brother, Danny.

"Hey," he said with a grin. "Watch where you're going there, ace."

"Oh. Hey." I gave him a quick kiss on the cheek. "I was just . . . leaving. See ya later!" I tried to pass him, but he grabbed my arm.

"Whoa, Vic, slow down. Can I talk to you for a minute?"

"Um, sure," I said, staring at the shiny badge on my brother's blue shirt.

He tapped my head. "I'm up here, sis."

"Sorry." I threw him a bright smile. "My head's in a million places."

"Obviously. Listen, I want to talk to you about Sofia."

Nooooh. Oh no, no, no. "What about her?" I asked cautiously.

"She hasn't been herself. She's too skinny, for one thing. And kinda quiet. And that's not Sofia."

"She said the heat's been getting to her."

"She told me the same thing, but I don't believe her." He crossed his arms, looked past me down the hall. "She's done for the day, right?"

"Oh yeah. We were just hanging out."

His eyes narrowed. "Hanging out or trying to solve a murder? You tellin' me Sofia doesn't have that red folder out and ready?"

Ready? It's already full. "No. I mean, not really. We're just tossing ideas around."

"Right. So you two haven't been going on any of your little recon missions?"

This probably wasn't the time to mention snooping around the Belmont Club. Or crossing a police line. Or attending an AA meeting under false pretenses, and rifling through a suspect's open garage. Some things were just better left unsaid. "Recon missions, ha ha!" I slapped his arm. "You're so funny, Danny."

"You may not have noticed, sis, but I'm not laughing." He crossed his arms more tightly and spread his feet apart, a clear demonstration of Tough Cop Swagger.

Which was just fine with me. I'd much rather field questions about our investigation than why his wife was sick. "Don't worry. Okay, Detective? It's an academic exercise."

"Sure it is." My brother leaned close, his hazel eyes boring into my own. "You may be considered the smart one in the family, but I'm not stupid, Vic. You stay out of this, or Sutton will be all over you." He jerked a thumb at his chest. "And maybe me, too."

"I will. Scout's honor." I held up the fingers of one hand and crossed them on the other. And made a mental note to go to confession for all the lying.

His face relaxed, but he didn't quite smile. "Okay. Is Sofia in her office?"

"Yup. She's . . . doing some paperwork." I stepped out on one foot, poised for a quick getaway.

"Uh-huh. Would there be a red folder involved?"

I spread out my palms in a *beats me* pose and shrugged. My brother rested a heavy hand on my shoulder. "Remember what I said, Vic ."

As I watched him walk down the hall, I thought about how glad I was to have my big brother around. And how I hated having to lie to him.

Chapter Fifteen

*T*hat evening, after a dinner of fresh pasta (courtesy of Tim, who makes it by hand in the restaurant) and fresh marinara sauce (courtesy of myself, as it's the first sauce I've perfected), I took my glass of Orvieto out to my deck. The sky was clouding up, turning from a dusky blue to a threatening gray; the ocean slapped the shore in fierce, foamy bursts, and the wind blew sharply across the dunes. I shivered a bit and tucked my knees inside my comfy old Rutgers sweatshirt. Storms at the shore filled me with a strange combination of unease and anticipation. We all live in fear of hurricanes, but who doesn't love a good old-fashioned thunderstorm on a summer night?

It's too bad I had no one to share it with at the moment, particularly on a Saturday night. I imagined that Tim and Lacey were together, but tried not to think about them cuddling in Tim's cottage on a rainy night. And what was Cal up to? Besides *not* asking me for another date? I'd seen him only once since Thursday, and while polite and friendly, there was none of his usual flirtatiousness.

I'd met Cal in May, and I knew little about him except what he'd told me. He was born in Baton Rouge,
but lived most of his life in New Orleans. (He'd gotten
a hearty laugh out of me saying New Or-LEENS rather
than New OR-lins.) He'd had a furniture-restoration
business that he lost in Hurricane Katrina; soon after,
he was divorced and came up north. When Sofia and I
had considered him a suspect, we'd done some digging, but didn't turn up much more than he'd told me.
Maybe he was simply a private person, and I'd been
too long around Italians who spilled every detail of
their personal lives with little prompting. But I was
convinced there was more to Calvin Lockhart than ap-
pearances. Though I did find that appearance attractive. *Let's face the unpleasant truth, Vic. A couple of months
ago, you were enjoying the attentions of two men. Now
they're both ignoring you.*

Well, if I couldn't have a man, I'd at least have a different kind of sugar; it was time for dessert. But I was
dismayed to find there were neither cookies in the
cupboard nor ice cream in the freezer. No way was I
going out in a thunderstorm, despite my sweet crav-
ings. Desperate times called for desperate measures: I
would bake. When I'd rented the cottage from Sofia
back in May, my mom, ever hopeful, had stocked me
up on staples, including a full spice cabinet and some
baking pans.

I preheated the oven and proceeded to open cabi-
nets. Flour, check. Butter, sugar, and eggs—check,
check, and check. As I reached into the fridge, I spied a
container of ricotta cheese. *Yess!* I would make my

grandmother's ricotta cookies, and eat as many as I damn well pleased. Okay, I had baking powder and salt, but no anise extract. Not even anise seeds. But as I was fond of an after-dinner digestive on occasion, there *was* anisette. I opened the bottle, taking a deep whiff of the licorice aroma. I poured myself a taste, then another (for inspiration, of course). Without a recipe, I was working from memory, but a quick look on my phone gave me the basics.

I sifted the dry ingredients first and then pulled out a hand mixer that hailed from Betty Crocker's early days. In a separate bowl I creamed the butter and sugar, which took forever, as I was too impatient to let everything come to room temperature. I finished with the ricotta cheese and a big splash of anisette, and tried a fingerful of dough. *More anisette,* I thought, and gave it another dash to bring it to *yum.*

I readied the first baking pan, and as I dropped spoonfuls of dough, spaced carefully apart, as Nonna had taught me, I pushed away thoughts of my nonexistent love life. Instead, I pondered Elizabeth Merriman's murder and what we knew so far. *Elizabeth was not a popular woman, but a micromanager who bullied her staff at the Belmont Club. At Merriman Industries, she made enemies of her husband's loyal employees and had to pay out on an asbestos lawsuit. But that was two decades earlier. On the night of her death, she has conflicts with Kate and Dr. Natale. William Fox and Toscano are also both present; both may have motives. We know that William Fox worked for Merriman, and he might want revenge for getting pushed out of the company. Toscano could gain finan-*

cially. I finished the first tray and slid it into the oven, poured myself more anisette, and sipped it while I mulled things over.

Okay, Elizabeth dies from a fall over the seawall, probably between twelve and one. According to Sally, Dr. C is still around at eleven forty-five that night, and Kate leaves at eleven thirty. Can we assume Sally is telling the truth? I cut a piece of baking paper for the second pan and started the next tray. *Dennis Doyle claims Elizabeth is still alive at eleven thirty; he also claims the Natale clan left at that time, but Sally says she saw Dr. C. later. Who's lying? And why?*

Startled by the oven timer, I dropped my spoon, sending a plop of dough across the table. I grabbed my oven mitt and took out the first tray, and the small kitchen was filled with the smell of licorice. *Dr. C. comes to see me and all but confesses to the embezzlement. After I find out Nonna attends Elizabeth's wake, she tells me the story of Elisabetta and Tommy Romano, and the birth of their blue-eyed baby. So is Toscano Elizabeth's son? What color are his eyes? Kate Bridges has blue eyes; could she be the lost child? Is a sense of abandonment the reason for her antipathy toward Elizabeth, or is there something else at work?*

I set the cookies on a cooling rack and examined my flat, misshapen results—not a final product I would show my grandmother, but one I would happily eat. As the first warm cookie melted in my mouth, I lost my train of thought. *Where was I? That's right, blue eyes. Dennis Doyle has blue eyes and an arrest record for assault. Could he be Elizabeth's grandson? Or might he have a different motive for murder, such as protecting his new in-laws?*

I ate three more cookies and slid the last tray into the oven, telling myself I would freeze the rest. As I washed the bowls and pans, my mind circled around the two possible motives in Elizabeth's death: revenge and gain. Unless she died in an accidental fall from that stairway. I shook my head. *Why would an elderly, half-blind woman walk out toward the beach so late at night?* It didn't make sense. And Sofia and I were so focused on Elizabeth's past. Were we missing something—or someone—with a more recent connection to her?

I scrubbed and rinsed, hoping to sharpen my focus. But I was startled by a sudden flash of lightning, followed by a crack of thunder. The bowl slipped from my hands, clattering into the sink. As the rain pounded the roof, the kitchen lights flickered, died, and came back on. My heart thumping, I grabbed two things I wanted at hand: a flashlight and the bottle of anisette. And prayed the lights would stay on.

I worked quickly, taking the last batch from the oven and wrapping the cooled cookies. Though the thunder had subsided, the rain was steady. Despite the warmth in the kitchen, I shivered in my sweatshirt. *Just nerves, Vic. Are you scared of a little thunderstorm?* I finished in the kitchen and headed out to the living room to close the windows. I shut and latched them, and looked out onto the dark street. The other houses were mostly dark, but here and there were signs of life. It was the height of the season; every cottage would have residents or renters. Why was I feeling isolated and a little scared? My attention was caught by a quick flash of light from a car across the street, as though someone had turned on an interior light. It was a beat-up sedan, but I couldn't tell its make. There was another brief flash from the car, and I pulled back from the window, my heart pounding again.

Okay, so somebody is sitting in his car. Maybe he's trying to read directions. Maybe he's lost or he's waiting for the rain to stop. So why wouldn't my heart calm down? Why did I have those warning prickles up and down my arms, the kind that tell you to listen to your instincts? So I did. Scooping up the flashlight and the anisette, I turned off the downstairs lights and scurried up the steps to my bedroom, locking the door behind me.

Sitting cross-legged on the bed with my phone next to me, I opened my e-reader and scanned the titles. Too many Gothics; this was not a night for the Brontës or Wilkie Collins. I was two pages into my favorite Dorothy Sayers, *Gaudy Night*, when I noticed the rain had stopped, replaced by a different sound. It was rough, rhythmic, like that of sandpaper against wood. Once, twice, and it stopped. I listened again and then I recognized it. That sandpaper sound was actually the muffled crunch of stones in my driveway. Someone was outside the cottage.

I shut off the light in my bedroom and sat on the floor. *He's not in the house,* I told myself. *He's outside, and you're locked in tight. Just wait.* But I had my phone ready. The sound faded, then stopped. Still clutching my phone, I unlocked my door and scrambled down the steps to the living room. I lifted one slat of the metal blinds. As my eyes adjusted to the darkness I watched a small, bent figure open his car door, the interior light shining off his shock of wild white hair. He drove away slowly, giving me enough time to see the letters and numbers I had written down on Thursday night. YRB-763.

I dropped into one of the mismatched chairs, exhaling in relief. I knew I wasn't in any danger now. But why the hell was William Fox lurking around my cottage?

Chapter Sixteen

Isabella stood at the door of the factory; through the window she could see the women at the machines, bent over their work, lines and lines of them filling the large room. Even standing outside, she could hear their unending noise . . .

As much as I wanted Isabella to make her way in America, I was having trouble concentrating on the story. I was hazy from a fitful night's sleep, and I kept stopping to look out the window for a return visit from William Fox. Which reminded me that I needed to call Sofia.

"Hey," I said. "How are you feeling?"

"Better today. Thanks. I heard you ran into your brother yesterday when you were leaving."

"I did indeed. He noticed that you're thinner, Sofe. He's worried about you."

"I know. I'll tell him soon." I could hear the resignation in her tone.

"Unless he figures it out first. He's not stupid, as he's fond of reminding me."

"Okay, is this why you called me?" she asked. "To nag me about your brother?"

"Nope. Not today anyway. I had a kind of a visitor last night." I closed my bedroom door behind me and headed down the stairs.

"A visitor?"

I stood at the front windows; the morning was sunny and clear, and last night seemed like nothing more than a bad dream. "Well, more like an intruder."

"Vic, are you okay?"

"I'm fine. The closest he got to me was the driveway. But get this: It was William Fox."

"William Fox? Maybe he figured out who you were from the meeting and wanted to be your sponsor or something."

"I don't think he came out at ten o'clock at night in the middle of a thunderstorm to offer me AA sponsorship. But he might know who I really am," I said, opening the front door but locking the screen. "Think about it. Toscano caught me at the club. Fox caught us at his house. If they're working together, it wouldn't take much for them to connect the dots, would it?"

She let out a long breath. "I don't like this. Maybe you should tell Danny."

"Not yet. And I'm not afraid of William Fox. Toscano, however, is another story. He gives me the creeps."

"Maybe you should stay with your parents for a while."

"God, no. I'll take my chances with either of those guys, thank you. But I'm not sure where to go with any of this right now. Back to Elizabeth's long-lost child? It would help if we knew whether Toscano, Kate Bridges, or one of the Doyles was adopted. It's not a thing you can come right out and ask people." I wandered out to the deck and watched the beach as it began to fill up with crowds of day-trippers. I normally avoided the beach on weekends, but today I was happy to have the company.

"I think you should go see Mrs. Natale," Sofia said. "She might tell you something about the Doyles."

"So what do you suggest? Do I ask straight-out whether one of Dennis's parents was adopted?"

"Maybe. But you never know what might come up in conversation. She was ready to blab about his arrest when she saw you at the wedding, right? Maybe you can find out more about that."

I took a seat in the sun and stretched out my legs, grateful for the sunshine after the storm. "So he was arrested for assault, but I'm having a hard time believing Dennis Doyle committed murder at his own wedding."

"It happened *after* the wedding, Vic. Which reminds me—we need to pin down the timing. When they left the club. The last time they saw Elizabeth. You've got Dennis saying one thing and that bartender saying another."

"Yes, assuming Sally the Bartender is not mistaken, or lying for some reason, Dr. Chickie was still there at eleven forty-five. So is Dennis lying to protect him?"

"Or himself. So, you'll go see Brenda Natale?"

"Yes, Sofia, I will go see Brenda. Listen, in the meantime, would you look into the adoption angle? Like which records would be open and which wouldn't?"

"I'll give it a shot. But see what you can find out

from the Natales. Because despite what your father thinks, and whether you like it or not, Vic, there's something we have to consider: Maybe Dr. Chickie really *was* the one who pushed Elizabeth over that seawall."

I didn't have to work that afternoon, and after getting Brenda's number and an admonition ("Don't upset her, honey") from my mother, I gave Mrs. Natale a call. She was home, and since Dr. Chickie was taking "his health walk," this would be a good time to come. The Natales lived on the bay side of town in a modern monstrosity of stucco and stone. It was a lot of house for two people, and I wondered if the Natales would be able to keep it.

I rang the front doorbell, and Brenda appeared immediately. "Hello, darling," she croaked. "Come in, please." She led me through the house to their back deck. "I thought we'd sit outside; it's restful out by the water—don't you think?"

"It's beautiful out here," I said, taking in an impressive view of the bay.

We sat at a large patio table, already set with a pitcher of iced tea, a bowl of fresh fruit, and a plate of Italian cookies. Brenda poured me some tea and slid plate in front of me. "Eat, Victoria, please."

She didn't have to twist my arm. I served myself some fruit salad and took a sesame-seed cookie. "Thanks for seeing me, Mrs. Natale."

"I'm just grateful you want to help him, dear." She didn't take any food, but instead lit a cigarette. "Terrible habit, I know," she said, blowing out her first puff with closed eyes. "Roberta is after me to stop. I'll try to keep the smoke away from you, hon. Now, how can I help you?"

"Well, I'm trying to piece some things together about the night of the wedding. I guess you could say I'm testing other theories about what might have happened to Elizabeth Merriman."

Brenda's heavy-lidded eyes were knowing. "You mean other than Chickie killing her?"

"Well . . . yes." I hadn't expected Brenda to state things so baldly, and I sipped my tea to fill the uncomfortable silence.

"Victoria, do you think I don't know what people are saying? I was never one to hide from things." She poured herself a glass of tea and looked up at me. "Did Chickie make some mistakes? Yes, he did. Did he kill that awful woman? No, he did not." She took a deep drag on her cigarette.

"I believe that, Mrs. Natale. And that's why I'm here today." Yet I could hear Sofia's words clearly: *Maybe Dr. Chickie really was the one who pushed Elizabeth over that seawall.* Was Brenda's blind faith in her husband misplaced? I took a bite of cookie for sustenance and readied my notebook and pen. "I have some questions. They may not make sense to you, and I'll understand if there's anything you prefer not to answer, okay?"

She waved her cigarette hand. "Go for it."

"Okay, when we were chatting at the reception, you mentioned Dennis's 'trouble.' His arrest is on record, so the prosecutor's office will have that information. But do you know the circumstances of the assault?"

Brenda's froggy eyes grew wide. "You don't think Dennis—"

"Of course not," I said hastily. "I'm just trying to get a picture of what happened."

"I don't mind telling you, because it was really kind of silly."

A silly assault? "Go on."

"It was a bar fight. A whole bunch of them drunk and banging each other around. He paid a fine and that was it."

"I figured it was something like that. I appreciate your telling this. I do have another question, though."

"Any way I can help, honey."

"Do you know if either of Dennis's parents was adopted?"

She frowned in confusion. "I have no idea. Is it important for Chickie's case?"

"It might be. But it's a long shot." *And please don't ask me to explain, Brenda.*

"Look, honey, if you think it will help Chickie, I'll see if I can find out." She bit her lip and frowned. "Though I'm not sure how you bring such a thing up to a person."

"I understand. Are you friendly with Mrs. Doyle? Maybe there's a way to get her talking about her parents."

But Brenda was staring out at the water. Then she turned back to me slowly and gripped my arm. "Hang on, darling. I just remembered a conversation I had with Maureen. We were talking about the kids, you know, and how we hoped we'd have a grandchild soon. So then Maureen mentioned what a big baby

Dennis was. Close to ten pounds, if you can believe it. Anyway, she had trouble delivering him."

"I'll bet," I said, resolving not to tell Sofia this part of the story. "What else did she say?"

"This is the important part. She said her mother-in-law had said the *same* thing about Dennis's father. He was also a very big man." She waved the cigarette smoke away from me. "His poor mother labored for days or something."

"That helps, Mrs. Natale. It really does." So Mr. Doyle was not adopted and could be ruled out. "Also, do you know how old Mrs. Doyle is?"

"She's younger than we are. Late fifties, maybe, but I know she's not sixty."

Assuming she wasn't lying about her age, Mrs. Doyle was too young to be the lost child. But I had to be sure. "Could I ask you one other thing? Does Mrs. Doyle have blue eyes?"

Brenda was not ready for the curve I'd thrown her, and paused with her cigarette halfway to her lips. "Maureen? Blue eyes?" She shook her head. "No, dear. Her eyes are brown."

Okay, I thought, *it's probably safe to say that Dennis Doyle is not Elizabeth's grandson. And the assault charge stemmed from a bar fight, not an attack on someone. He's probably not a violent guy. But is he lying about when they last saw Elizabeth Merriman? And if so, why?* "Mrs. Natale, there's one other thing. What time did you all leave the reception?"

Almost at once, Brenda Natale shifted her eyes back to the water. "We left at eleven thirty," she said.

"And you're sure about that?"

She nodded and looked down at her tea. "Yes. Elizabeth was still in her office. We could see her through the window."

It was the same story Dennis had told me, nearly word for word. And if I asked Roberta, she'd probably tell me the same thing. And I had no doubt it was rehearsed. "Okay, then," I said. "Eleven thirty it is."

"We did leave at eleven thirty," said a voice from behind me. "But I went back." Dr. Natale kissed his wife, who only shook her head. "I have to tell her, Brenda," he said.

Brenda stubbed out her cigarette and sighed. "Then have some tea first," she said, and poured him a glass.

I waited, pen poised and heart fluttery. Was I about to hear a confession? "Dr. C.," I said, "maybe you shouldn't—"

"It's okay, Victoria. Johnny told me not to talk about any of it, but this is different. Your father's like my family." He passed his hand over his eyes and rubbed the stubble on his chin. "I think I'll feel better if I tell the truth."

I put the pen and notebook away, and Dr. Chickie gave me a faint smile. "Thank you," he said. He drank down half the tea, set the glass in front of him, and folded his hands. "As I said," he began, "we all left the reception at eleven thirty. And Elizabeth was still in her office. But I had Dennis take Roberta and Brenda in his car, and I stayed behind. I wanted to try to plead my case with Elizabeth one last time. I went to her office and laid an envelope of cash on her desk. I said it was the first installment of the money I owed. I told her I'd pay back every cent of the money, but would she please not press charges."

"What did she say?"

"She said no. Then she said, 'It's too late, Charles. The wheels of justice are already turning.'" He shook his head. "That's how she put it. 'The wheels of justice.'"

"What do you think she meant, Dr. C.? Had she begun the process of pressing charges?"

"I'm not sure." He slumped in his seat, turning his glass from side to side. When he spoke again, his voice was barely audible. "But I would expect an arrest is imminent."

"You don't know that, Chickie," Brenda said, gripping her husband's arm.

"It's probably a good idea if you don't say any more about this, Dr. C." I started to gather my things, but glanced longingly at my uneaten fruit. It would be tacky to stuff my face while my orthodontist's life was falling apart.

"Wait a minute, Victoria," Dr. Natale said. "I do have one other thing to say before you go—and this you *can* write down. When I left Elizabeth Merriman's office at eleven forty-five last Saturday night, she was very much alive." His bloodshot eyes held my own. "And that's the last I saw of her. So help me God."

Chapter Seventeen

*T*hat evening, after a quick dinner in my cottage, I called Sofia. After a pregnancy update—morning sickness a little better, and, no, Danny didn't know yet—I filled her in on my visit to the Natales.

"So, it comes down to who was still around that club at midnight," Sofia said.

"And if any of them had motive," I added.

"So let's think about this logically, Vic. Assuming Dr. Natale is innocent, Elizabeth was probably murdered for one of two reasons: revenge or money."

"Right," I said. "Revenge points us to somebody tied to Merriman Industries; money points us to the lost child."

"There might be a Merriman connection we're missing," Sofia said.

"There might," I agreed. "But I'm leaning toward the lost child. If that child felt abandoned, he or she would have another reason for murder besides Elizabeth's money."

"Absolutely. And here's a thought: What if the biological child approached Elizabeth and was rejected?"

"You might be onto something here. It would be like being abandoned twice, wouldn't it?" As I pondered this theory, I remembered Kate's nearly irrational dislike of Elizabeth. "Hang on, Sofe. Remember I told you I overheard Kate and Elizabeth fighting the night of the murder? I couldn't make out much of it, but I clearly heard Elizabeth say something like, 'Out, out! Do you hear me?' What if Kate is the biological child and chose that time to tell Elizabeth? What if that was the rejection?"

"Hmmm." There was doubt in that one syllable. "I don't know, Vic. That's a weird time and place to say, 'Hey, I'm your long-lost daughter,' don't you think? It sounds more like she was getting fired."

"Very shrewd, Ms. Delmonico. You've given me something else to think about, and maybe given Kate Bridges another motive for murder."

After I got off the phone, I took a walk on the beach to think about my next course of action. It didn't take me long to realize there was only one thing to do. But I needed Tim to do it.

"I really appreciate this, Tim," I said, glancing at his stony profile. "I know you don't get that much time off." *And that I'm taking you away from Lacey. Sadly.*

"This is a stupid idea, Vic. You know that, right? Chef Bridges is probably gonna throw us straight out of her kitchen. *If* she's even there." He'd insisted on driving my Honda to the Belmont Club. (Apparently, I drive like an old lady.)

He was keeping his eyes on the road, his brows

knitted into a permanent frown. Though Lacey would no doubt turn it upside down later this evening. "I can't believe you would get yourself involved in something like this again," he said. "After last time."

It occurred to me that *After Last Time* would make a great movie or book title. Too bad I was sick of hearing it. "Tim, I didn't get myself involved. It happened the minute I overheard that conversation between Elizabeth Merriman and Dr. Chickie. And please don't repeat that to anybody, okay?"

"Who am I gonna tell?"

"I don't know. Your girlfriend, maybe?"

"We're just dating. She's not my girlfriend."

Somehow a bitter little laugh escaped from my lips. "Does she know that?"

But Tim chose not to answer. We rode in silence for a few minutes; then I noticed Tim curl his lip, as though he'd thought of something distasteful. "So, what about you and Lockhart?" he asked.

"What about it? We've been out on one date and taken one walk together. Hardly a relationship."

"But you're going out with him again?"

"If he asks."

He grunted, still frowning, and I thought the better of this line of conversation. "You know what, Tim?" I said. "I think we need another rule: no talking about our love lives."

"Fine by me." He pointed to the now familiar white building in the distance. "We're just about there, Vic."

As we approached the Belmont Club, I developed a nice case of the stomach flutters. Toscano had just warned me off, yet here I was, back for another spot of investigating. "Hey, Tim? Would you wait in the car a minute after we park?"

"What the hell for? You just dragged me all the way down here to give you an excuse to get in."

"Hang on, will you? I just need to check in with Sally at the bar for a minute, okay? We should probably make sure Kate is here. I'll meet you back in the kitchen." I neglected to tell him that if Jack Toscano was anywhere around, I planned to abandon the whole idea. But Tim was already cranky. "Wait for me to text you."

He made his displeasure evident by screeching to a stop in the rear parking lot. "I told you we should have called first."

"Kate never would have said yes."

"There's no guarantee she'll even see us, Vic."

Trying not to notice his impressive biceps, I patted his upper arm. "Just turn on the old Trouvare charm, pal."

The delivery entrance to the club was open. Once inside, I skirted around the kitchen and made my way down the long hallway that led to the bar, sending up a quick prayer to St. Jude, the patron of lost causes. He must have been listening, because I got to the bar unhindered. I popped my head in, and was rewarded by a wave and a grin from Sally.

"If it ain't the mystery writer! How ya doing, Victoria?"

"I'm good, Sally, thanks. Listen, is Kate here?"

She nodded, drawing a slow circle in the air around

her ear. "Crazy Kate's here all right. And today's lipstick is brought to you by the color purple."

"Oh, good. I mean that she's here, not the purple lipstick." I peered inside the bar to make sure it was empty. "Uh, one more thing. Is Toscano around?"

She shook her head. "Did you need to talk to him?"

"No! Definitely not." I pulled my head out of the doorway. "So, I'm just gonna go look for Kate."

"Good luck with that!" she called after me.

I was in the middle of texting Tim when my head shot up at the sound of a deep, accented voice. Chef Etienne Boulé, he of the silver hair and bedroom eyes, stood blocking my passage in the hallway.

I flashed him a hopeful smile. "Chef Boulé, you may remember me from an event last weekend. I'm from the Casa Lido restaurant?" As his expression didn't change, I made a desperate attempt at charm. "You may not recognize me without my hairnet," I said, smiling wider and patting my freshly styled hair.

He nodded briefly. "You still have not told me why you are here."

"Oh. Well, our sous chef, Tim Trouvare, was hoping to observe Chef Kate at work, since she is a renowned *pâtissière*," I said, murdering the French with my high school accent. I tried not to notice him wince.

"I don't know what you think you are doing, *mademoiselle*," he said, "but Chef Kate will not take kindly to someone attempting to, shall we say, *imitate* her work."

I gasped. "Did you think we were here to steal her recipes? I promise, Chef, we would never do such a thing. Truly. Tim and I simply want to watch her work."

He stood in the middle of the hallway, arms crossed. I was close enough to catch the faint scents of sandalwood and tobacco, and I was arrested by his dark eyes. "Let us hope that is the case," he said. One side of his mouth lifted in amusement, and just as I was thinking how attractive he was, I caught sight of his wedding ring. Some girls had all the luck.

"No more than one hour, *mademoiselle*," he said, holding up a finger. "If you last that long. Now, if you will excuse me." The moment he was past, I finished the text. *Coast is clear.*

But just because the coast was clear didn't mean I was comfortable sailing it. I slunk down the quiet hallway toward the kitchen, hoping Tim would get there ahead of me. Even if Kate was immune to Tim's charms, he still stood a better chance with her than I did. I pushed open the heavy doors slowly, a sense of dread shadowing me as I entered the spacious kitchen. We would probably get kicked right out on our behinds. Even if we could stay awhile, there was no guarantee I'd find out anything about Kate's past or her argument with Elizabeth.

Inside, a few of Chef Etienne's staff were prepping at various stations, but none appeared to notice me. That is, except for my old friend Antoine, who greeted me with some dubious French words and an expressive leer.

I hurried past him, thinking I'd take my chances with Crazy Chef Kate, whose voice boomed from the dark recesses of the kitchen. "What the hell are *you* doing back?"

I heard Tim's deep tones, but not his words, as he tried to calm her. "No way," she responded. "I work alone."

Once I was within earshot, I paused to listen. "But, Chef," Tim said, "I just want to observe. Everybody in the business knows your pastry work is primo."

Primo? You couldn't have come up with a better one there, ace? Just as I entered Kate's lair, she wheeled around and pointed a shaking finger at me. "And what are *you* doing sneaking around?"

Whoa. That *was* some purple lipstick. She was also wearing purple eye shadow and two bright spots of blush. That and her green head scarf gave her the look of an oversized grape. "I'm . . . I'm not," I stuttered. "I mean, I'm with Tim."

"Well, you can both turn around and go home. I'm not interested in babysitting either one of you. I've got work to do."

Tim dialed up his smile from charming to blinding. "What are you working on today, Chef?"

Kate let out a sigh. "Not that it's any of your business, but I'm making puff pastry for a peach *tarte tatin*."

"Oh, my gosh," I said, "we just did a peach *torta*, didn't we, Tim?" But Tim only rolled his eyes.

"What a coincidence," Kate said, her hands on her hips. "Considering peaches are in season and all." She stalked past us to the large refrigerator and I gave Tim a look: *Should we stay?*

He lifted his chin slightly, which I took as a yes. I took a place at the corner of her work counter, and Tim stood a respectful distance behind her. Holding the wrapped dough, she looked at us in disgust.

"All right," she said. "I can see I'm not gonna get rid of you. You, Casa Lido Chick, stay right where you are." She frowned deeply, her snaky eyebrows wiggling in her forehead. Then she turned to Tim, her expression softening by a fraction. "You, Mr. Charming, you can watch. But stay outta my space."

"Yes, Chef," he said, brushing me away with his hand as though it were a tiny broom and I was a dust bunny. I frowned at him, but moved down a bit.

Why was she willing to let us stay? She didn't seem to need her ego stroked, despite Tim's flattery. Chef Massimo had talked about her passion for her work; maybe she wanted to share it with an audience. As I watched her clownish face furrow in concentration, I had a different thought. Did she suspect we were here for a different reason? One that had to do with Merriman's death? Maybe she was simply trying to figure out how much we knew. Whatever her reasons, I had one chance to move the conversation in one of two directions: the night of the murder and her fight with Elizabeth or her own past. Which would get us thrown out faster?

Kate worked on the pastry with mechanical precision, folding it and then smacking it down again with her hands. As she worked—fold, smack, fold, smack— the sweat beaded across her forehead and her breathing was labored. She was tiring quickly. I didn't know much about puff pastry (except that it made a mess when I crunched down on it) but Kate was working up a sweat with it. I opened my mouth to ask her about it, but Tim shook his head.

"Have you always wanted to work in pastry, Chef?" he asked.

Kate grunted in assent, grabbed a towel, and swiped it across her forehead, leaving a streak of orange makeup behind. "I started out doing deliveries for a bakery. Then worked my way inside the kitchen."

Thank you, Tim, for that opening. "Were you young? When you started, I mean?" Both heads swiveled in my direction; both faces bore the same expression: *Who invited you?*

But Kate answered me. "I was fifteen when I worked there."

"I was about that age when I was bussing tables at the Casa Lido," Tim said.

"I worked there every summer," I piped up, but neither of them paid attention.

"Where were you trained, Chef?" Tim asked.

"Paris," she said. "And New York," she said breathlessly.

"Wow," I said. "How does a kid who starts out working in a bakery end up in Paris?"

Kate looked up from her work, her arms rigid. "What do you mean?"

"Oh. Just that it's sort of a huge leap. I mean, that was an amazing opportunity for you."

Her eyes shifted to Tim, the dough, and back to me. "Yeah," was all she said.

I had to push the conversation in a more personal direction; it would be a strain, but probably the only chance I'd have to learn anything about Kate's past. Without looking at Tim, I took the plunge. "You must have gotten a lot of support from your parents."

Her hands tightened on the wooden pin. Tim mouthed *What the hell?* over her head, and the silence that followed hung like dark cloud. When she spoke, her tone was deadly. "What do my parents have to do with anything?"

"Nothing. Just . . ." My voice trailed off at the sight of her face. Her painted-on brows smudged from sweat. Her eyes darkened in fury. The orange make-up streaked, her face yellow pale in the places she'd wiped it clean, the lipstick that made her mouth look bruised. What had Sally said about Kate? *That there was something off about her.* And that was especially true at this moment.

"That's right," she said. "Nothing. And that's what I have for the two of you. Nothing. Now get the hell out of my kitchen."

"Sorry, Chef," Tim started to say, but she stopped him with a warning hand. I backed away from the counter, spun around, and pushed through the kitchen doors into the hallway. The car was parked out back, but I took the long way around through the front of the building. There'd be hell to pay when Tim caught up with me. But I would happily deal with it.

While I hadn't learned anything definite, one thing was clear: The mention of Kate's parents had caused her to react with anger and possibly a hint of fear.

Why? Was she adopted? Or had she been abandoned? Was she, in fact, Elizabeth Merriman's biological child? If so, she stood to gain a fortune from her death.

Tim was waiting for me when I got to the car; I steeled myself for a lecture, but he was strangely quiet. He had pulled off his bandanna, leaving his curls askew. For just a second, he was my Tim again, and I had to sit on my hands not to touch him.

"Look," I said, "I know you put yourself on the line for me today. But I did find out something that may be important."

"Good for you." His hands rested on the wheel, but he didn't start the car. He sat unmoving, staring out the front window. Finally he turned to me, his expression dark. "You know that was stupid, right?" he said softly.

"I know, Tim. She might have been somebody who could help you in your career, and now we've alienated her—"

His hands tightened on the wheel and his eyes widened. "Is that what you think I'm upset about? Myself?" He shook his head. "You have some opinion of me, Vic."

"Well, why *are* you upset? I don't understand."

He pointed to the building behind us. "In case you haven't noticed, that woman in there is a psycho. I don't know why you had to ask her about her parents. For all you know, she could have been the one who killed Merriman, and you just pissed her off big time."

He was worried about me. A strange thrill took hold of me as the truth dawned: Tim was actually putting me ahead of himself. I rested my hand on his arm, and at least he didn't shake me off. "I don't intend to have anything else to do with her," I said. "And I won't come anywhere near the Belmont Club ever, ever again." *Unless I get married someday*. But that was a thought best kept to myself.

He patted my hand and sighed. "You have to cut it out with this investigation BS. Stick to the books, okay? You can solve as many mysteries as you want in them."

With that, the moment was broken, as Tim climbed back on his high horse of condescension and I bit back a retort: *Thanks for your permission, boss*. He started the car, and as we left the lot, a sleek black car was pulling in. A late-model Lincoln, it slowed as it passed us. The driver and I turned simultaneously, and I looked into the dark face of Jack Toscano.

Chapter Eighteen

*T*he next morning, I woke to a vibrating phone and a voice mail. When I saw that it was my favorite reporter, I held it as far away from my ear as possible. "Hell-o, Victoria!" The trill of Nina LaGuardia's not so dulcet tones cut through my quiet morning. "Just calling to let you know that late last evening, Dr. Charles Natale was arrested for embezzling funds from the Belmont Country Club. He should be released on bail later today. Be sure to call me back with a comment. Toodles!"

I erased the message, but this was one development that would not go away. Poor Dr. Chickie. So the wheels of justice had turned after all. But his arrest wasn't a surprise—except perhaps to Brenda. I had to hope he'd pay back the money and get a lighter or suspended sentence. The real concern, however, was Dr. C.'s now-obvious motive for murder. He claimed that when he'd left Elizabeth at eleven forty-five, she was still alive in her office. Sally, at least, could corroborate the time. Was there someone else still in the club who'd seen Elizabeth alive after Dr. C. left? Assuming Dr. Na-

tale had told me the truth yesterday. And what of Toscano and Kate? Sally saw Kate leave at eleven thirty,
when Elizabeth was still alive. But where was Toscano
between eleven and twelve that night? And how could
I get that information without arousing his suspicions?

When I got to the Casa Lido later that morning, I
started by checking the phone messages. There were
two asking about reservations. But the third one had
nothing to do with the restaurant.

"This is a message for Victoria Rienzi," said a man's
voice in a deep whisper. "Be careful. Please." And then
silence.

The caller ID read "private number." I played the
message three times, and each time it unnerved me
more than the last. I didn't recognize the voice, but
there was a slight sibilance on the "s" sounds in "message" and "please." Had I heard that sound in a voice
recently? I scribbled down the reservation information
and erased the messages. I did not want Mama Nicolina hearing it; she worried enough as it was. Who was
trying to warn me? The voice didn't *sound* threatening,
but that didn't mean the person wasn't a threat. It was
clearly a man, and the first man who came to mind
was Toscano. He'd seen me at the club again yesterday.
Had he left this warning in the guise of one who was
concerned? Or was the person genuinely concerned
about me? That "please" at the end of the message
wasn't Toscano's style. Could it have been Dennis
Doyle?

But my thoughts were interrupted by an entrance

from my mother, this one more dramatic than usual. "Oh, honey," she said breathlessly as she came in the door, "they've arrested Dr. Chickie."

"I heard, Mom." I gave her a quick kiss. "But he'll be getting out on bail, right?"

She nodded, and I could see that she'd been crying. "Poor Brenda," she said. "I can't even imagine what this must be like for her."

"I think she's pretty tough. She seemed to be holding it together yesterday."

"I don't know why you had to go over there, hon."

"I needed to clear up a few things."

"*You* do not need to clear up anything," she said, shaking her finger from side to side like a metronome. "That's a job for the police and the prosecutor. I won't have you involved in this, Victoria."

Thank God I erased that message. "Mom, as I've noted a dozen times already, I *am* involved in it."

"Not to this extent. Running around and asking questions that could get you in trouble, or worse. And I know Sofia is egging you on. What if you tipped off the real murderer?" She grabbed my upper arm in an Italian Death Grip.

I pried her fingers loose and patted her hand before giving it back to her. "Mom, Sofia and I are just gathering information." If my mother only knew the information Sofia was sitting on. I felt a small rush of warmth at the thought of the new baby.

"What are you smiling at?" my mother asked. "This is not funny."

"I'm not laughing, I promise. And I'm not doing anything dangerous." *I hope.*

"I still don't understand something, honey. I know you have to talk to Prosecutor Sutton, but in the meantime, why can't you just leave it all alone?"

It was a good question, and one to which I hadn't given much thought. Why *couldn't* I leave it alone? Dr. Chickie was already in custody; he was likely to serve time. If he were innocent of murder, as I believed, Sutton's team would find that out. And if Toscano, Kate, Dennis Doyle, or someone still unknown to us was guilty, they'd find that out, too. So what was I doing? More importantly, why was I doing it?

Oh, cara, said the voice of Bernardo Vitali, *the truth is closer to you than you are aware. But which truth, Bernardo?* The truth of the murder? Or my own motives for getting involved in it? Both were pretty murky right now. I looked at my mother's worried face and gave her a quick hug.

"What was that for?" she asked, rearranging her mussed curls. But she was smiling and her cheeks were pink.

"Just because."

"Victoria, promise me you'll be careful. Please," she said, using exactly the same words as the unknown caller.

"I promise, Mom." It was one I prayed I could keep.

Today's special was vegetable lasagna *al forno*, made with produce from the garden and thin sheets of Tim's fresh pasta. As usual, much of the vegetable prep fell to me, but today's dish required some skills I wasn't sure I possessed. All the veggies had to be sliced one quarter inch in thickness, and in approximately the same-sized pieces so they would roast evenly. At least focusing on the vegetables helped me put that unnerving phone call to the back of my mind. I pulled the zucchini ribbon from the mandoline, wondering if it would pass muster with my grandmother. As I was studying it, Lori stuck her head inside the kitchen.

"Hey, Vic, there's a guy out there asking for you."

"I'm kinda backed up here, L.J., so unless Matt Damon's looking for me—"

Lori made a sound between a snort and a laugh. "He's no Matt Damon—that's for sure. And he's kinda creeping me out with these dark glasses he's got on."

I covered the vegetables with a towel and turned, my stomach thumping from nerves. "Actually, I think I should go talk to him."

"Should I stick around?" Lori asked, as she walked me back to the dining room.

"Just do what you need to do out here. I'll be fine."

Toscano was waiting by the door. "Ms. Rienzi. I was hoping I might catch you here." He held out a hand, which I took reluctantly.

"Mr. Toscano. This is a surprise." *Unless you're the mystery caller.* But my instincts were telling me he wasn't.

He glanced at Lori, who'd stopped working to listen to every word. "Might we sit for a moment?" he asked.

"Yes. Would you mind following me to the bar? I

think we won't be disturbed there." As long as Cal didn't show up early. But there was a part of me that was hoping he would. I didn't relish being alone with Toscano, even in my own restaurant.

We each took a seat, and I waited. The light in the bar was dim, and I was hoping Toscano would take off the glasses. But he merely smiled in a sharklike way that raised the hairs on the back of my neck.

"Why are you here?" I asked, breaking the silence.

"I'm here to set the record straight about Elizabeth Merriman's death."

Well, Jack, you sure get to the point. "But you don't need to talk to me to do that," I said. "I'm sure you had to make a statement with the prosecutor's office, and—"

He held up his palm. "Miss Rienzi, I know that you've been asking questions about Elizabeth's death. And doing a little investigating of your own out at the club. Twice now, if I'm not mistaken." He crossed his arms and lowered his brows, his disapproval obvious. "Look, I know that you're friendly with Dr. Natale's family. And while I feel for him in this . . . predicament, it's one of his own making." He took off his dark glasses, and for the first time I could see that his eyes were the same cloudy blue as Elizabeth Merriman's. "I didn't kill my mother," he said simply.

My heart beat with excitement. Here was a key mystery solved; we could now rule out Kate as Elizabeth's lost child. I tried to feign surprise. "She was your mother?"

He nodded. "I had known about her for some time, before I served in Afghanistan, in fact. I did two tours of duty in the Sandbox. But you probably know that, don't you?"

I shook my head. I *didn't* know this, but it made sense. I'd pegged Toscano for a military man the minute I'd seen him. As I took in his fake smile and falsely polite manner, I tried to summon some admiration for a man who'd served his country. I had to give him at least that much. But I still found his presence disturbing.

"While I was overseas, I had time to take stock of my life," he said. "After all, I was in danger every day. More than ever, I had to learn about my birth parents. When I came back, the first thing I did was track her down. At first, she was skeptical, as you can imagine." His mouth twisted in a small smile. "But of course I was ready to do a DNA test." He pointed to his eyes. "And like her, I'm troubled with cataracts. Once she realized I was telling the truth, we began to get to know each other. She told me a bit about my late father, how he served in Korea. I think it pleased her that we were both military men." He shook his head. "Look, my mother was not an easy woman, but I think she cared for me in her way, and I for her." He spread his palms out in front of him. "What possible reason would I have for killing her?"

"I would think that's obvious." I took a breath looked him straight in the eye. "She was a very wealthy woman, Mr. Toscano."

"Yes, she was. But she settled most of her assets on me some months ago. The rest was going to her charities. And I have provided the police with all the official paperwork to prove it." He smiled again, satisfied and triumphant. "So you see, Miss Rienzi, I had no motive for killing my mother." He put his glasses back on and leaned toward me. "And I would appreciate it if you would stop your little investigation. You're not helping Charles Natale." He was close enough for me to smell his aftershave. "Being a mystery writer does not give you license to stick your nose where it doesn't belong. And while you're a charming young woman, you're trying my patience. Do you get what I'm saying?"

I nodded, unable to speak, rooted to my seat. This was the second warning I'd received in the space of an hour. You bet I was getting it.

"Good," he said. "Just so we understand each other." He stood up from the barstool, turned a sharp military left, and marched off. Despite the summer heat, I shivered in my shoes. Maybe Jack Toscano wasn't a murderer. But I had no doubt he was a dangerous man.

I headed back through the dining room, but before I could make it to the kitchen, some fresh hell came through the door in the person of Lacey Harrison. Dressed casually, she made a T-shirt and jeans look chic.

"Hi, Lacey," I said, trying hard to sound friendly. "Tim's not here yet."

She held her purse in front of her, as though she didn't know what to do with her hands, and, unusual for her, she wasn't smiling. "I know that, Victoria," she said. "I came to talk to you."

I was popular today. And not in a good way. "Okay," I said. "Do you want to sit down for a minute?"

She shook her head. "This won't take long, and I know you're busy. I do have to ask, though: Would you please not mention to Tim that I was here?"

"Of course. But why do you want to talk to me?"

"I know that Tim helped you out with something yesterday; he wouldn't say what, and it's not really my business."

So Tim had kept his word. Even though he hadn't approved of our trip out to the Belmont Club, he hadn't shared the information with his new girl-friend. It gave me a sense of relief, and though it was unbecoming, a touch of satisfaction, as well. "I'm sorry if I kept him," I said. "I know you guys had plans."

"I didn't mind that he was late. And I didn't mind that he was helping an old friend."

An old friend. Ouch. I looked into her sweet face and saw that she was telling the truth. "But you do mind something, don't you?" I asked her.

She nodded. "He spent a good part of the evening talking about how worried he was about you. He was clearly preoccupied." She looked away from me and back again. "I know you guys were involved a long time ago. I know you're still close. And I'm okay with that. I really am. But my gut is telling me there's a deeper connection between the two of you—maybe deeper than you both realize."

I nodded in agreement with her words. And in the hope it would prompt her to say more.

"And I can imagine how this sounds," she contin-ued. "I mean, I've known the guy for what, ten days?" She smiled for the first time. "It's a little early in the game for confronting the old girlfriend, right?"

Ouch again, I thought, but smiled back. "Could we make that *former* girlfriend, please?"

"Sure," she said, and laughed. The sound was deep and pleasing, not the giggle of a vapid girl. And not for the first time, I thought, *I really like her. I don't want to, but I do.* Then her face grew serious again. "As I said, Victoria, I just met Tim. But I like him. A lot. And if there's still something between the two of you, I want to back away now, before I get any more involved."

"I understand, Lacey. Tim and I have a history, it's true. And that history has deep roots. But when I came back to Oceanside, I made it clear to Tim that both of us needed to move on." *Which is not the same as saying we don't have feelings for each other.*

"Okay." She nodded, still clutching her purse. "As I said, it's early days yet for Tim and me. But . . ." She paused, as though deciding what to say, then took a breath before she spoke. "Look, I have a broken en-gagement behind me, and I'm still feeling bruised. I don't want to get hurt again."

"Of course." And then I did something that sur-prised us both. I gave her an impulsive hug, my sec-ond of the day and a record for me. "I'm sorry about the engagement," I said. "I've been there, sort of." I wondered how much Tim had confided in Lacey about our past. I couldn't imagine him telling her that eight years ago, he'd dumped me for somebody else. Not in the first week, anyhow. "Listen, Lacey, I think you'd like a chance with Tim, right? And maybe you feel like I'm standing in the way of that?"

Two pink spots appeared on her cheeks, but she looked me in the eye. "In a sense, yes."

I shook my head. "You don't have to worry about that, okay? I have no designs on Tim. We are old friends, and we do work together, but that's as far as it goes." *You're lying, Vic,* said a voice in my head, but I ignored it.

"Thanks, Victoria. I really appreciate you talking to me about this." She smiled. "I know it's a little awkward. And you won't say anything to Tim, right?"

"I won't tell him."

"You're the best," she said, and I could hear the relief in her voice.

I watched her go, lean and lithe in her white T-shirt and skinny jeans. She was a woman with a lot to offer a man, and she'd been hurt badly once before. We had more in common than I cared to admit, and I wished her the best. But a dark little part of me hoped she wouldn't find that best with Tim.

I was still staring after her when I heard Cal's voice. "How you doin' on this fine morning, Victoria?"

I turned, smiled, and took a good, long look. Eyes that were a warm, woodsy green. A face that was browned by the sun and lined by experience. A grin that was two parts wicked and one part kind. Not to mention a bod that wouldn't quit.

"I am very well this fine morning, sir," I said. "And I was hoping you'd answer a question for me."

"Ask away, *cher*." He set his toolbox on the floor and crossed his arms. "You have my full attention."

"Good," I said. "Because I intend to keep it." I took a breath and looked straight into those sleepy green eyes. "Will you go out with me?"

Chapter Nineteen

*T*hat afternoon I stood outside Sofia's studio, watching through the window while she took a group of ten-year-olds through the five ballet positions. Though my own career in dance had been mercifully short-lived, I found myself shifting my feet into first, second, and third along with the kids. But I did manage to get my sister-in-law's attention before I executed a plié out on the sidewalk. She motioned me inside, and I waited while she said good-bye to her small charges, most of whom stopped for hugs at the door.

"You'll make a great mom, SIL," I said as we walked back to her office. "You have so much patience. With the kids, that is."

She grinned. "With you and your brother, not so much, right?" She took two water bottles from a small refrigerator and handed me one. "I got your e-mail about Kate. Is there more since then? Sit down and fill me in."

"Well, I have had quite the morning." I started with the phone call from Nina and the news of Dr. C.'s arrest, moved on to the mysterious phone message, Toscano's visit, and my chat with Lacey. "Oh, and then I finished by asking Cal to go out with me."

She raised one eyebrow. "You *have* been busy. Save the Lacey and Cal stuff for later, though. It's Kate and Toscano I'm interested in at the moment. So, you and Tim went to see Kate at the club yesterday."

"Right. And it wasn't very pretty. Our pretext for being there was flimsy, and she's not a stupid woman. I think she let us stay to figure out why we were there in the first place."

"And she freaked out when you mentioned her parents?"

I nodded. "It was strange. But, then again, *she's* strange. Now that we know Toscano is Elizabeth's son—"

"According to him, Vic."

"And according to DNA proof he gave Elizabeth and the cops. I think we should operate under that assumption."

"If you say so. So, if he's Elizabeth's son, Kate had another reason for her reaction to your question about her parents."

"Which could be anything. She might be estranged from her parents. She might have been abused. Or maybe she's just a private person." I shook my head.

"Or she's a little unbalanced. Could she have been the one who left the message, Vic? Think about the timing of the call. Maybe she disguised her voice?"

"Hmm. It's possible, but I was sure it was a man. Also, there was a slight hiss to this voice. And I wouldn't imagine Kate saying 'please' to anybody." I shook my head. "I'm pretty sure it wasn't her."

Sofia took a pad from the red folder. "Putting the phone call aside for a minute, I'd like to know what Crazy Kate and Elizabeth were fighting about the night of the murder. You heard something like 'Out, do you hear me?' Which still sounds to me like somebody getting fired."

"So, do you murder someone for firing you?"

"Maybe. You said yourself that she loves what she does. And she still has her job at a fancy club, doesn't she?"

"Yes, but she's talented enough to get a job anywhere. It doesn't make sense as a motive. I keep coming back to Toscano," I said, shuddering at the memory of his veiled threat.

"Except that he already had her money. If what he says is true, he had no reason to kill her."

"So you think Kate and Toscano are both dead ends?" I pulled some notes from Sofia's folder and looked again at the information about Merriman Industries.

"I'm not sure. Neither seems to have a clear motive. Somebody had to have a damn good reason to push an old woman over that wall. Think about how cold-blooded that is."

"'Cold-blooded' describes Jack Toscano to a T."

"True, but right now he doesn't fit." She looked up from her notes. "Are we back at William Fox? Did he wait twenty years to take revenge on the woman who ruined his career? And he was there that night."

Then I heard the voice. *Are you ladies looking for me?*

A male voice with a dragged-out hiss on the end of "ladies." I met Sofia's eyes. "Oh my God, that was *his* voice on the phone. I'm sure now it was Fox."

"How do you know?"

"The way he pronounced the 's' on 'message.' The night we were at his house and he asked if we were looking for him—do you remember the way he said 'ladies'?"

"You're right. I noticed it when he was speaking at the meeting." Sofia shook her head. "I don't like this, Vic. He was also sneaking around your house in the dark. Now he's leaving anonymous messages to warn you off."

"He just doesn't strike me as dangerous, Sofe. He said 'please' on the message, as though he was concerned. I think the phone call might have been a genuine warning."

"You don't know that. And he's tied up in some way with Toscano." She scribbled on the pad as she spoke. "Are they working together, maybe? Did Jack hire William Fox to knock her off?"

"For what reason? She'd handed over her assets to Jack already. She was an old lady. Why take that kind of risk if you don't have to?"

Sofia shook her head. "Unless there's another reason he wanted her dead that we're not seeing."

"It's possible. The question is: What *else* are we not seeing?" I pictured Elizabeth in her beaded gown, chatting with guests, chiding the kitchen staff, waving her cane around with that one-carat emerald sparkling on her hand. Was it simple robbery, after all? "I wonder," I said. "Was that ring still on her hand when the body was found?"

"You think somebody killed her for it?"

"I think it's a long shot, but possible. The only thing is, her hands were arthritic. I remember wondering how she took that ring on and off with swollen knuckles."

"Sounds like another dead end to me," Sofia said, but wrote it down anyway.

I spread out the papers from the red folder and studied them. My gut was telling me the answer was here, but I was missing it. "Sofe, you said you thought this case had deep roots. And I agree that Elizabeth's murder is somehow tied to the past. But how far back do we go?"

"Well, maybe we work chronologically." She pulled a sheet from the pile. "Here are the notes from your conversation with Nonna." She scanned the page, frowning. "Are you feeling okay, by the way? You look a little funny."

"I'm actually better." She pointed to her face. "This is me thinking, not me feeling nauseous."

"The expressions are similar."

"Funny. Hey, Vic? Maybe we need to approach things a different way." She tapped the sheet in front of her. "Tommy's younger sister would be around seventy. I think we should try to track her down. If Toscano spent time looking for his mother, wouldn't it follow that he'd look for his father's family, too? He might have found his aunt; if he's been in touch with her, she might have important information for us."

"It's a thought." I turned the sheet to look back at the notes. "Though she could be anywhere," I said. "And *Romano* is a common name. She could also be married. If that's the case, where do we even start?"

But Sofia was already at her computer. "We take a chance and look up *Romano*. Do we have a first name?" she asked from behind the screen.

"No," I said. "But I can check with Nonna."

I heard Sofia's nails clicking on the keys. "I figure we'll start right here at home," she said. "How many seventy-year-old females named Romano can there be in the state?"

"In Jersey?" I said as I got to my feet. "Thousands. Listen, Sofe, I'll leave you to it, okay? Text me if you find anything."

She stuck her head out from behind the computer. "Where do you think you're going? We've got work to do."

"*You* have work to do," I said. "I have a date."

It was a relief to take a break from investigating for a while to concentrate on getting pretty for my date. But the harder I tried to dismiss thoughts of long-lost children, mysterious phone warnings, and emerald rings, the more forcefully they returned. Had Toscano known about his father? Had Elizabeth spoken to him about Tommy? And had he tracked down Tommy's sister? If so, would she be able to shed more light on this man? I stopped primping long enough to write down a reminder: *Ask Nonna for Romano sister's first name!*

Back at my mirror, I gave myself a critical once-over.

I'd treated myself to a little black dress at our local boutique, a V-necked sleeveless number that revealed my tan and hinted at a few other things. My hair was pulled back into a sleek ponytail, the band wrapped in gold mesh. I had darkened my brows and used a smoky eye shadow and liner that Victoria the Waitress wouldn't dream of wearing during the day. But Victoria Who Finally Had a Date was pulling out all the stops, including a final touch of lip gloss in a flattering shade of plum.

I put on my great-grandmother's gold earrings, and rummaged in my jewelry box for a vintage cocktail ring I'd bought in the city. As I slipped it on my finger, the question revealed itself to me, appearing hazily in my mind like the answer at the bottom of a Magic 8 Ball. A question that grew until it blocked out all thoughts of prepping for my date. A question that could rule out a possible motive, and one to which my grandmother might have the answer. But it would have to be asked in person, as Nonna hated telephones, including landlines.

I glanced at my phone. I had less than an hour before I was supposed to meet Cal for our date. I could probably squeeze in a visit to my grandmother and still get to the restaurant on time. Maybe. I slipped off my heels, slid into flip-flops, and grabbed my purse. If there was traffic, I might not make the restaurant for seven. But it was a chance I had to take.

"So, why are you so dressed up?" The question was laden with suspicion. "And that makeup is too dark."

I ignored the dig as we each took a seat at the kitchen table. "I have a date with Cal."

Her face cracked into a rare smile. "Calvino. How nice. Better than that Tim."

Since the spring, my grandmother had been on an Anti-Tim Campaign, which provided a nice counterpoint to my mother's Anti-Cal Campaign. "I'm glad you think so. But before I go, I need to talk to you a minute. Would you mind telling me Tommy Romano's sister's name?"

"What for?"

"Well, I got so interested in the story of Tommy and Elisabetta that they inspired me to do some research about them. For my book."

Her eyes narrowed behind her bifocals. "I told you that in confidence."

"I know," I said. What I *didn't* say was that the story might well come out, anyway, during the investigation. "I'll be changing names and details. You don't have to worry about that. I just thought that if I could talk to Tommy's sister, I'd have more, uh, insight."

"Is that so?" She tilted her head. "And by 'insight' do you mean 'information'? So you can find out more about how Elisabetta died?"

I slipped both hands into my lap and crossed all available fingers. Then I lied straight to my grandmother's suspicious face. "No."

She only grunted in reply, but then switched tactics. "How 'bout a nice peach?"

"Thanks, Nonna, but I'm about to go to dinner. And you know me—I'll end up dripping juice all over my dress."

"That's true." She pointed to my ears. "You're wearing my mama's earrings."

"I wear these a lot when I get dressed up. Which reminds me. I have something else to ask you."

"What now?" Her frown said a multitude of things, none of them encouraging.

I would have to put this delicately, but how? "Um, at wakes when there's an open casket"—Lord, this was a grim subject—"do people normally have their jewelry on?"

She pinched her thumb and fingers together in Italian code for *What, are you crazy?* "Why would you ask me such a thing, Victoria?"

"It's just that when Grandpa died, I remember seeing his wedding ring on his hand. But you didn't actually, uh, bury him in it. Because Danny wears it now."

She let out a huff. "How disrespectful are you to speak of your own grandfather in this way? What does your grandfather's ring have to do with anything?"

So, this is going well. "It doesn't, actually. I guess what I'm asking is: Is that a typical practice?"

She narrowed her eyes at me again and then crossed herself, just in case what she was about to say was sacrilege. "Yes, I suppose." She held out her left hand. "When it's time to lay me out, you leave these rings on my hand. They can be yours afterward. And make sure your mother finds me a nice dress. On second thought, I'll buy it myself ahead of time."

"Nonna! I don't want to think about that, please. I'm not asking about you. Actually, I'm asking about

Elizabeth Merriman. At her wake, was she wearing a ring? A big emerald?"

She shook her head. "No. No jewelry."

"Are you sure?"

"Of course I'm sure," she said. "An emerald, I would remember. I have some nice emerald earrings your grandfather gave me. You'll get those when I die, too."

I clapped my hands over my ears. "Stop it, please. Enough about this." I grabbed my keys and stood up. "I have to run. But thank you for the information." I sneaked a kiss, which she didn't wipe off. Progress anyway.

I scarpered down the steps as fast as my flip-flops would carry me, my head reeling with this new information. If that ring wasn't on Elizabeth's finger, where was it? And was the person who now possessed it a murderer?

I had made reservations for us at the Shelter Cove Inn, a tiny place along the bay. Getting a table there was no small feat in July, and I was nearly thirty minutes late. Had they given up our reservation? More importantly, would Cal be angry at having to wait for me? Before leaving the car, I slipped on my gold sling-backs and did a last touch-up on my face, firm in the belief that the better I looked, the less angry he would be. As I hurried into the restaurant, I nearly collided with a maître d' whose icy expression froze my heels to the floor. With his slicked-back hair and practiced sneer, he exuded the air of a snooty gatekeeper. As one who was used to Frank Rienzi's swingin' charm as restaurant host, I was taken aback by the chill.

"May I help you, madame?" Though he said it with the accent on the second syllable, he was about as French as a plate of fries.

"Yes," I said, attempting to sound the right note of haughtiness. "I am meeting a friend here this evening and I wonder if he's been seated."

"I believe the gentleman is waiting in the bar." He stepped back behind a lighted podium and opened a leather portfolio. "I assume you have a reservation," he said without looking up.

"Of course. It is for seven o'clock." For some reason, I was enunciating each word like a New Jersey version of Eliza Doolittle.

"It *was* for seven o'clock," he said with a sniff. "It is now seven thirty-four."

In a futile attempt at chumminess, I leaned my elbow on the podium. "You know what traffic is like in the summer." I threw him a brilliant smile, but it had no effect on Sniffy.

"I do indeed, madame, which is why I suggest that our guests leave ample time to get here. I'm afraid we shall be unable to seat you until nine thirty."

"That's unacceptable." But one look at Sniffy's flared nostrils had me rethinking my indignation. "I mean, couldn't you find us something a bit earlier?"

He closed the book. "I'm afraid not. Now, if you'd care to wait with the gentleman at the bar, I'll happily show you the way."

And I'd like to show you an Italian gesture or two. Instead, I smiled through my teeth. "I'll find it. Thank you."

As I stood in the doorway of the bar, it wasn't hard to find Cal. Though he was dressed in a dark suit, he was the only man in there with hair that reached his shirt collar. He was sipping a drink—probably whiskey—and I enjoyed the contrast of his large, rough hands against the starched white cuffs of his shirt. He turned around on his stool, a slow grin forming as he looked at me.

"I'm so sorry," I said, and reached out my hand.

He pulled me closer, keeping my hand in his. "You show up looking like that, a man forgets where he is, let alone what time it is. And in case you haven't noticed, *cher*, I'm a patient guy." He raised his glass. "Would you like one?"

"Please," I said as I sat down. "But a small one, okay? I'm still getting used to the taste."

He gestured to the bartender and took my hand again. "You look beautiful," he said, his green eyes holding mine.

"You clean up pretty nice yourself there, sir." I squeezed his hand lightly, but slipped mine out of his grasp. It was too early in the night to get disoriented by the Lockhart charm, and his signals that were jamming my personal navigation system. "Cal, I'm sorry I'm late. I had to stop and see Nonna."

He lifted a brow in my direction. "You went to see Giulietta?"

"Uh huh." I nodded, keeping one eye out for that Scotch. "I had to ask her about . . . a recipe." The bartender slid a glass in my direction, and I sent him a grateful smile. *Thanks for the distraction, pal.* "I'm trying to get her to teach me how to cook." I lifted my glass to Cal's; he tapped mine lightly, and I heard the unmistakable *ping* of crystal.

"Can I ask you something, Victoria? If you grew up in that restaurant, how's it only now that you're gettin' cooking lessons?"

"Now, there's a question." I took a sip of the Scotch; I would need it for this story. "Well, you're right. I did grow up there. I helped out in the dining room from the time I was ten years old. Danny and I both waited tables when we were in high school. I think the plan was for my brother and me to take over the business."

"But you guys had other ideas."

I nodded. "Once Danny decided on a career in law enforcement, he was let off the hook."

Cal swirled the amber liquid in the bottom of his glass. "And all eyes turned to you."

"Yup. I studied business at Rutgers with the idea that I'd run the restaurant someday. In the summers, I'd wait tables, hang out in the kitchen with Nando and Chef Massi. I was allowed to do some vegetable prep, but that was it. Nonna promised I'd eventually learn the sauces and our core dishes, but once I took over, I'd be strictly front of the house."

Cal frowned slightly. "Did you *want* to be at the restaurant?"

"Another loaded question, Mr. Lockhart." I shook my head. "I was conflicted about it. Until . . ."

"Until when?"

I looked straight into his smoky green eyes. "Until Tim came back from culinary school and my parents hired him as a line cook."

He tilted his head, his face holding an expression of warmth and something akin to sympathy. "And then the restaurant business didn't look so bad anymore."

"No. I think my parents had hopes that we'd get married and run the place together."

"And what about you, *cher*? What were your hopes?" He took my hand and held it lightly, as though I might snatch it away from him.

"The same. But that, sir, is water under the Driscoll Bridge." I let my hand rest in his briefly, savoring the moment of comfort.

"Is it?"

"Yes. It is." I lifted my glass for another sip of Scotch, which went straight to my head. I needed to eat something and get off the subject of Tim as soon as possible. "May we talk about something more interesting, please?"

He grinned, and that went to my head, too. "Fine with me," he said, and as if reading my mind, pushed a bowl of cashews in my direction. "But you still haven't told me why you never learned to cook."

"Ah. That would be the Revenge of Nonna."

"Meaning?"

"Meaning that after Tim broke up with me, I decided to leave Oceanside. And once I did, Nonna locked up her recipes for good." I grabbed a handful of cashews, but forced myself to eat them like a lady, one at a time.

A glint of amusement shone in his eyes. "You're kiddin' me."

I shook my head. "Nope. She made it clear that there would be no cooking lessons unless I came back to run the Casa Lido. And we both dug in our heels," I said with a sigh. "For eight years. So now I'm consigned to meatball maker and escarole chopper. But I'll wear her down."

He tapped the end of my nose and smiled. "You're a lot like her, you know. Why do you think her and me are such fast friends?"

"I would say mainly because you're not Tim." I downed the rest of the Scotch, and my head spun like a boardwalk ride.

"Truer words were never spoken." He lifted my chin and held my eyes with his own. "'Cuz that guy was stupid enough to let you go. And that's his loss."

I blinked, wondering if he was about to kiss me. Instead he emptied his drink and handed the bartender his credit card. "Victoria, would you like to get out of here?"

I looked at my watch. Dinner was still an hour and a half away, and I needed something in my stomach besides a bowl of nuts. I'd have been happy with a burger, but I also wanted this meal to be special. "My plan was to take *you* to a nice dinner," I said.

He waved his arm. "This is all a little stuffy for my taste anyway. And I think you could use a little fresh air, no?"

"Actually, yes." I stood up, a little shaky on my sling-backs.

He took my arm and tucked it under his, leading me gently through the crowded bar. And despite the fact that I am an independent woman, it felt pretty nice to be taken care of.

It was also nice to tell Sniffy we were leaving. His only reply was to purse his lips and make a great show of scribbling out my name. *Way to make your customers feel welcome, pal.*

Once outside, I took deep breaths of the clean sea air.

"Better?" Cal asked.

"Uh huh. My head's a little clearer. But I don't think I should drive."

"I'm in complete agreement. In fact, I'll drive ya back here later. After we get some food in you." He led me to the parking lot, where I expected to see his work truck. Instead, we stopped in front of black BMW.

"Wow," I said. "Nice car." And what I didn't say was, *Woodworking must be paying better than I thought.*

"Thanks," he said briefly, holding my door open.

I slid into the black leather seat, getting a whiff of New Car Scent mixed with Hunky Guy; it was nearly as intoxicating as that whiskey I'd downed. I leaned forward, noting the walnut dash, arrayed in dials and colored lights. I turned to Cal and grinned. "Hey, did 007 own this before you?"

"Nobody owned it before me." He pressed the button for the ignition—a revelation for me, as my lowly Honda requires a key—and the engine started with a soft growl. I glanced at his profile as we pulled out of the parking lot, but his expression told me very little.

"Where we going?" I asked.

"You like jazz? There's a club not far from here in Messina Beach. Nothin' fancy, but they make a great burger."

"Well, I don't know much about jazz, but I do know my burgers. Do they use Angus beef?"

"Not sure about that, Victoria, but they taste mighty good. And there happens to be a trio playing there to-night that hails from my hometown."

"Really? They play New Orleans jazz?"

"Yup. Seen 'em play Preservation Hall back in the day. Sat so close I had to duck the trombone spit."

"Eww," I said, wrinkling my nose. "Can we get a seat in the back, please?"

"Wherever you like, ma'am." We had reached the town, and he pulled into the driveway of a familiar, low-roofed building.

"Oh, this used to be the train station in town. We'd come here sometimes to go to Rahway and then into New York." We got out of the car and I studied the dark red shingles and black shutters on the windows. "It looks just like I remember it."

"Well, it's a club now." Cal held out his hand. "Shall we?"

We got there in time to hear the group play a rous-ing version of "When the Saints Go Marching In," in-spiring a number of audience members to sing along. The atmosphere was lively and loud, and about as far from the Shelter Cove Inn as you could get. But I was glad we'd come.

The trio was ending its set, and after Cal got me

settled, he headed to the stage, where he engaged in much hand clasping, man hugging, and backslapping. He was still grinning when he came back to the table. "Pretty cool they remembered me," he said.

"Well, you're a pretty memorable guy, Calvin Lockhart."

He dipped his head in acknowledgment. "I'll take that as a compliment."

We got our drinks—beer for him and wine for me this time around, which I sipped slowly. After a waitress brought us our burgers, I asked Cal a few questions about jazz.

"I like all kinds," he said. "Charlie Parker's the king, in my book, but I also like me some Chet Baker and John Coltrane."

"I've heard *of* them," I said, "but I don't think I've heard their music."

"I got a Chet Baker CD in the car; I think you'd like him."

"Sorry if this seems like I'm stereotyping you," I said, "but I assumed you'd like country music."

He took a deep swig of his beer. "Not particularly. Unless you count the Allman Brothers. Don't get me wrong, though; I'm a big fan of the Man in Black." At my blank look, he grinned. "That would be Johnny Cash. You know, 'Ring of Fire'?"

"Ah. I saw the movie about him. But you'll have to excuse my ignorance. In my house the twin musical gods are the Men in Blue—collar, that is. Sinatra and Springsteen."

He raised his glass. "Ain't nothing wrong with that.

I'm a fan myself." He gestured to the stage. "I think they'll be back in about ten minutes. Would you like to stay to hear some more?"

"Sure. I'm still working on this burger anyway. And you were right—it is good."

"Glad you like it." Then he leaned toward me, his face serious. "In the meantime, wanna tell me what you and Miss Firecracker are up to?"

I looked down at my wineglass. "We're not up to anything."

"Right. But you happened to be at the country club the night that woman was killed. And you're tellin' me you're not running around asking questions. Doin' research that you're pretending is for some book you have no intention of writing?"

"Maybe a little."

"A little, huh?" He rested his chin in his hand, studying my face.

"Okay, maybe more than a little." I stopped as a memory from our last date suddenly surfaced. "Hang on, Cal. Remember the night we were up on the boardwalk? You told me you worked at the Belmont Club. Before you took the job at the Casa Lido."

There was now a wariness in that green gaze. "Yeah. Back in the spring. Why?"

I sat forward in my chair. "Did you know Elizabeth Merriman? I mean, did you have any dealings with her?"

He shook his head. "It wasn't a big job and I wasn't there very long. I saw her maybe one or two times. But I never talked with her. Anyway, she didn't strike me as the type to chat with the hired help." He looked away from me and sipped his drink.

From what I knew about Elizabeth Merriman, she was exactly the type to chat with—no, make that *order around*—the hired help. "I'm surprised." I said. "I mean, the night I was there, she was micromanaging for sure."

He shrugged. "All's I know is I never spoke with her. So I can't really help you."

I couldn't shake the feeling that Cal was hiding something. But maybe he was just a private guy, as lots of guys are. "One more quick thing, if you don't mind. Do you remember seeing a large ring on Elizabeth Merriman's hand?"

He looked at me carefully. "Think so. A big ole rock, right?"

"Right." I waited to see if he would describe the ring, but decided he needed some prompting. "According to my grandmother, she wasn't wearing it when she was laid out."

He lifted a shoulder. "Coulda been stolen, *cher*. A diamond of that size would bring somebody a pile of money."

"That's possible," I said. "It's . . . quite a rock." Only it wasn't a diamond. I had spotted that emerald from across the Belmont Club kitchen the night I met Elizabeth; there was no way it could be confused with a diamond. But maybe Cal was mistaken. Or maybe his memory was faulty. Or maybe he'd never seen Elizabeth Merriman's ring at all. Had Cal worked at the Belmont Club or hadn't he? *I should ask Dad about his references*. I felt guilty for even thinking such a thing;

for all I knew, Elizabeth had any number of rings. Still, there were things about Cal that didn't add up. Like a brand-spanking-new BMW, for example.

"Well, thanks anyway," I said.

He wiped his mouth on his napkin and smiled. "Sorry I can't be more help." He'd finished his burger but pushed the fries to the side.

I pointed to his plate. "Are you going to waste those tasty fries?"

"Gotta watch my waistline," he said, patting his stomach.

"Please, you don't have a spare ounce on you."

He cocked an eyebrow. "So you've noticed."

"I suppose you could say that." My face grew warm, the result of a glass of wine and the memory of Cal in a pair of tight jeans. But I was saved by the appearance of the musicians coming back to the stage, and we were treated to another half hour of raucous New Orleans jazz.

At the end of the set, I motioned to the waitress for the check, but when she brought it to the table Cal slapped his hand over the black billfold. "I got it," he said.

"But this is my treat. I asked you, and I screwed up our dinner reservation. At least let me pay."

"Tell you what." He took my hand, turned my palm up, drew small circles there with his finger. "We can wrestle for it. First person with a pin pays the check." His face split into a grin and he raised an eyebrow. "That's a win-win all around, wouldn't you say?"

With my free hand, I took the last gulp of my wine and felt my face—as well as a few other body parts—suffuse with warmth. "Fifty-fifty?" I said weakly.

"You drive a hard bargain, girl," he said, giving my hand a final squeeze.

We each seemed lost in our own thoughts as we rode back to the Shelter Cove Inn. Mine were a winey whirl of questions: Did I like this guy enough to see him again? *Yes*. To get involved in a relationship with him? *Maybe*. Did he have genuine feelings for me or was he merely hoping for a fling? *Too soon to tell*. As he pulled up to my car, I worried about that moment of awkwardness—the possibility of a good-night kiss—and took the coward's way out.

"This was really fun, Cal. Thanks." I gestured to the building. "I'm kind of glad we didn't get in there. Thank you so much." I opened my door, about to jump out, but he put a hand on my arm.

"I'm not saying good night yet, Victoria. I'm following you back to your house and making sure you get inside safe. I don't like all this snoopin' around you're doing."

It was on the tip of my tongue to tell him about William Fox, but I didn't. He helped me inside my car and pointed to my door, which I dutifully locked. As we pulled out of the lot, he stayed behind me. On the way home, when I'd glance at the rearview mirror, he was always there, a safe distance away. It was reassuring. He was watching out for me, so why was I hesitant to tell him about William the Intruder or about Toscano's veiled threats? I still had to talk to Sutton, so I had to be discreet. But there was also more to it. There was a part of me that didn't quite trust Cal.

Granted, he was a private person, but there was so little I knew about him. He'd referred once to an ex-wife, but not by name. And he'd never talked about any other family. True, the Rienzis were close to the point of smothering, but I'd expect a guy to occasionally mention a parent or sibling. For all I knew, he had a kid somewhere. And now there was the issue of Elizabeth's ring.

As I turned down my block, I remembered the last date we were on. We'd been talking about accents, and, without warning, he'd launched into a perfect New Jersey voice. If my eyes had been closed, I'd never known it was Cal speaking. *So what, Vic? He's got a good ear for voices. Does that make him untrustworthy?*

"Maybe," I said aloud. I pulled into my driveway, Cal still following behind.

"Cute place," he said as he came up the front walk. "Good location, too."

"Thanks," I said. He walked me up the steps, his hand under my elbow and we stopped in front of the door. Then came the ultimate question: *Should I ask him in?*

"I have an early day tomorrow," he said, "so I'll say good night right here, if that's okay."

Well, viewers, tonight's forecast is steamy, followed by a mixture of relief and disappointment. "Sure."

He stepped closer, put one finger under my chin,

and lifted it slowly. My eyes lingered on his mouth, which was moving ever closer to my own.

All at once I tasted whiskey and wine; somewhere in the back of my head a jazz sax was playing and a tiny Mardi Gras parade wound its way up and down my spine. My lips softened against his, and I slid my arms around his neck. *How long?* I thought. *How long has it been since I was well and truly kissed?* He pulled me closer, but gently. He wasn't rushing the kiss and he wasn't rushing me. I slid my hands into his hair, and he pressed his palms against my back, moving his lips to my chin, the side of my face, my neck, and back to my mouth. My knees buckled slightly, and I could feel his smile against my lips as he tightened his hold.

Abruptly, the music in my head stopped, and in the silence I could hear my heart pounding. He traced the line of my mouth with his finger. "If I don't leave this very minute, I'm likely to forget my mama raised a gentleman. I had a lovely time, *cher*. I'll see you in the morning."

He turned, lifted his hand in a wave, and stepped into his black car, flashing me one last grin. Breathless and shaky, I leaned against my front door and watched him go, knocked flat by the force of Hurricane Calvin— with all my doubts and suspicions about him blown out to sea.

Chapter Twenty

"**A**re you even listening to me?" Sofia shook my arm a tad more forcefully than necessary.

"Uh huh." I stared out the car window dreamily as we headed south on Interstate 95.

"Then what did I just say?" Sofia demanded.

"You asked did I put Louise Romano's address into the GPS."

"That was two questions ago. I asked what you said to her on the phone."

"Oh." Back in the moment, I shook my head to clear it of all thoughts of whiskey-flavored kisses and well-muscled arms. "I said the usual. That I'm doing research for a book."

"Well, that's sort of true this time."

"I guess," I said with a sigh.

"Okay, was that an *I'm tired of lying* sigh or a *Mr. Down on the Bayou is a good kisser* sigh?"

"Kinda both."

"Vic, how much do you really know about this guy?"

"What do you mean?"

"It's a simple question. We looked into his past and

couldn't find a thing. You only know what he's told you. We couldn't even confirm the furniture business he talked about."

"He lost it in Hurricane Katrina! And that was in 2005. Why would you expect to find anything about it now?"

"Because the Internet leaves a long trail, and you know it."

The rational part of my brain told me she was right. It also reminded me about the BMW and Cal's mistake about the ring. I told it to shut up. But Sofia was still talking.

"And you shouldn't throw away all reason just because a guy's a good kisser."

"He's not just a good kisser. He's a FAB-u-lous kisser. They don't come along every day."

"If you say so. Here's our exit." She shook my arm again. "Can you please snap out of it, Vic? We need to be focused."

"I've got it together—really. I'll ask her all about her brother, and hopefully we'll find out whether she knows she has a nephew. You'll take notes, right?"

"Yes," she said firmly. "You talk and I'll write. This way I know we won't miss anything." She glanced at her dashboard and back at the road. "The turn's coming up."

In about five minutes we were parked in front of the small colonial belonging to Louise Romano. Sofia's hunch that she still lived in Jersey proved correct; she was also still using her maiden name, which made my job easier. I'd started working the phone at nine this morning, and by ten I'd found the right Louise.

As we walked up to the door, Sofia grimaced and pressed a hand to her stomach. "Here we go again. Ugh."

I put my hand on her arm. "Are you sure you're up to this?"

"I'm fine," she said, and rang the bell. "What about you? Are you sure you can see with all those stars in your eyes?"

The woman who answered the door was about seventy, with cropped salt-and-pepper hair. She was still striking, particularly her bright blue eyes. I knew without a doubt that we were looking at Tommy Romano's younger sister.

"You must be Victoria," she said. "I'm Louise. Please come in."

"It's nice to meet you, Louise," I said as I stepped inside. "This is my sister-in-law, Sofia. She's here to help me take notes, if that's okay."

Louise smiled. "Of course. Come sit in the sunroom."

We followed her to a small room at the back of the house. It had glass panes on three sides, but the fourth wall was lined with books. A black cat streaked from under the couch, and I jumped. "That's just Edgar," she said with a grin. "Don't mind him."

I couldn't help smiling back. "As in Poe, right? You did say you were a mystery fan."

"Yes," Louise said, "but I'm a bit embarrassed to say that I haven't read yours."

"Please don't be," I said. "But I'll send you an advance copy of the new one—how's that?"

"That would be lovely. Please sit." Sofia and I took

seats on the couch, and Louise sat across from us. "But this new project you're working on isn't a mystery, is it?"

That depends upon how you define "project," Louise. I pulled out my pad and pen, but then hesitated. I hated lying to this nice woman who'd welcomed us into her home. As always, when faced with guilt, I led with a partial truth. "Not really. It's more of a historical based on my family's history, so I'm seeking out people from their old neighborhood. My grandmother, Giulietta Rienzi—you probably knew her as Giulietta Catenari— told me some great stories about Oceanside Park in the forties and fifties."

"I remember your grandmother," Louise said. "And your great-grandmother, Ida. We would go to her when we were sick sometimes. Your grandmother and my brother, Tommy, were in the same class in high school."

I was grateful to see Sofia already writing, as I was in danger of getting lost in Louise's story. I didn't want to stop to take notes. "Yes, Nonna said wonderful things about your brother. He seemed so alive when she spoke about him that it struck me he'd make a compelling character." *And he would,* I thought. *Once I learn more about you, Tommy—and about your son, who- ever he is—I promise I'll put you in my book.* So this, at least, would not be a lie.

At the mention of her brother, Louise's face held an expression of warmth tinged with sadness, much as Nonna had looked when she spoke about Tommy. "My brother was a special young man," she said. "Larger than life, you know? In fact, hold on a minute. I'll be right back."

The second Louise left the room, Sofia turned to me. "You're gonna ask her about Elizabeth, right?"

"Eventually, Sofe. But give me a minute, will you? I feel bad enough being here on false pretenses—"

But Louise was returning with a large framed photo. "I think you'll have a better sense of him if you see this. This was his official army portrait."

Sofia let out a long breath. "Wow," she said.

I held the picture out in front of me. "Wow is right." The young Tommy Romano wore his hat back far enough to reveal the dark curls that my grandmother had talked about. But his eyes were an arresting blue, rimmed with black lashes. Only his broad shoulders and strong jawline saved him from being pretty. And while Jack Toscano was an attractive man, this guy was movie-star material. *If this man is your daddy, Jack,* I thought, *you don't look a whole lot like him.* I handed the photo back to Louise. "Now I know what all the girls saw in him," I said with a grin. "Including my grandmother."

"Aside from the fact that he was handsome," Louise said, "he was smart, athletically gifted, and kind. So kind."

Sofia gave me a quick nudge, and I thought I knew why. It was hard to imagine the stiff and reserved Jack Toscano as the son of this extraordinary boy. But how much is nature and how much is nurture? Toscano's experiences with his adoptive family were more likely than his DNA to have shaped his personality. Maybe we needed to track them down next.

"Tell us more about Tommy," Sofia said.

"Well, he was ten years older than I was," Louise said. "And, of course, I trailed behind him everywhere. But he let me. He'd use his pocket money to buy me ice cream or take me to the movies at the Paramount." She stopped. "I heard the Paramount still shows movies."

"It does, yes," I said. "It's kind of an art house now."

Louise looked out one of the large windows and sighed. "I haven't been back to Oceanside Park in all these years. Not even to walk the boardwalk." She shook her head. "I can't do it. It's just too painful. Is your family's restaurant still there, by the way?"

"Still going strong," I said. "I'm working there this summer while I do my research."

"Good for you," Louise said.

"Not really," Sofia piped up. "Nonna's running things now."

Louise laughed. "I didn't know her well, but even as a young woman, Giulietta came across as strong willed."

"That's putting it mildly, Louise," I said. "But I'll tell you what—when she talked about your brother, I saw a different side of her."

"He had that effect on people," she said. "He was . . . *beloved* in that town. There's no other way to put it."

It was time to move the conversation in a more sensitive direction. How much would the nine-year-old Louise have remembered about her brother's great romance? And would she connect the young Elisabetta with the Elizabeth Merriman, whose death had been all over the news? "Speaking of love, my grandmother told me that Tommy had a serious girlfriend before he left for Korea."

She nodded. "Elisabetta Caprio. She was as pretty as he was handsome. They were a striking couple. But her parents didn't approve of her dating at all, and *our* parents didn't approve of Tommy sneaking around. So I'm not sure how much time they were able to be together."

Long enough to conceive a child. "I have to say, it makes a romantic story."

Louise met my eyes; hers were tear filled. "Until its ending."

"Yes," I said. "Would you mind talking a little about that?"

"Not at all," she said. "There are so few people left I can talk to about Tommy. If he'd lived, he'd be eighty. It's so strange to imagine him as an old man. In my mind, he's forever nineteen."

That's how it would have been for Elizabeth Merriman, I thought. She would advance further into age, year after year, while Tommy Romano stayed a boy. Sitting on that couch in Louise's house, I was struck by a wave of sadness and sympathy for Elizabeth. "He'll always be that young man in the photo," I said.

Louise nodded. "We got word early in 1952 that he'd been killed. My mother took to her bed. My father just shut down. I was a little girl, alone in my grief." She shook her head. "We moved away about a month later. To this very house, in fact. And here I stayed."

By now my guilt was eating holes in my stomach. "I'm sorry if this has been difficult for you, Louise. I so appreciate your talking to me today."

"I'm happy to do it. I adored my brother, Victoria. And I didn't have him for very long. That's why I was so grateful to have known his son."

I felt Sofia stiffen on the couch next to me and kept my face averted from hers; we couldn't give anything away. "Tommy had a son?" I asked, trying to keep my voice neutral.

Louise nodded. "Yes, he and Elisabetta had a son. I didn't know at the time, of course. We'd moved by then and we cut all our ties with Oceanside after that; as I said, it was just too painful."

At this point, Sofia could no longer contain herself. "How did you find out about Tommy's son?"

"He found me about two years ago. Once his adoptive parents passed away, he began searching for his birth family; I'm his father's last living close relative."

"Do you know if he ever tracked down Elisabetta?" I asked.

"I'm not sure." She shook her head. "I think his feelings about her were conflicted. He told me he assumed she was dead. He didn't talk to me about her much, and, of course, I didn't really know her. Over the years I thought about trying to find her myself, but never followed through."

Sofia elbowed me again, a quick, sharp shot that said *tell her*. "In fact, Louise," I said, "she passed away recently."

"Did she?" Louise looked thoughtful. "I'm sorry to hear it."

I was about to ask her nephew's name when Louise

stood up. "Would you like to see a picture of Tommy's son?"

"Very much."

Louise walked to the bookcase and took down one of the framed photographs. She passed it to me, and I stared at the image of four men in combat fatigues, all wearing dark glasses. "This was taken in Afghanistan," she said. "It's a shame you can't see his beautiful blue eyes; they were exactly like Tommy's."

I grasped the frame so tightly my knuckles whitened. The four men in the photo were of varying ages; the two on either end appeared to be middle-aged. Louise pointed to the one on the left. "That's my nephew," she said. "The two young guys were in their company, and the guy on the right is their commanding officer. Thomas was very close to him."

The guy on the right. He stood a little apart from the other men, holding himself rigidly. There were deep lines in his forehead, and his skin was leathery. Despite the dark glasses, it was possible to read his expression: serious to the point of grim. *Jack Toscano.* Sofia peered over my shoulder, saw my face, but stopped herself from asking. I needed to make sure. I pointed to the other middle-aged man on the left side of the photo. "So that's your nephew," I said.

She nodded, and I watched in surprise as her lower lip trembled and tears rolled down her face. "That's Thomas," she whispered, her voice breaking. "He was a hero, just like his father. And like his father, he died serving his country."

Chapter Twenty-one

Sofia gripped the wheel as she drove just a bit too quickly down I-95. "That was like the mother lode of information right there."

I nodded. "My mind is spinning. Toscano's an imposter, and he's probably a killer. His eyes, Sofe—remember I told you they had that cloudy look? He said he had cataracts—"

"Contact lenses," Sofia interrupted. "I bet you anything he wears blue contacts. Did you ever see somebody with dark eyes wearing colored lenses?"

"Exactly, I know! They always look a little off. And, of course, Elizabeth wouldn't have gotten a good look at his eyes."

"And even if she did, she would have seen the blue lenses," she said.

"But he told me he took a DNA test. Which means he—"

"Took something from the dead son. Hair or fingernails. We never asked Louise how Thomas died, but Toscano had to have been there, right?"

"I would think so," I said with a small shudder. I had

a sudden image of Toscano leaning over the body of his dead comrade, taking a sample of his hair. "God," I said, "what a cold-blooded, greedy, opportunistic—"

"Creep," Sofia said.

"Yes, a creep for sure. And would you stop finishing my sentences, please?"

Sofia grinned and turned to me. "I wonder if Elizabeth was onto him, Vic, and he killed her to make sure he inherited. That's how it looks, doesn't it?"

"Probably. But there's got to be more to this. Louise said that Thomas assumed his mother was dead. What if he just told *Louise* that? He had to have known something about his birth mother that Toscano got wind of somehow. I wonder if he found documents or something."

"Vic, when we were looking at the picture from Afghanistan, Louise said that Thomas was very close to his commanding officer. They were the same age in a place with a lot of younger guys. Maybe Thomas confided in him; maybe he was planning to contact his mother all along."

"And once Thomas was dead, Toscano saw a way to make a fortune." I shook my head. "It's so tragic, this whole story."

"It would make a great subplot in your book, Vic," Sofia said. "I mean the early stuff, about Tommy and the young Elizabeth."

"Well," I said, "it's helped me see Elizabeth in a different light—that's for sure. Maybe she turned into an Iron Lady, but she didn't start that way."

"And she didn't deserve to get shoved off that seawall."

"No, she didn't." I looked out the car window at the swiftly passing greenery and the cloudless July sky. Though I tended to be skeptical about the existence of heaven, I found myself hoping that Tommy and Elisabetta and Thomas had found one another again. "Too many lives cut short," I said. "Too much sadness all around." Whatever it took, I would make sure that Toscano was brought to justice. I wasn't doing this for Dr. Chickie anymore—I was pursuing the truth for those long-ago teenagers and their dead son.

That night I took a walk along the beach. It was growing dusky; the day-trippers were long gone and except for a single fisherman, I was alone on the wide expanse of beach. The solitude and sound of the waves would help me think this through. I was due in Sutton's office in the morning to give my statement. And I was hoping to have some answers by now. I would have to tell them what Elizabeth had said to Dr. Chickie the night of the wedding; those damning words constituted a threat and gave Dr. C. a motive for murder. He was already in custody for one crime. Would my statement bring on an arrest for another?

I stood at the water's edge, watching the tide recede. I stooped to pick up a scallop shell, and under it was a piece of green sea glass, maybe from an old Coke bottle. I brushed the sand from its rough triangular shape and slipped it into my shorts pocket. Sea glass was a treasure these days; maybe it would bring me luck when I faced the Tiger Lady tomorrow.

Besides my formal statement, I would have to tell

Sutton what I'd learned about Toscano, but I would be risking her displeasure and a whole lot more. Giving her information about Toscano might take the focus from Dr. C. But doing so was an admission that I'd interfered in her investigation. I thought about my fictional detective, who at dark moments seemed more real to me than the characters in the drama all around me. I imagined his expression, his dark eyes serious under his Panama hat: *You must do the right thing, Victoria. Ah, but what is the right thing, Bernardo?*

I rolled up my jeans and stuck my toes in the surf. Still a little chilly for July, but at least there were no jellyfish yet. As I watched the water, I remembered long summer days on this beach, digging in the sand with my brother, watching him and his friends—including Tim—surf for hours. I was more of a splasher than a swimmer, though Danny had spent many an afternoon trying to teach me. *Danny. Of course.* I would call my brother. He wouldn't be happy about my involvement the case, but he could help me navigate the swift currents of events that threatened to drown me.

But my brother wasn't picking up his cell, which meant he was either at work or on his boat. It was nearly dark now, and I shivered in the cold surf. I walked back up the beach to my cottage, rinsing my feet in the outdoor shower before I went inside. The house was dark, and I fumbled for the light switch in living room. Still jumpy from my experience with William Fox, I turned on every light downstairs. *You're being silly, Vic,* I told myself, but locked the front door anyway. It was time for some fortification. I opened the fridge and poured myself a large chardonnay. I told myself I would sip it slowly and mull over our visit to Louise Romano. And then try to figure out what to do next. I sighed. I'd have to tell Sutton everything I knew; there was no way around it. I headed out the patio doors.

But no sooner had I sat down on my deck when I spied a distant figure making his way up the beach. He wasn't wearing dark glasses, but his stiff gait and upright bearing gave him away, and my stomach clenched in fear. Jack Toscano was walking up the beach toward my cottage. (Maybe I needed to talk to Landlord Sofia about an alarm system.) I had seconds to decide what to do. He knew I was here and probably knew I was alone. Even locking myself in was no guarantee I'd be safe from him, and I couldn't risk being trapped in the cottage with a dangerous man. *Please, God, let this be the right move.* I locked the door behind me and stood out on my deck. I would be safer out here, with a better chance of getting away or attracting attention. A wave of nausea washed over me as he made his way across the sand. I turned from his line of sight, took out my phone, and texted my brother: *Toscano at cottage. Feeling threatened. Come if you can, pls.* Then I hit the record function. *Please let there be enough power,* I prayed, as I slipped the phone back into my pocket. Then I turned to face him, crossed my arms, and willed my heart to stop pounding.

"Are you looking for me, Mr. Toscano?" I called.

He was no longer wearing the glasses, but it was too dark to see his eyes anyway. Stopping about ten yards from my deck, he stood with his hands jammed into the pockets of his windbreaker. "Yes, I was, Victoria."

"You can stop right where you are," I called back. "You can talk to me from there."

"What I have to say is not for anyone else's ears." He took two steps closer.

Should I tell him the police were on their way? I wasn't sure that was true; I hadn't gotten a return text. But even if Danny *was* on his way, I wanted to hear what Toscano had come to say to me. I just had to hope he wasn't there to kill me. "Don't come any closer," I said sharply.

"There's no reason to be afraid. I'm not going to hurt you."

"Then take your hands from your pockets and show me they're empty." What the hell was wrong with me? I was acting like a character in a police drama. I had no weapon, no way to protect myself against a former military man who could probably kill me with a well-placed karate chop. And I was giving *him* orders.

He slowly lifted both hands from his pockets, patted them quickly, and then spread his fingers wide. "See? No weapon. I'm just here to talk."

"So you've said." My hand still in my own pocket, I gripped my phone, willing it to vibrate in my hand. *Text me back, Danny. Please text me back.*

Toscano pointed at me and I flinched. "Now as a show of good faith," he said, "why don't you put that phone down on your deck? Right where I can see it."

I took it from my pocket and, bending down slowly, let it rest on my deck.

"Good girl. I don't want you doing anything stupid now."

Oh, right. 'Cause I haven't done anything stupid yet. Like scrounging for evidence at the Belmont Club. Like getting involved this mess in the first place. Dr. Chickie owed me big time for this one. "I . . . I won't," I said, unable to keep my voice from shaking. "Just say what you came to say."

"I will. But this isn't the first conversation we've had, Victoria. When I saw you at the club, I knew you'd been over by the beach path—how else would you get a splinter in your hand and grass in your hair? But I chalked that up to curiosity. And then I told you about my relationship with Elizabeth, and the fact that I had no motive to kill her. I assumed that would be the end of it. I tried to warn you." He shifted slightly in the sand, inching closer to the deck. "But then you returned to the club, didn't you? Why? So you could listen to Sally's gossip and snoop around the kitchen? For what—evidence?" He smirked, and I shuddered in a wave of dislike for this man. *Thank God you're not her son*, I thought.

I lifted my chin, determined not to be afraid *and* to keep him talking. "Not that it's any of your business, but I'm doing research for a book."

He let out a harsh laugh. "Ah yes. I forgot I'm speaking to the famous mystery writer Vick Reed. And your visit to Louise Romano—was that research, too?"

My arms stiffened at my sides. "How did you know about that?"

"Let's just say that William Fox has been doing a little work for me as a private detective."

So that was why Fox had shown up that night. "You had him following me, didn't you?"

"It's amazing what that man will do in anticipation of a great big payout. Too bad he'll never see that money."

I had a sudden image of the little man standing outside his sad house in his bathrobe and pajamas, and felt a lurch of pity. "Did something happen to William Fox?"

Toscano's voice had an edge. "William Fox is not your concern." He shuffled his feet in the sand, bringing him a few inches closer to the edge of my deck. "What *is* your concern, however, is that visit to Louise Romano. And now it's mine, as well."

Because I know your secret, Toscano. I know you're not Elizabeth's son. I tried to keep my emotions under control—if only I'd inherited Frank Rienzi's famous poker face. "You don't need to be concerned about my conversation with her, Mr. Toscano."

His face split into a sneering grin. "Oh, Victoria, do call me Jack. But I'm not sure I believe you." He took a step forward, and I glanced around wildly, first to the empty beach and then the quiet street behind me. Where was my brother?

"Why so skittish, dear?" he asked. "I'm only here for information. And you're going to give it to me. *What* did Louise tell you?" He bared his teeth like an aggressive dog, and I clamped my hands to my thighs to keep them from shaking.

"She told me that . . . that her nephew had served courageously in the Middle East." I let out a breath.

"That he looked a lot like his father. That she was grateful she'd found him and that she'd gotten to know him."

"Interesting choice of language there. But you're a writer," he said, edging closer to the cottage. "And words are your thing. And I'm sure you've been telling yourself all kinds of stories about me and Elizabeth Merriman."

I shook my head. "I don't know what you're talking about. I went to see Louise Romano because I'm doing research for a book. I . . . I've told you everything. She barely mentioned you." Which was true. But of little comfort at this moment.

"I'd like to believe you, Victoria. I really would." With that, he stepped close enough for my outside light to flash on. He froze in the sand as the light fully illuminated his face—including his dark brown eyes.

Startled by the bright light, Toscano threw his arm over his face. I was about to make a run for it when I heard the roar of a motorcycle coming down my driveway. There were two men on the bike, one of them in police blues. It was still moving when my brother jumped off, tore off his helmet, and aimed his service revolver at Toscano.

"Hands in the air, Toscano. Now."

Toscano complied, but affected an injured air. "Officer, you're making a mistake. I was just speaking with Miss Rienzi."

"Right," Danny barked. "And William Fox locked himself in the trunk of your car. Now keep your hands where I can see them."

What had Toscano done to William Fox? And why? Maybe Fox had gotten cold feet about following me and tried to call off the deal. But my thoughts were interrupted by the sound of the other man cutting the bike's engine. In the dark, I assumed he was a fellow officer in plainclothes, but when he took off his helmet, I got a clear look at his curly hair. *Tim, coming to my rescue.*

Was it shallow of me—not to mention foolhardy— that the sight of Tim barreling toward me banished any fear I had of Toscano? As I threw myself into Tim's arms, I went from starring in a police drama to a chick flick in the space of about three seconds. He was holding me so hard I couldn't breathe, but I didn't care.

"Are you okay, Vic? He didn't hurt you, did he?" He pressed his hands flat against my back, and I could feel his heart banging in his chest.

"No, he didn't hurt me. I'm okay." I slid my arms around him, rested my cheek against his chest, and, for the first time in days, felt truly safe.

He grabbed my face in both hands, and I was sure he was coming in for a kiss. I was about to close my eyes when I saw the look on his face. "You have to stop doing this, do you understand?" he said through his teeth. "You're not a cop. You're not a goddamned detective." He let go of my face and stepped back, ran a hand across his face, and shook his head. "You have to stop doing this," he said again. "My heart can't take it."

"But—" I started to say, but was interrupted by the appearance of two squad cars, lights flashing, one of them from Belmont Beach.

"Your brother called for backup," Tim said. "You know, 'cause *he's* the professional."

As Danny led Toscano to one of the cars, he paused just long enough throw me a look of cold fury. My eyes were pleading *please don't tell Mom*, but he merely shook his head. Tim and I stood in my driveway in silence, watching both cars drive away, one of which held a murderer.

I was still hanging on to Tim when a white van swung around the corner. I had seen that white van before, and as it approached my cottage, I could see its NEWS 10 logo and the equipment sticking up from the top of it.

"Oh no," I said, as it screeched to a halt in front of my house. In a flurry of activity, doors opened, tech guys jumped out, and my old friend Nina LaGuardia appeared, already in full makeup. Even in the dark, I could see the glint of triumph in her eyes as she shoved her microphone under my nose.

"Ms. Rienzi," she said, "how does it feel to apprehend a murderer—*again*?"

Chapter Twenty-two

*L*ater that night, I was sitting with my parents at the restaurant when my brother appeared in the dining room. "I thought you'd all like to know that Toscano's in custody," he said as he took a seat. I noticed he made a point of not looking my way. *He's still mad*, I thought. *How much will he say in front of them?*

"Well, that's a relief," my mother said. "At least poor Chickie won't have to deal with people thinking he's a murderer, too."

My Dad had his laptop open in front of him. "I don't see anything about it online, Dan."

"Not yet, Pop," Danny said. "But it will be."

Thank you, I said with my eyes, but my brother only frowned. "Has Toscano been formally charged, Danny?"

"Well, not with murder," he said. "They've got him on kidnapping and fraud, though."

"So they know he's not Merriman's son?" I asked.

My parents both looked up in confusion. After a quick glance at Danny, I decided to tell part of the story. "Elizabeth had given a baby up for adoption sixty years ago," I said. "Toscano was pretending to be her biological son to defraud her of her fortune."

"That's terrible!" my mother exclaimed. "What a cruel thing to do. Did they find the real son?"

"He's dead, Mom," I said, earning another frown from my brother, who was clearly wondering where I'd gotten this information. "So, Dan," I said, "have they made Toscano take a DNA test?"

He crossed his arms and stared at me. "Yes. And there's an exhumation order in for Merriman's body. But in the meantime, he's got a sister in Maryland who came forward and swore Toscano hadn't been adopted. Even offered to do a DNA test herself. They'd been on the outs for years."

"Such a shame," my mother said. "A brother and sister being estranged like that."

"It is, isn't it?" I said, looking pointedly at Danny, who only shrugged.

"But what's really sad," my mom continued, "is that poor woman thinking she'd found her son after all these years. How lonely she must have been."

"You're right, Mom," I said. "I'd been thinking the same thing." I turned to my brother, whose tight expression told me I was still not forgiven. "Danny, when you got to my house last night, how did you know about what happened to William Fox?"

"When I called Belmont for backup," he said, "they were already looking for Toscano. He'd forced Fox into the trunk of his car."

"Is Fox okay?" I asked. "He's the reason for the kidnapping charge, right?"

He nodded. "Fox is okay. A neighbor heard him screaming and kicking from the trunk. The neighbor called nine-one-one and Belmont's guys got him out pretty quick. Luckily, he was willing to talk. He admitted that Toscano was paying him for information about Merriman Industries."

"I guess Toscano was trying to fill in the gaps about Elizabeth's life," I said.

"Fox was also supposed to be spying on you." Danny pointed to me accusingly, as though I had invited William Fox to lurk outside my cottage at night.

The less said on that subject the better. So I spoke a different thought aloud. "I wonder if Toscano had planned to kill Fox to get him out of the way."

Danny shrugged. "Could be. Throwing him in that trunk was an act of desperation."

I nodded. "You mean just getting him out of the way for the time being until he figured out to do with him." *And what might he have done to me?* The thought made me shudder. "Dan, is Toscano saying anything at all?"

"Not much. Except that he insists up and down that he didn't kill Elizabeth Merriman. And claims he's got an alibi."

"Does it check out?"

Danny shook his head. "Don't know yet; Belmont's on that now."

Something about this didn't make sense. Why would Toscano clam up about the kidnapping and fraud yet talk about the murder? Did he really have an alibi for that night? But I was too tired to think it out. I stood up and grabbed my purse. "Listen, I need to go, guys. To-

morrow's my appointment with Regina Sutton," I
said.

My brother crossed his arms and narrowed his eyes
in my direction. "Guess you'll have a lot to tell her."

County Prosecutor Regina Sutton stared me down
from across her desk, her amber eyes blazing. "Ms.
Rienzi," she asked, "do I show up at your house, sit
down next to you at your desk, and tell you how to
plot your latest novel?"

I swallowed audibly. "Of course not, but—"

"But what? There is no *but*. Once again, you have
involved yourself in a criminal investigation. *My* investigation. And you are a hindrance to it. You understand what 'hindering an investigation' means, do you
not?" She clasped her hands in front of her, leaning
toward me as if to say *Let's see you get out of this one.*

So I tried my only weapon at hand—diversion. "I
thought I was here to give a statement about the night
of Elizabeth Merriman's death. And I've already done
that. Your assistant took it. It's all signed and everything." *And it makes things look so bad for Dr. C.*

She nodded and smiled tightly. "That is so, but now
it is my turn to speak with you. And I have a question
or two. First, what was Jack Toscano doing at your
house last evening?"

Okay, this one I can answer. "He just showed up. I
was out on my deck—it faces the beach—and I saw
him approaching."

"From the beach side?" She pulled a pad toward her
and began taking notes.

"Yes. He said he wanted to talk to me."

"About what?"

Now here's where things might get dicey. *Stick to the truth, Vic.* "He found out that I went to interview Louise Romano."

She looked up from her pad, frowning. "Who is Louise Romano?"

Was it possible that Sutton's team had not dug into Elizabeth's past? If Sutton knew about Toscano's masquerade as young Tommy, she might not be so quick to arrest Dr. Chickie for murder. I decided to take a big gamble. I sat up tall in my chair and looked straight into the Tiger Lady's eyes. "I sought out Louise Romano as part of my research for a book about my family. My grandmother had knowledge of Elizabeth Merriman's past, and I thought it would make a good subplot. Louise is the sister of Tommy Romano, a young man who died in the Korean War."

"So that visit was research for a book, eh? Would that be like the research you were doing back in May, Ms. Rienzi?"

The *doing research for a book* excuse was growing increasingly flimsy. I shook my head. "No. The story of Elisabetta Caprio and Tommy Romano was a tragic one, and it *is* worthy of a book." That, at least, was true. "But after I heard it, I realized it might have bearing on her murder." I paused deliberately, praying I could carry this off.

Regina Sutton's head snapped up, setting her dangling earrings shaking. "If you have information critical to this case, I insist you share it with me now."

"I fully intend to cooperate with your investigation, Ms. Sutton, but I, uh, have a concern."

She narrowed her eyes. "And what might that be?"

Now or never, Vic. "My concern is that you might perceive my research as a hindrance. Particularly as I have been speaking with people who are involved in this case. And I know that hindering a criminal investigation carries certain . . . consequences. But I would hope that the information I provide might be perceived as a gesture of good faith that could, uh, mitigate my actions."

Sutton sat back in her chair, crossed her arms, and tilted her head, a smile playing about her mouth. "Are you trying to cut a deal with me, Ms. Rienzi?"

"Yes," I said, letting out a large breath. "Look, I know it looks bad for Dr. Natale right now, but I don't believe he's a murderer. And I stumbled across some background information on Elizabeth Merriman that I think might build a case against Jack Toscano. I know I'd be compelled to give you that information anyway, but, frankly, I'm terrified of getting in trouble or causing problems for my family. And I don't know who scares me more: you or my grandmother." The words sped recklessly from my mouth; I was talking the way Sofia drove, and praying I wouldn't crash and burn.

Still leaning back in her chair, Sutton shook her head. "Now, if this were a police show on television, this is where you and I would bond, right? We'd shake hands, exchange some clever banter, and team up to put a murderer behind bars. Is that how you see this little scene playing out?"

"N-not exactly."

She flattened her palms on the desk, revealing ten glittery nails worthy of my mother. I stared at them while she spoke. "Well, this is not a television show," she said. "This is not one of your books. And I don't make deals with people who make my job harder."

I hung my head, feeling like a third-grader who'd just gotten caught stealing the milk money. Only third-graders didn't end up in jail. "I understand," I mumbled.

"However," she said with a sigh, "I don't believe your intentions were malicious. And I might even believe that *part* of what compelled you was research. And since Toscano isn't talking, I'll take any information we can get." She opened a drawer and set a small voice recorder on her desk. "So, tell me your story, Ms. Rienzi. But understand, I make no promises."

It was too soon to give in to relief, but I did breathe a bit easier. I started with my grandmother's story of the young lovers and the baby put up for adoption, and ended with my visit to Louise Romano and what Toscano had said at my house the night before.

Sutton paused the recorder. "So, Toscano might well have had knowledge of Merriman's biological son? Enough to pass himself off as Thomas Romano Jr.?" I nodded and she pressed the record button.

"They served together in Afghanistan until Thomas was killed," I said. "Louise, his aunt, indicated the two were close. So it's quite possible that Thomas confided in Toscano. Then when Thomas died in action, Toscano saw an opportunity. He got the blue contact lenses and presented himself as Elizabeth's long-lost son."

Sutton nodded. "Go on."

"He knew the blue contacts wouldn't fool anybody but Elizabeth, who's partially blind herself. So he came up with 'eye trouble' of his own and wore dark glasses as much as possible. Toscano also told me he passed a DNA test; if that's true, he must have taken something from the body."

She raised an eyebrow. "Try to limit your theorizing, Ms. Rienzi. What else did Toscano tell you?"

"He said that at the time of her death, Elizabeth had already settled sizable assets on him and that he proved that to the police. He indicated to me that he'd have no reason to kill her." As I spoke, I had a sense of disquiet. What was it about Toscano and Elizabeth that was nagging at me?

"And he told you this last evening?"

I started at her sharp tone, and she paused the recorder again. "Did he or did he *not* tell you this last night?"

"Not exactly," I said. "He came to see me at the restaurant a couple of days ago."

"You've spoken to him before?" She pointed a glittery finger at me. "And you're still claiming you did *not* seek him out?"

"Absolutely not. He struck me as dangerous, and I steered clear of him." I didn't add that that I was aware of the kidnapping charge or his association with William Fox; there was no way I could pass off knowledge of Fox as research. I had to pray she wouldn't ask me about him.

"At least you had that much sense," she muttered,

and hit the RECORD button again. "Getting back to last evening, Ms. Rienzi. Please recount for the record what transpired between you and Toscano."

I finished up with a description of my conversation with Toscano, up to the moment the light flashed in his face and I noted his brown eyes. "And that's when my brother arrived," I said.

She turned off the recorder and folded her hands. "While I acknowledge that this information is helpful, Ms. Rienzi, as I said before, I make no promises." She leaned across her desk, fixing me with her feline gaze. "And I had better not hear of any further involvement in this case. Do I make myself clear?"

I jumped to my feet. "As an unmuddied stream, Ms. Sutton."

"Writers," she said, shaking her head. "You're dismissed, Ms. Rienzi. *For now.*"

I left her office with shaky knees and very wet armpits. I was pretty sure I'd escaped being arrested. And maybe bought Dr. Chickie some extra time.

But I had barely left the county office when a slow dawning of light rose in my brain. Toscano already had control of Elizabeth's fortune. The only reason he would have for killing her was if she'd been onto him; he'd want her dead before she could change her will and expose him as a fraud. But I'd seen them the night of her death. I closed my eyes, straining to remember what I'd witnessed between the two of them. Elizabeth across the room, deep in conversation with Toscano. His head bent close to hers, and she smiling up at him. *Smiling.* Would she smile at a man who'd defrauded her of a fortune? The implication was clear—as late as a couple of hours before Elizabeth's death, she still believed Toscano was her son. And if this assumption was correct, I'd just punched a great big hole in the case against him.

I got into my car automatically, sat unmoving with my hands on the wheel. Should I go back inside and talk to Sutton? Didn't this information change things— and not in a good way—for Dr. C.? Just then my phone vibrated, and Nina LaGuardia's name appeared on its screen.

"Damn," I said, but answered it anyway. "Wow, Nina, it's ten thirty. You're late this morning."

"Ever the wit, aren't you, Victoria?"

That would be to make up for your lack of them, Nina. I sighed. "What is it you want? I'm cooperating with Regina Sutton's investigation; you know I can't talk to you—on the record or off."

"Yes, dear, I remember. I'm actually calling with some news for *you*."

I should have picked up on the sly tone in her voice, but I was too busy grabbing a pen and a pack of sticky notes from my purse. "I'm listening," I said.

Her trilling laugh drilled into my ear, and I winced. "Good," she said. "Because one of my sources gave me a *very* interesting piece of information last night." She paused for effect.

"Just say it, Nina, would you?"

"Now you write this down, darling, okay? I'll speak nice and clear so you don't miss a word. Here it is: A witness has come forward from the night of Elizabeth

Merriman's death. Apparently, he was out for a midnight stroll on the beach. And guess what he saw?"

Now I really was listening, my pen poised and ready. "Go on."

"Well, this witness claims he saw Elizabeth and another person walking on the path between the club and the beach."

Cradling the phone, I scribbled some notes and waited. "Another person?"

"Uh huh. Another person described as short, stocky, and bald. Wearing a dark suit. And leading Elizabeth by the arm."

"That doesn't mean anything," I said. *Except doom for Dr. Chickie.* "Did the witness see anything else?"

She laughed again, and I held the phone farther from my ear. "You mean did he see the Embezzling Orthodontist shove Merriman over the seawall? Sadly, no. But he saw enough. Enough to put Dr. Charles Natale in an extremely sticky position, wouldn't you say?"

The answer was obvious. Had my parents heard this news? And then another thought occurred to me, one that had probably crossed Nina's usually obtuse mind as well: Dr. Natale was a close friend of my dad's, and Frank Rienzi was a well-known figure in Oceanside Park. If Dr. Chickie was arrested for murder, the Casa Lido would once again be dragged into a murder investigation, this time at the height of the summer season. I pressed my fingers to my eyes, trying to sort out what I should do next.

"Victoria?" Nina said sharply.

"I'm here."

"What's the matter, dear? Did I catch you off guard with that little tidbit? Now, while I have you on the phone, I have a question or two for you. How close is your father to Charles Natale? And how does it feel to find yourself, once again, in the middle of a murder investigation?"

"I have no comment, Nina," I said through my teeth.

"Oh, but you will, Victoria," she sang out. "You will."

Chapter Twenty-three

Sofia met me at the restaurant, where I filled her in on my adventures, starting with the encounter with Toscano and ending with my visit to Prosecutor Sutton. Dressed in her dance clothes, she sat with her chin in her hands, giving me more attention than I was used to. At least from her.

"So, Danny and Tim came to your rescue last night? I'm jealous," she said.

"You're kidding me, right? Tell me you'd want to be caught alone with a criminal." I stopped short of calling him a murderer, however.

"If it meant two hot guys roaring up on a motorcycle to save me? Hell, yes." She took the red folder from a large messenger bag and set it on the table. "Guess we can mark this 'case closed,' huh?"

"I'm not so sure, Sofe. Something struck me as I left Sutton's office and—"

We were interrupted by the sound of the front door and turned around to face my mother, who walked straight to our table. "Hello, honey," she said to me.

"Hello, Sofia," she said quietly. Was there a softening in her tone?

"Oh, hi, Nicolina," Sofia said. "How are you?"

"I'm well, hon, thank you." My mom moved closer to her daughter-in-law and frowned. "But you look thin, Sofia. Are you feeling all right?"

The air around us was suddenly charged. I watched Sofia's eyes widen slightly, her throat move as she swallowed nervously. "I'm . . . fine."

Still frowning, my mother took a closer look at Sofia's face. "There are little shadows under your eyes," she said. "Are you getting enough sleep?" Her eyes flicked to Sofia's V-neck leotard. My sister-in-law had always been curvy, but now her breasts swelled over the opening of her top. I guess there are some signs of pregnancy you can't always hide. In the growing silence, I glanced at Sofia, who sat frozen in place. "It's . . . it's the heat," she finally said.

"Probably." My mother's face gave nothing away. "Well, I need to get started in the office, girls." She looked at Sofia. "You take care of yourself, now," she said.

After her footsteps died away, my sister-in-law looked at me with panic in her eyes. "I'm so busted!" she hissed. "She knows, Vic. I can tell."

"You're probably right. But is that such a bad thing? You've found the absolute surest way to get back into my mother's good graces, and you're upset?"

She leaned closer, lowering her voice. "What if she tells Danny?"

I shook my head. "She'd never do that, even if she suspects. But don't you think it's time to tell him?"

She hung her head. "Yes. I can't avoid it anymore."

I grabbed her two hands. "I'm so glad, SIL. I know you guys will work things out. And in the meantime, I'm about to run out and buy little Bernardo or Isabella a whole bunch of presents."

"Bernardo? Isabella? Do you really think I'll name this baby after a character in your books?" She let out a laugh, sounding just like her old self. She packed the red folder and pushed in her chair. "My first class is in a few minutes, so I'd better hit it. And I'll talk to Danny today. I promise."

"That's great, Sofe. And let me know how it goes, okay?" She was out the door before I realized I hadn't told her what I remembered about Toscano. Or about Nina's phone call. And how that information changed everything about this case.

But things got busy quickly once lunch preparation was under way, giving me a convenient excuse to avoid sharing what I now knew: that Toscano might not be Elizabeth's murderer, and that Dr. C. was looking guiltier by the minute. Even cleaning lettuce at the salad station was better than facing that uncomfortable truth. And I would have to go back and tell Sutton what I'd remembered about Toscano and Elizabeth the night of the murder if I wanted to stay out of trouble myself. But at least I could try to talk to Sofia about it first. I glanced at the clock; if I hurried, I might be able to catch her between classes. Wiping my hands on my apron, I whirled around to come face-to-face with my mother.

"Were you going somewhere, Victoria?" My mother's normally cheerful expression was questioning, one might even say suspicious.

"Uh . . ." If I told her I was off to call Sofia, that would open a line of conversation I was not about to pursue. I was sure she had her suspicions about her daughter-in-law's pregnancy, but no way would I confirm them. "Actually, Mom," I said, "I was coming to see you. Could we talk in the dining room?"

My mind raced as we walked down the hallway from the kitchen. What *did* I want to see her about? It had to be pretty big to keep her away from the subject of whether or not Sofia was pregnant. Maybe I should tell her what Nina had shared—she would find out soon enough from Brenda, anyway, and the news *did* have ramifications for us and the restaurant. I led her to the family table, where we both sat down.

"Listen, Mom," I said. "You know I spoke with Regina Sutton this morning, right?"

Her eyes narrowed, her radar turned up high. "Are you in trouble, Victoria?"

"No." *Not yet anyway.* I put my hand on her arm. "I just want you and Daddy to be prepared—"

"I know," she said nodding. "Chickie could be under suspicion for murder."

Could be? "It's more serious than that, Mom. Nina LaGuardia—you know, that reporter who drives me crazy—called to tell me that there's an eyewitness."

My mom's hand flew to her mouth. "To the murder?"

"Not to the actual murder, no. But somebody saw a short, stocky bald man leading Elizabeth down that beach path."

"No," she breathed. "It must be a mistake. Someone's lying—Chickie would never hurt anyone! And what about poor Brenda—"

"Mom," I interrupted, "right now I'm concerned for you and Daddy."

"I don't understand."

"You're friends with Dr. Chickie. He and Daddy play cards together. There could be a . . . a *taint* on you guys or the restaurant. Don't you see?"

She dropped her voice and leaned closer. "You mean because of what happened before Memorial Day?"

"Right. We could find ourselves associated with a murder yet again. At least in people's minds."

My mom let out a breath. "That's ridiculous. Your father and I weren't even there!"

"But I was, don't forget. And I heard that exchange between Dr. Chickie and Elizabeth Merriman. She threatened him, Mom. If this goes to trial, you understand I'll probably have to testify."

She shook her head, her auburn curls jiggling. "This just gets worse and worse."

I took her hands. "Whatever happens, we'll weather it. I'll do whatever I can, and so will Danny. We all know Dr. C. is innocent." But as I spoke the words, I felt a flicker of doubt.

She squeezed my hands briefly and stood up. "Thank you for letting me know, honey. But don't worry about Daddy and me. I think it will all be okay in the end." Her eyes took on a dreamy expression, and her lips curved in a slight smile. "I think there are good things ahead of us."

She means the baby, I thought, and I smiled back. "Me too," I said.

I waited until she closed the door to her office before I got moving. We were only a few minutes from opening for lunch, and I had to get through to Sofia. But when I took out my phone, there was a text from my brother that made my heart sink:

Toscano alibi checks out

So Toscano had been telling the truth about that, at least. He hadn't threatened me because I was about to expose him as a murderer, but as a fraud. I slipped my phone back into my apron pocket and sneaked into the one place I knew I'd have privacy: the Casa Lido restroom. Lovingly decorated by my mom with prints of the Amalfi Coast and Italian landmarks, and scented with dried lavender from the garden, it was actually a pleasant place to hang out.

Once I got her on the line, I filled Sofia in on what I remembered about Toscano and Elizabeth from the night of her death, what Nina had told me, and Danny's text confirming Toscano's innocence. I studied the pictures of the Ponte Vecchio in Florence and the Spanish Steps in Rome while Sofia talked.

"Natale must have done it, Vic," she said. "He's on the scene. He's got a motive, and his only alibi is from his family."

I leaned against the sink, making sure not to mess up the pristine state of the restroom. "But there's no proof that the man seen with Elizabeth was Dr. C. Maybe it's someone we don't know about or haven't considered."

But Sofia was insistent. "C'mon, Vic. A short, stocky bald man in a dark suit is seen leading Elizabeth Merriman down that walkway to the platform. Where else is there to go with this? Especially since Toscano's alibi checked out?"

I dropped my voice in case someone was outside the door—and by "someone," I meant my grandmother. "Eyewitness accounts can be wrong. Think about all the people who are wrongly accused or convicted of crimes because witnesses were mistaken."

But she wasn't buying it. As Sofia continued to repeat the litany of evidence against Dr. Chickie, I focused on one question: Were we missing something or someone? And then I had a thought.

"Hey, Sofe," I interrupted. "William Fox is a short man."

"With a head full of hair!" She laughed. "Did he shave his head to commit the murder? I suppose he's been wearing a wig this whole time."

At Sofia's words, the first moment of apprehension came as a tingling sensation, a tiny biological nudge to my system. Then I raised my eyes to the print on the bathroom wall, read the words across the bottom, and the tingle grew to a full-out shiver. "I have to go, Sofe," I said, my voice echoing in the small space. I cut off the call before she had a chance to ask me anything else, tore off my apron, and ran like hell.

Chapter Twenty-four

I double-checked the address I'd written down as I pulled up to the house, a modern bi-level overlooking the sea, in a pale peach color that suggested the last rays of the sun at the end of the day. There was no doubt that its owner was a person of wealth. And now I had a pretty clear idea of where that wealth originated. I walked up the stone path to the door, thinking that I should have been nervous. Instead, a sense of sadness tugged at me.

She answered the door without her wig. She was completely bald. Her face was devoid of makeup. A few sparse hairs marked where her brows should have been, but her eyes were lashless and ringed in dark, purplish circles. Her skin had a yellow cast, her lips pale, her blue eyes faded. She didn't seem surprised to see me; without a word, she motioned me inside.

She sat with a grimace, and I imagined that by now she was in a lot of pain. Next to her chair was a small table that held a glass of water, hand sanitizer, tissues, and several prescription bottles. This spacious, modern living room had become a sickroom.

I took a seat across from her and leaned forward in my chair. "You must know why I'm here, Kate."

She nodded, took a tiny sip of water, and briefly closed her eyes. "You know," she said in a raspy voice.

"I don't know everything. But a couple of minutes ago some things finally fell into place. The scarf you always wore. The heavy makeup. Your weak grip when we shook hands. How you seemed to tire easily. And you wore black the night of the murder. And here's something else I know: There are two men—both criminals, I'll admit—who aren't murderers."

Kate looked me straight in the eye. "I'm the one who caused her death."

"Because of your dad," I said. I pointed to her table of medicines. "And because of you. Because you've got nothing to lose."

One side of her mouth lifted in a strained attempt to smile. "You're right on that score. I got nothing to lose. Except my life, of course." She shifted in her chair and winced. "And that should be happening anytime now."

"Kate, if you can't do this, it's okay. I shouldn't even be here—"

She held up her hand. "Just let me tell it, okay? It will be a relief." She took a sip of water, then a painful breath before she spoke. "My father worked for Merriman for more than thirty years before he died," she said, "first for Mr. Merriman and then for her. Asbestos was in a lot of things they used all the time, like house siding and roofing, for example. Insulation for housing and pipes. It was in cement and joint compound—almost any building material you could think of. In the early days, they didn't know how dangerous it was to handle the stuff. But by the time Elizabeth took over, there were clear guidelines. Ones she didn't follow." She shook her head slowly. "Not even something as simple as using face masks to protect them from breathing that crap in."

She paused, and I spoke. "Your father was one of the plaintiffs in the suit—Lorenzo DePonti."

She grinned again, a real one this time. "That was brilliant of me, huh, calling myself Bridges?" I couldn't help smiling back at her, but there was a part of me that was screaming: *You're smiling at a murderer, Vic!*

"Actually," I said, "it took me longer than it should have. My family speaks Italian. I felt like an idiot when I finally made the connection."

She shook her head. "What does it matter now? But, yes, I was born Catherine DePonti. And I invested my father's settlement from Merriman and became a rich woman." She lifted her arm and gestured at the paintings, the fireplace, and the expensive furniture. "For all the good it did me," she said. She looked out a window toward the ocean and then turned back to me. "I don't think I have to tell you that I'd trade it all to have my parents back. To buy myself even one more year."

I was puzzled at her choice of words. "Did you lose your mother, too?"

"So that didn't turn up in your research, Victoria?" Her mouth twisted. "Yes, I lost my mother, too. Elizabeth Merriman killed us all, just as if she'd used a gun. Except that bullets are quicker and the pain is short-lived."

"I don't understand," I said.

Her eyes fluttered closed again, and I could see she was trying to conserve what was left of her energy. She opened her eyes, and when she spoke, her voice was strong. "I was an only child. Italian family—you know how that is. It's not like I was spoiled, but I got lots of love and attention. We were close, all three of us. In fact, it was our closeness that killed us. Every day when my dad came home from work, my mom and I would wait by the door, and before he did anything else, he'd hug and kiss us both." She took a sip of water and rested her head against the back of the chair. "My dad worked with that stuff for years. He'd come home with it in his hair, on his clothes. Clothes my mother would shake out and launder. And there was enough of it to make her sick. In fact, she got sick first. I don't know if you found this out when you were digging, but family members of people exposed to asbestos can get sick, too, and it's always fatal. It wasn't long before she died that my father started developing tumors, too, and I watched it all again. You might even say I had a ringside seat to my *own* death."

I blinked, feeling the tears start behind my eyes. But something told me that if I showed any emotion, I'd never get the full truth from her. I swallowed hard and took a breath. "When were you diagnosed?"

"A little over two years ago."

"I'm confused about something," I said. "Your parents died more than twenty years ago and—"

"Why did take so long for me to get sick?" she interrupted. "My doctors tell me the latency period for mesothelioma is long, decades sometimes. But once those tumors take hold, you're done. All the chemo does is buy you time." She pointed to her bald head. "This round was the last try. But I'm out of options."

"So you knew when you came here a month ago . . ."

"I knew I was dying. Yes. In fact, I had hardly any time left. That's what helped make up my mind to do it."

"Kate," I said quietly, "can you answer some questions for me?"

"Okay." She sighed, and even that seemed to cause her pain. "I'm gonna have to answer to the police soon enough, right?"

I nodded. "I'll try not to tire you out, okay? I think I've pieced most of it together. When you came to work at the Belmont last month, you knew she was president of the club?"

"Yes. I worked my ass off to rise as a pastry chef, just so I could eventually get the chance to get close to her. And then I did," she said simply. "If you're asking did I come here to kill her, the answer is yes."

Her words were chilling, but I couldn't help being fascinated by them. "So you planned it all?"

She looked at me with sunken eyes. "Yes, I planned it. I've wanted revenge on her long before I got sick myself."

"That night," I said, "I overheard you both fighting. Was it anything specific?"

Kate gave a small, crooked smile. "That was just me pushing her buttons and her threatening to can me. We did that once a week."

"When I saw you after that, you said—"

"That somebody should put her lights out. And you're wondering why I'd say that when that was actually my plan."

"Right. Why call attention to yourself in that way?"

She rubbed her eyes. "You know, I'm not sure myself. Maybe I was just that cocky that I wouldn't be caught. Or maybe I didn't care if I was caught."

"Or maybe you *wanted* to be caught," I said. "Like calling yourself Bridges, which is essentially your real name. And then giving yourself a really obvious alibi at eleven thirty when you left the bar in such a loud and public way."

"I don't have time for psychoanalysis," she growled, and for a minute I saw a glimmer of the feisty Chef Kate.

"Maybe not," I said. "But I think implicating Dr. Natale didn't sit right with you."

She sighed. "I didn't like having to do that to him. But here was a short, stocky bald guy who'd just gotten caught taking money from the club. He was handed to me on a silver platter."

"I'm not sure his family would see it that way. But you're right—your builds are close. All you had to do was wear black that night, wash your face, and take off your scarf and wig. From a distance, it would look as though a short bald *man* in a dark suit was leading Elizabeth down that walkway."

She nodded. "After I went out the front door at eleven thirty, I went only as far as my car, where I wiped off the makeup and took off my wig. I waited until I saw the Natales leave. I knew Elizabeth would go back to her office, as she did every night after an event. She's often the last to go. Well, her and Toscano."

I leaned forward in my chair. "Wouldn't Toscano have been the one to drive her home that night?"

"Usually. But I told him she'd called a cab. And I told *her* he'd left without her."

"And you offered to drive her home?" My heart sank at the thought of the old woman accepting an offer of a ride from her killer.

"Yup," Kate said. "And she wasn't happy about it, believe me. But she had no choice." Her voice hardened. "I didn't give her one."

"But once you left the club, she must have realized you weren't going out to the parking lot. Her eyes weren't that bad."

"Oh, her eyes were pretty bad, believe me. But I wanted to make sure, so I cut the lights. I threw the breaker for the part of the kitchen that included that side-door light. She was standing in the dark kitchen, panicked. I took her arm and told her I'd lead her out."

"But that cane was like an extension of her senses. Once her feet hit those wooden boards, she would have known where she was."

Kate nodded. "Oh yeah. And of course she could hear the ocean, too. She knew just where I was taking her."

I suppressed a small shiver, followed by a flicker of fear. No matter how sorry I felt for this dying woman, she was still a killer. And I was alone in a house with her. And then it hit me that Elizabeth Merriman would have fought for her life; she might well have used her cane. Kate was in a weakened condition, and a smaller woman than Elizabeth. Something still didn't add up. "Once she knew that, Kate, did she fight you?"

"She started to, all right. Lifted that cane like a weapon. But I stopped her." She took a sip of water, then a slow breath.

My hands tightened on the arms of my chair and I stared at the sick, exhausted woman across from me. "How?"

"I told her I had information for her." She met my eyes, a small spark of defiance in her own. "Information about her son." I gasped, and she cocked her head in my direction. "You think you're the only one who can do research? I've spent my life studying Elizabeth Merriman. It was an obsession." *She probably knows more about Elizabeth than I do.* "What did you tell her when you were out on that platform?" I asked.

She shrugged. "The truth. That Toscano was a liar. That he was not her long-lost son and that he'd been taking her for a ride."

"How did you know that?"

"I didn't. But I found out she'd had a baby sixty years ago, and he was the right age. I never believed the boyfriend rumors, anyway. So I took a chance, and I was right."

"But did you tell her—?"

"The rest of it?" Kate dropped her head and rested her hands on her knees. "You mean did I tell her that her real son was dead? Yes," she said. "I did."

"That was cruel," I said, my anger rising. "Maybe telling her that was revenge enough."

"It should have been," she said. "I watched her face crumple up like a piece of old newspaper." When she raised her eyes, they were full of tears. "And that's when I knew I couldn't go through with it."

"What do you mean you couldn't go through with it?" My voice grew louder, echoing in the quiet room. "A woman is dead."

"Victoria, I said I'd caused her death, not that I'd killed her." She took a tissue, wiped her eyes, and then blew her nose. "I don't blame you if you don't believe me, but Elizabeth Merriman's death was an accident."

"An accident?"

Kate nodded. "She slipped off that platform."

"How?" I whispered.

There was a pause while Kate took a breath and again rested her head on the back of the chair. "After I told her about her son, she asked why I was doing this. She actually said, 'What have I ever done to you?' That's when the anger came back, so I told her the story of what happened to my father. What happened to our family. What happened to me." She closed her eyes then, clearly exhausted.

"What did she do?"

"She started to cry. Loud, deep sobs. The kind of crying that comes from somebody who's not used to it. She wasn't a crier." She paused. "Neither am I." She wiped her mouth with a tissue and kept it clutched in her hand. "Then she started twisting her hands. It was dark and I couldn't tell what she was doing. But she was struggling to take off that big ring. She held it out to me," Kate said through her teeth, "like it was some kind of payment for what she did. She begged me to take it."

"Did you?"

She opened her eyes then and looked at me. "Yeah, I took it from her. And then I chucked it across the beach. For all I know, the tide came in and got it."

So the mystery of the missing ring, at least, was solved. "What did she do then?"

"She just cried harder. She was leaning over the side railing and dropped her cane. I tried to calm her down. Like I said, she was loud, and I figured someone might hear us. So I tried to take her arm, but she shook me off and moved closer to the stairway." Kate swallowed audibly. I tried to hand her the water, but she shook her head. Her voice dropped to a whisper. "So I tried again, and she got mad. She jerked her arm back—she was pretty strong—and slipped. I was reaching my hand out to her when she went over. I can still see her falling." She dropped her head in her hands. "I wasn't gonna go through with it," she said through her fingers. "I really wasn't."

"I believe you."

She lifted her head from her hands and looked at me. "What do you plan to do?"

"Well," I said, "I was hoping I wouldn't have to do anything. That you'd go to the authorities yourself. Both Toscano and Dr. Natale broke the law. But they haven't killed anybody. And you said it was an accident."

She put her head back and closed her eyes. "Like the cops will believe that."

"Listen, Kate, get a lawyer and tell your story the way you told it to me. You might even get a suspended sentence, considering your situation. . . ."

She opened one eye, grinning slightly. "My situation? You mean because I'm dying, don't you?"

"Yes," I said quietly. "And I'm so sorry. But doesn't that make it even more imperative to tell the truth?"

She let out a long, exhausted sigh. "I'm *so* tired. I just want it all to be over." Then she lifted her head and looked at me. "Will you give me a couple of hours? I promise I'll square everything away, and I'll text you afterward." She held out shaking hand. "Do we have a deal?"

I took her hand and held it gently. "Okay, Kate." I wrote down my cell number and left it on the table next to her medicines. "But I'm trusting you to do the right thing."

"I will," she said. "In fact, I'll write it all down."

And I left her sitting there in the darkening room, holding a pen over a sheet of white paper. A little more than an hour later, a text of only two words came through: *It's done*.

Chapter Twenty-five

*T*he next day, the atmosphere at the family table was subdued. My mother's face was thoughtful, a little sad. Without his hat, my dad lost his carefree Rat Pack persona, and he read the paper in silence. I sat between them, my coffee and biscotti untouched. We all looked up when Danny came in the door. He sat down across from me and rested his hand over mine.

"They found her body, sis. Right beyond the rock jetty. She left a letter explaining everything." His hand tightened on mine. "You might have to corroborate it at some point."

I nodded, my throat thick. "I didn't think she'd do that. I thought she'd turn herself in."

"Oh, sweetheart," my mom said, "you did the right thing by going to her. You gave her a chance to make it right."

My dad put his arm around my shoulders. "And in her mind, she did. She admitted everything in writing, so now Chickie won't have to face murder charges. And she ended things the way she wanted. You said yourself that she was suffering."

"You know what's strange? Nonna told me that when Elizabeth was a young girl, pregnant and desperate, she tried to jump off the jetty to kill herself. I guess it's all come full circle," I said, and then sighed. "Except for the loose ends, of course. I'll probably have to talk to Sutton again. And I can't escape an interview with Nina."

My mother smiled. "And your agent will be calling to say that your book sales have gone up again."

"Maybe. Speaking of books, I think I've got a great plot I can use in my historical. Remember I told you that Elizabeth had given up a baby?" And while I wasn't sure my grandmother would approve, I shared with my family the rest of the story—of Elisabetta and Tommy and Thomas. When I was done, my mother was wiping her eyes.

"Oh, Victoria, what a moving story. And so terribly sad. But it helps me understand Elizabeth Merriman better."

I nodded. "It does, doesn't it?"

"Wow," my dad said. "I never heard any of this till now. All these years, and Ma never said a word."

"No," I said. "She's kept this secret for more than half a century. She felt responsible for Elisabetta." I shook my head. "I hope she's not mad at me for telling you."

My mother patted my hand. "She won't be, honey. Nonna's responsibility to Elizabeth ended a long time ago."

"I guess so. I hope she sees it that way." I stood up and pushed in my chair. "Is Tim in the kitchen? I'd like to fill him in on some of this."

When I pushed through the doors, I stood for a moment, watching Tim from behind as he prepped for the day. And just as I thought *I have to get over him*, he turned around.

"Did they find Chef Kate?" There was concern on his face, but I couldn't tell whether it was for me or himself.

"Out by the rock jetty."

He winced as though something hurt him. "That's a real loss."

"She was dying, Tim. And she was suffering. That was clear when I went to see her."

He wiped his hands on his apron and rested his back against the sink. "You okay?"

I nodded. "I'm okay. Isn't this where you lecture me about getting involved with murders?"

He laid a hand on my shoulder, and I was comforted by its warmth. "Not right now." He shot me a crooked grin. "Not that I won't at another time, though."

I smiled back. "You know, Tim, when I think about this case, there are some striking parallels. Elizabeth Merriman, Kate Bridges, and even Roberta Natale—they're all only children with essentially loving parents. But so much of this was set in motion by the actions of those parents, whether intentional or not."

Tim nodded. "Dr. C. stole a bundle to give his daughter that wedding."

"Right. And the young Elisabetta lived under such strict rules that she had to give up her baby. And poor Kate—what did her parents ever do except love her?"

Tim was watching me carefully, and in the pause he asked me a question. "Vic, do you ever think about—"

I dropped my eyes, unwilling to have him see the emotion there. "The wedding we didn't have? The kids we didn't have? Yeah, I do sometimes. You?"

"Sometimes." He reached for my hand. "If I could change what happened, I would. In a heartbeat."

"I know you would." *But we can't change the past, Tim. And as much as I care for you, I'm not sure I can trust you with my heart again.* I gave his hand a squeeze before letting it go, and plastered a smile on my face. "C'mon, dude, it's ancient history. And you have a lovely young woman in your life."

He grinned. "And you have a not so lovely old man. Where is Lockhart today anyway?"

"Haven't seen him yet."

"But you plan to."

I looked into his slate gray eyes and told the truth. "I do."

Tim shook his head. "He doesn't deserve you."

I let out a laugh. "That's funny—he says exactly the same thing about you."

But Tim didn't laugh with me. Instead he took my hand again. "I want you to be happy. You know that, right?"

"I know." I slipped my hand from his. "I want the same for you. Listen, I need to get out there and set tables before Nonna shows up."

"Yup," he said. "And there's a meat stock that's calling my name." He turned back to his work and I left the kitchen, a heaviness settling around my heart.

Out in the dining room, it was soothing to fold napkins, wipe glasses, and smooth the freshly laundered linens out over the tables. In a few hours, hungry people would be coming in for lunch. Good smells were already wafting from the kitchen, and my mood lifted at the thought of serving plates of pasta and pouring glasses of wine. *Feeding people helps,* I thought. So did the small tasks involved—setting places and lighting candles and cutting flowers for the tables. *You're a regular Mrs. Dalloway, Vic.* But anything that kept me from thinking about Tim or poor Kate Bridges was welcome.

And at that point, I was actually smiling, until I turned to face my grandmother.

"So it's true what I heard?" she said. "That woman who killed Elisabetta drowned herself?"

I nodded. "Yes, Nonna. But Kate didn't kill her; it was an accident."

"Is that what she told you? And you believed her?" She crossed her arms and frowned, the picture of skepticism.

"I did believe her. I don't think she had anything to lose at that point."

My grandmother lifted a broad shoulder. "Except her soul."

"I guess that's true," I said quietly. "But it's all over now."

She turned to go but stopped and looked back at me. "Victoria, would you take me to see Louise Romano?"

"Of course. I think she'd like that. You can talk about Tommy and young Thomas and even Elisabetta."

"Yes." My grandmother blinked behind her glasses—was it possible there were tears in those tough old eyes? But she held herself straight, patted the pocket of her sweater, where I could make out the square shape of the funeral card. "Yes," she said again. "And may they all rest in peace." Then she crossed herself and walked out of the dining room.

Chapter Twenty-six

$\mathcal{F}$or the next two days, I nagged Sofia to talk to Danny. I understood why she was hesitating to tell him about the baby: it would mean the end to her plans to enter the police academy, at least for now. But by the second day (and fourth phone call) I sensed a change in my sister-in-law's mood.

"Hey, Vic," she said cheerily. "What's up?"

"You know what's up. The same thing that was up this morning and the day before that. You *need* to talk to my brother."

"Relax, SIL. I got it covered."

"So you say. But how long do you think Future Grandma Nicolina will be able to sit on this information? And if she shares her suspicions with my father, it's all over. He'll be taking out an ad in the *Press*."

"I have to do this in stages and handle your brother just right. One thing at a time. Vic, seriously, I have it all figured out."

"Wait," I said slowly. "There's *more* than one thing? And what is there to figure out? I'm confused."

She let out a sigh at my obtuseness. "It's not just the

baby. It's my career, too. Because I finally figured out a solution. I'm not entering the police academy. I'm doing something different." Her voice rose in excitement. "I'm gonna get my PI license."

"'PI' as in 'private investigator'? As in 'seedy guy in a rumpled trench coat'? As in 'my brother will never go along with this'?"

"It's not your brother's life we're talking about; it's mine. And I'm good at being an investigator. Look at how I helped you solve your cases."

"Okay, first of all, they're not *my* cases. Second, you understand that being a PI is not very glamorous, right? Do you really want to spend your time chasing down cheating husbands?" I had a sudden image of Sofia hanging out in hotel parking lots in unmarked vans.

"There's more to it than that. I've been researching it," she said excitedly, sounding more like her old self than she had for a month.

"So, are you planning to drop both little bombs on Danny at once?"

"No way. Baby first. Which is how it should be, right? There's plenty of time to tell him the other thing. But you won't say anything, right?"

I sighed. "No, I won't say anything. But you know that I hate keeping secrets from him, right?"

"I know. Actually, Vic, he's coming over in a little while, so I need to get pretty. Today's definitely the day; I'm telling him for sure. Maybe we'll catch you later at the restaurant."

How will that conversation go? I wondered. I suspected that my brother would be overjoyed about the baby. I so wanted things to work out for them. But why *couldn't* Sofia pursue a career and be a mother? Well, my brother was traditional in his thinking, but not unreasonable. He'd married a woman who owned her own business and her own home (now my cottage). But what might he make of this new scheme? I shook my head. It was hard to imagine Danny going along with anything that might put his wife in danger. So I had to hope that my brother and his wife were truly solving their troubles—and not merely postponing them.

No one was in the dining room when I arrived at the Casa Lido, but there were muffled voices coming from the kitchen. When I pushed open the door, a strange sight met my eyes. There was Cal, of all people, stirring something with a wooden spoon. And not just any wooden spoon—my grandmother's *personal* spoon, the one made of olive wood imported from Italy. At his elbow was my grandmother, watching intently. There was Nonna, watching Cal cook with *her* spoon in *her* kitchen. Had I somehow entered another dimension? I sniffed. If I had, they used butter on this side of the universe.

"Calvino," Nonna said, pointing inside the pot, "that is much too brown."

Cal shook his head. "That's the way it's gotta be, Giulietta. Can't make gumbo without that base bein' good and dark." He stopped stirring, turned his head, and met my eyes. I hadn't seen Cal since our date—

since that kiss, the memory of which was still fresh and warm. It wasn't just the heat in the kitchen that brought a deep rose color to my face. And while I find the scent of butter intoxicating, it was not quite enough to set my heart pounding like a drum. One side of his mouth lifted in a slow grin; I smiled back, my cheeks burning.

"Hello, Victoria," he said, still stirring the butter. "And how are you on this fine morning?"

"I'm well, thanks." *If you ignore my red face, fluttery tummy, and shaky knees.*

My grandmother crossed the kitchen and grasped my arm. "Come, Victoria. Let Calvino show you how to make the gumbo like his mama does."

"Uh, okay," I said, as she propelled me toward the stove. "You want me to . . . cook?"

"*Sì.* Calvino will show you what he knows." She beamed at him in a way I've never seen her look at another human being, except maybe Danny. "And now I will go check things in the dining room."

After she left, Cal looked over at me. "Well, *cher*, you heard the lady. I think this is where I'm s'posed to show you everything I know." He slid an arm around my waist and pulled me close, setting me in front the stove, then handed me the spoon. "We'll start with how to make a roux. I'll save the rest for later."

Trying not to get distracted by wondering what "the rest" might entail, I stirred the brown paste around the pot. "Did you say 'rue'?" I asked. "As in 'I rue the day I set foot back in this town'?"

"No. Roux as in r-o-u-x. It's a butter-and-flour base

for gumbo." He stood behind me, both hands at my waist. He kissed the top of my head. "You smell amazing, by the way." He stepped closer and bent his head, his breath warm on the back of my neck.

"Hey," I said, "I'm stirring here."

"You certainly are, sweetheart," he murmured, leaving a trail of kisses from my ear down the side of my neck.

"Okay, you need to, uh . . . s-s-stop." I shivered and leaned against his chest, my hand still gripping the spoon.

"You heard what your grandma said. I'm supposed to be givin' you the benefit of my experience." He uncurled my fingers from the spoon and turned off the heat under the pot. "And I've hardly taught you a thing yet."

I turned to face him, and the look in his green eyes gave me a small jolt. "I'm sure your knowledge is . . . extensive, Mr. Lockhart." He tightened his hold on me and grinned. "However," I said, "I'm not sure I'm ready for school just yet." I took his hands gently— albeit reluctantly—from my waist.

"I told you I was a patient man, particularly for things that are worth waiting for." He rested his forehead against mine. "Did I tell you what a nice time I had the other night?"

"You did." I wondered if he were about to ask if we might do it again when the kitchen door swung open. I jerked my head up to see Tim scowling darkly at us.

"Hope I'm not interrupting," he said, "but I have work to do in here."

Cal looked up and gestured to the stove. "All yours, brother." He cocked his head and crossed his arms across his chest. "The kitchen anyways."

Tim's answer was a muttered curse and a clatter of pots in the sink.

It was pretty clear Cal was staking a claim on me, and I couldn't tell if I was offended or flattered. I stepped away from him and frowned. "The kitchen," I announced, "belongs to the Rienzis." I looked from one to the other and smiled sweetly. "Just a reminder, boys."

I left the kitchen with Cal on my heels. "Hey, slow down there," I heard from behind me.

I paused in the hallway between the kitchen and dining room and turned back to Cal. "I could say the same to you, Cal."

He held up both palms. "Point taken, Victoria. You need me to take it slow, I'll do just that."

"Thank you. I appreciate it."

"Not at all. From here on out, I will comport myself as a total gentleman."

He pushed a strand of hair from my eyes. His face was serious, but there was a suspicious light in those green eyes. "No more suggestive jokes," he said. "No more nuzzlin' on your neck. And certainly no long clinches outside your front door on a warm summer night."

Hmm. The neck nuzzling was pretty nice. Not to mention the good-night kiss that left me weak-kneed. Perhaps my call for caution had been a bit hasty. I opened my mouth to say so, but Cal simply nodded, gave me a small salute, and walked past me toward the dining room.

"What just happened here?" I muttered to myself.

"I don't know, honey. You tell me."

I slapped my hand against my chest and swung around. "Good Lord, Mom. Where'd you come from?"

"My office." She pointed a long fingernail in the direction of the bar. "Are you seeing him?"

"No. Well, sort of, I guess." I sighed. "We've gone out on a couple of dates—that's it."

She narrowed her eyes. "I don't think so. You should see the look on your face."

I glanced at the kitchen doors, lowering my voice to a whisper. "What would you have me do, Mom? Spend my life waiting for Tim to grow up?"

"He *has* grown up. Don't get me wrong—I haven't forgotten how he's hurt you. But people make mistakes, and, if they're lucky, they learn from them."

I looked back at the kitchen doors. "And you believe that about Tim?"

She nodded, her curls bouncing. "I do, hon." She rested her palm against my cheek. "I wouldn't even be talking to you about this if I didn't think you still had feelings for him."

"Even if I do, Mom, we've both moved on." I patted her shoulder. "Don't worry about me, okay?"

"No chance of that, my darling. I'll worry about you and your brother until I go to my grave."

"Okay, on that happy note—" But we were interrupted by voices from the dining room, one of them a deep baritone. My brother.

"Where is everybody?" he shouted. "Get out here, will you?"

He and Sofia stood in the doorway, holding hands, their faces flushed and eyes shining. *Guess he knows*, I thought, and as if reading my mind, Sofia grinned at me and nodded.

"Hey." Without letting go of his wife's hand, my brother kissed us both. "Where's Pop and Nonna?"

"They're in the bar, honey," my mom said, barely concealing her excitement. She, too, had read the signs. "I'll go get them." She skittered across the dining room, her heels clicking away on the wood floor.

She's been waiting for this, I thought. *And it has the bonus of keeping her mind off my love life.* I led them to the family table, making a conscious effort not to look at my sister-in-law. In moments, my parents and Nonna joined us.

Danny turned to look at his wife. "Do you want to tell them?" he asked softly.

She shook her head and patted his cheek. "You know you're dying to," she said with a smile.

My mother was fit to burst. My grandmother nodded as understanding dawned. My father merely looked confused, and turned all his attention to Danny.

The words were barely out of my brother's mouth before my mother leapt from her seat. "I knew it!" she shrieked. "Oh, darlings, I couldn't be happier." As she captured the two of them in her maternal grip, Sofia grinned at me over my mother's shoulder.

"I'm *so* happy for you guys!" I said a shade too loudly, but it was my way of acting surprised.

"Thank God," my grandmother said, her hands

clasped as though in prayer. "And now you're together, as it should be."

I noticed that Nonna uttered those last words as a commandment. She took Danny's face in her hands and kissed his cheeks, then did the same for Sofia. Through it all, my dad sat wearing a dazed smile.

"So, Grandpa Frank?" I asked him. "What do you think of this news?"

"Ah, honey, it's wonderful," he said, turning to me. "A baby's just what we need around here. In fact—" He stopped and dug a paper from his back pocket and flattened it. A racing form. "Hah!" he said, slapping his palm down on the paper. "I knew it—there's a horse running at Monmouth named Bambino." He rolled the paper up and pointed it at me. "It's a sign, I tell ya." He reached across the table and squeezed Sofia's hand. "How're you feeling, baby?"

"Pretty good most of the time," Sofia said. "But I'm a little queasy right now."

"Ugh, sorry you're still sick," I said. "Can I pour you some water?"

But Sofia's eyes widened, and too late I realized what I'd said. Danny's eyes bored into mine and I froze in my seat.

My mother, who'd somehow missed the silent exchange, started listing various cures for morning sickness. "A nice dry biscotto in the morning, hon. Before you even get out of bed."

"Never mind that, Nicolina," Nonna said. "Some fresh mint is what she needs. We have some right in the garden."

"Oh, I heard that works," I said. "I'll go get some." I jumped up from my chair, almost knocking it over in my haste to get out of that room. I scurried out the back door and crossed the parking lot in record time. But it wasn't long before my brother found me. I bent over the mint, studying each leaf in a lame attempt to pretend I didn't know he was there.

"Hey, Vic?" I could hear the edge in his voice. "What did you mean back there?"

"What do you mean what did I mean?" Stalling for time, I kept my back to him and continued picking leaves.

"Look at me," my brother barked. "You know what I'm talking about. You told Sofia you were sorry she was still sick. You knew, didn't you? You knew she was pregnant."

I straightened up and sighed. "Yes, Dan, I knew."

"Before I did." He crossed his arms and glared at me, his mouth tightened in a grim line.

"It's not what you think."

"It's not, huh? It's not you two keeping stuff behind my back? Right." He turned quickly and started back to the house.

"Danny, wait. Let me explain, okay?" I called after him. But he just kept walking.

When I got back to my cottage at the end of the day, I was still thinking about the confrontation with my brother. And there was only one thing that would make me feel better: the ocean. I threw on my shorts and headed outside. The beach at six o'clock was my favorite time. Day-trippers had long gone home, and the renters were usually packing up their things. Here and there a few lone couples, mostly older year-rounders, were sitting with towels wrapped around their legs, their noses in paperbacks, maybe one of them even a Bernardo Vitali mystery.

I dragged my beach chair close to the water's edge, stretched my legs out in front of me, and tipped my head back to soak up the last rays of sun. And to think. Remembering my conversation with Tim about Kate and Dr. C., I thought about the ties of family. How they bound us and comforted us but sometimes chafed. When I looked in the mirror, I saw an independent woman with the first faint lines of age marking her face. But inside I was still Danny's kid sister and Frank and Nic's little girl. Not to mention Nonna's head-strong granddaughter. Well, Cal had said she and I were alike. I shook my head. How can you care about people so much and yet want to escape them at the same time?

I loved that we were all together at the restaurant this morning, celebrating the baby, but I hated the friction with my brother. *He's right to be angry*, the voice of my conscience said. *He should have been the first person to know*. I trailed my fingers in the wet sand, suddenly aware of a shadow hovering over me. A literal one. When I opened my eyes, my brother was standing next to my chair.

"Thought I'd find you down here," he said, and plopped down next to my chair. In a T-shirt, shorts, and flip-flops, he was Brother Danny, as opposed to Cop Danny, which came as a relief.

"You know me well, brother." I shaded my eyes and looked into his face. "You still mad at me?"

He grinned and shook his head. "I'm not allowed to be." He scooped handfuls of wet sand, piling them idly while he spoke. "The minute we got home, my wife ripped me a new one. Said if I should be mad at anybody, it should be her, not you."

I put my hand on his arm. "You had a right to be mad."

He shook his head, still scooping sand. "No. I should've let you explain. She told me how it happened. That you caught her throwing up."

"You have no idea how I nagged her to tell you, Danny."

"Oh, I think I do. Anyway, I'm in no mood to be mad at anybody." His face brightened, his grin growing wider. "Do you believe I'm gonna be a father?"

I shook my head. "Not really. But it's Frank as a grandfather that's really got my head spinning. He's probably out buying a whole bunch of lottery tickets and laying bets on Bambino right now. And setting up a pool on the birthdate and the baby's weight."

Danny threw back his head and laughed; it was a sound that did my heart good. "So, you're back home, I assume," I said.

He nodded. "Where I belong. And where I plan to stay. From here on out, we work out our problems like grown-ups."

"That's good to hear. And anytime you guys need time alone, be sure to call Aunt Victoria to babysit."

"I'm holdin' you to that," he said, pointing a finger at me. He paused, still piling sand. "Hey, Vic?" he asked. "Were you ever so happy that you felt like you didn't deserve it?"

"Hell, no!" I said. "I deserve every millisecond of happiness that comes my way. I figure I earned it."

"Well, that's true." Danny said. "And I want you to be happy."

"Funny. You're the second man who's said that to me of late."

"Tim?" he asked without looking at me.

"The very one." I cupped some wet sand and dribbled it on top of Danny's pile.

"Has it been okay working with him?"

"It's been fine. You know he's seeing somebody, right?"

He nodded. "The redhead?"

"Yup. She's actually nice, despite her unfortunate hair color."

"Maybe." His face tightened. "But are you sure—?"

I held up my hand to stave off the rest of the question. "Yes, I'm sure. Whatever you were going to ask me, I'm sure."

"Okay," He grinned again, his face taking on a dreamy look. "A baby," he said, shaking his head. "Still gettin' my mind around it."

"*La famiglia,*" I said softly.

"*La famiglia,*" he agreed.

I squinted into my brother's face; his eyes were suspiciously bright. "Hey, Mr. Tough Guy, is that a tear I see?"

He stood up, brushing the sand from his hands. "Nah. Sun's in my eyes." He gripped my shoulder and squeezed. "Later, sis."

"Later, bro," I said to his retreating back, and wiped away a small tear of my own.

Recipes from the
Italian Kitchen

There are many variations on Italian Wedding Soup, but the one element they all share is polpetti, or tiny, flavorful meatballs. The meatball recipe here is based upon my mom's, and one I have been using my whole adult life—the secret is the blend of ground meats. (If you can't find the meat blend prepackaged at your grocery store, ask the butcher to prepare it for you.) While many self-respecting Italians wouldn't dream of mixing meatballs with anything but their own two hands, I prefer the food processor for this messy job. If you don't have homemade chicken stock on hand, a good quality prepared stock is fine for the soup. If escarole is not to your taste, use spinach, Swiss chard, or any other green you like. This recipe makes a large batch. I generally freeze half the meatballs and cut the soup recipe in half, but if you have a big family, go for it.

Nonna's Famous Italian Wedding Soup

For the meatballs:

1-2 small cloves garlic, according to taste
⅓ cup chopped fresh parsley leaves
½ pound ground beef
½ pound ground pork
½ pound ground veal
½ cup flavored Italian bread crumbs
½ cup freshly grated Pecorino Romano cheese
¼ cup milk

1 large egg, lightly beaten
1 teaspoon salt
½ teaspoon freshly ground black pepper

For the soup:

2 tablespoons good-quality olive oil
1 cup finely chopped yellow onion
1 cup diced carrots (3 carrots), cut into ¼ inch pieces
¾ cup diced celery (2 stalks), cut into ¼ inch pieces
½ cup dry white wine
*16 cups homemade chicken stock or four 32-ounce
containers of good-quality prepared broth*
2 cups small pasta, such as orzo or ditalini
*2 ounces escarole, washed well and torn into bite-sized
pieces*

1. Preheat the oven to 350° degrees F.

2. With the food processor running, drop the peeled garlic cloves and parsley through the feed tube, and process until finely minced. Scrape down the processor. To the parsley-and-garlic mixture add the ground meats, bread crumbs, cheese, milk, egg, salt, and pepper. Pulse until all ingredients are well combined, scraping down the bowl once. With a melon baller or small cookie scoop, drop meatballs of about one inch in diameter onto a sheet pan lined with parchment paper. (You should have about 60 meatballs. Roll them in your palms to smooth them, if you wish, but they don't have to be perfect.) Bake for 15 to 20 minutes, until cooked through and lightly browned. Set aside.

3. In the meantime, make the soup by heating the olive oil over medium-low heat in a large heavy-bottomed soup pot. Add the onion, carrots, and celery and sauté until softened, 5 to 6 minutes, stirring occasionally. Stir the wine into the vegetables; add the chicken stock and bring to a boil. Add the pasta to the simmering broth and cook for 6 to 8 minutes, until the pasta is tender. Add the meatballs to the soup and simmer for 1 minute. Taste, and add salt and pepper as needed. Stir in the escarole and cook for 1 to 2 minutes, until it is just wilted. Ladle into soup bowls and sprinkle each serving with extra grated cheese.

Even Vic knows that the secret to a good ragu (to-mato sauce with meat) is a long, slow simmer, either on top of the stove or slow-cooked in the oven. This recipe makes a deeply flavored sauce, even with the cheapest cuts of beef. It freezes well, and is best served over sturdy pastas such as rigatoni.

Rosie's Easy Beef Ragu

1 to 1½ lbs. beef chuck, cut into large cubes (or precut beef for stew)
2 tablespoons olive oil
Salt and pepper to taste
2–3 large cloves garlic, roughly chopped
2 tablespoons tomato paste
¼ cup full-bodied red wine
1 28-ounce can imported chopped tomatoes
1 28-ounce can imported strained tomatoes or tomato puree
2–3 teaspoons salt
6–8 large basil leaves, snipped into small pieces
2 tablespoons fresh parsley, roughly chopped (frozen herbs may be substituted for fresh)

1. Press cubed beef dry with paper towels, then put into a large bowl with the olive oil and mix until all the meat is coated. Lightly season with salt and pepper.

2. Coat a heavy-bottomed 4-quart pan with cooking spray. Brown the beef in batches over medium-high heat and set aside. Pour off excess fat, if you wish.

3. Lower the heat to medium, and cook the garlic quickly in beef fat. Add the tomato paste and red wine and deglaze pan. Stir thoroughly to pick up all the browned bits. When the mixture reaches a high simmer, add tomatoes, salt and pepper, and fresh herbs.

4. Put the meat and any juices back into the pot. Bring sauce to a slow boil, about 10 minutes.

5. Reduce heat to low, cover, and simmer the sauce on the lowest heat for 2½ to 3 hours, or until the beef is fork tender. Stir occasionally. (For oven cooking, set the temperature to 275° F. Make sure you use an oven-proof pot, and let the sauce come to a boil on top of the stove first. Set on the middle rack in the oven for 2½ to 3 hours. Check the sauce once per hour during cooking to stir and add liquid as needed.)

Though Nonna makes these for a wedding, in our house this cookie is a Christmas staple. (The smell when they are cooking is heavenly!) My own grandmother, Maria Genova, made these regularly, and my aunt Marie Genova Abate provided the recipe here. For some, anise is an acquired taste, so if you don't like that licorice flavor, vanilla or almond extract may be substituted. This recipe makes about three dozen cookies.

Nonna's Ricotta Cookies

2 cups flour
2 teaspoons baking powder
¼ teaspoon salt
1 cup sugar
½ cup butter (do not substitute)
2 eggs
1–2 teaspoons of anise extract
1 cup fresh ricotta cheese

For topping:

confectioner's sugar
nonpareils or colored sugars

1. Preheat the oven to 350° F. Sift the flour, baking powder, and salt in a bowl and set aside.

2. In a larger bowl or stand mixer, cream the butter and sugar until fluffy. Add the eggs and anise extract.

3. Add the dry ingredients and ricotta alternately to the butter mixture until well blended.

4. Drop by rounded teaspoonfuls, two inches apart, on parchment-covered cookie sheets, and bake for 10 to 12 minutes. Do not overbake; the bottoms should be a light golden brown.

5. Let cool, and top with confectioner's sugar glaze and nonpareils or colored sugars.

Read on for a sneak peek at the next
Italian Kitchen Mystery,

A Dish Best Served Cold

Coming in fall 2015 from Obsidian.

A mingled blast of garlic and alcohol hit me as soon as I opened the back door. The reek was emanating from Pietro Petrocelli, known colloquially as "Stinky Pete." Naturally, I never called him that to his face (or in front of my grandmother, who knows him from the old country). Pete listed to one side, then the other, blinking his bloodshot eyes and grinning at me with his nearly toothless mouth. Recoiling from the stench of unwashed skin and lack of dental hygiene, I took two steps back into the restaurant kitchen.

"Uh, hi, Pete. Nonna's not here at the moment." I started to close the door, but Pete, who was pretty quick for a drunk, held it fast.

"It's *La Signorina Scrittrice*," he slurred. "The Lady Writer. How you do, *signorina*?" He stuck his unshaven face inside the door opening, treating me to another whiff of garlic breath. "Is your papa here?"

"No," I said firmly. My dad, Frank, who had a soft spot for Pete, would sometimes give him a glass of home-made wine, but only when my grandmother wasn't around. Nonna would feed Pete if he was hungry, but she drew the line at liquor.

"Hokay," he said with a sigh. "So, maybe, Lady Writer, could you do an old man a favor?"

"Not if it involves wine." I gripped the side of the door, trying unsuccessfully to push it closed.

"C'mon, *signorina*. I am parched in the heat." He pressed his free hand against his chest. "I have a great thirst."

"I'll bet you do," I said. "You can have some water. And if you're hungry, I'll give you a panini. But that's it. And then you have to go."

He finally let go of the door and shook his head. "It is not for water that I have the thirst. But I will take, how you say, a 'suh-nack.'"

"One 'suh-nack' coming up. But you have to wait there, okay?" I said, closing the door. I grabbed a roll, threw on some salami and cheese, and wrapped the sandwich in a paper towel.

When I handed it to him, Pete stuck the sandwich into the pocket of his tattered shirt and winked at me with one droopy eye. "For later," he whispered. Taking advantage of the open door, he pushed his head inside again; I tried very hard not to inhale as he spoke. "If you give me *il vino*, I can tell you stories. For your books." He raised his hand in a scribbling motion to illustrate.

"I can't, Pete. It's not good for you. Nonna won't let me."

"Oh, your grandmother, she is a saint," he said, clapping his palms together as though in prayer.

"Uh huh." *She's a saint, all right.* "You need to go, Pete." I shoved harder against the door.

He tapped the side of his head. "Me, I know t'ings. Many t'ings I could tell you for your murder books."

"I'm sure you could, but you really have to go now."

Pete nodded, pulled his head back from the doorway, and patted his breast pocket. "Thank you, *signorina*. And remember what I said," he called as he stumbled off. "I have stories to tell."

Stories involving the grape, no doubt, but probably little I could use for my "murder books." I bolted the door behind me and grabbed a handful of basil from the refrigerator, stuck my nose in it, and sniffed deeply.

"Victoria," my grandmother called out sharply, "what are you doing to that basil?"

She stood in the doorway to the kitchen, her hands on her hips and a frown on her face—her usual pose when greeting me.

"What does it look like? I'm clearing my nasal passages. Pete was here."

"That's Mr. Petrocelli to you. Have some respect."

"Ugh, Nonna, he's disgusting. He came around hoping Daddy was here to give him wine."

She shook her head and made a *tsk*ing sound. "A terrible affliction. Pietro was once a cabinetmaker, a craftsman. And a man like that turns to drink. Such a shame."

"Why are you nice to him? Why do you even let him come around?" I asked, giving the basil a quick rinse at the sink.

"Back in Naples, he knew your grandfather." At the

mention of her late husband, Nonna crossed herself and looked at me expectantly.

"May God rest his soul," I said quickly.

She nodded her approval and resumed her story. "Pietro's older brother, Alfonso, was also close to your grandpa's *fratello*, your great-uncle, Zio Roberto. But such troublemakers, those two." She shook her head again. "Got in with criminals. Your grandfather's family never talked about Roberto."

I put the basil away and gave my grandmother my full attention. A long-lost great-uncle who "got in with criminals" and was a forbidden subject for the Rienzi family? This was rich material for my novel, a historical I was writing based on my family. I grabbed my waitress pad and a pen from the pocket of my apron; they would have to do in lieu of my computer.

"What happened to him?" I casually set the pad down on the counter, trying to keep it out of her sight. If she thought I was writing instead of prepping vegetables for lunch, I'd be in for it. I set the bin of carrots on the counter for effect.

"He died in the old country. No one was sure how." Nonna, who'd been scrubbing vigorously at the sink, dried her hands on a towel and tied an apron around her waist. "Have you chopped the onions and garlic?" she called over her shoulder.

"Uh huh." I scribbled away in secret on the other side of the carrot bin. "So, did he just disappear? I mean, did they have a funeral for him? Is there a death certificate?"

She pinched her fingers and shook her hand in the classic Italian gesture. For as often as I'd seen it, I was surprised her hands weren't frozen in that position. "What are you, the police?" she asked. "Why all these questions?"

"I want to know about our history."

"Well, I want to know about the vegetables. Bring me that onion and garlic so I can start the sauce."

I brought her the open containers from the refrigerator, my eyes tearing up at the smell. I was still learning about cooking, but I knew the garlic and onion had to be kept in separate containers. You have to start with the onions, as they take longer to cook; garlic burns if you're not careful, so that gets added later. A perfectly sautéed onion-and-garlic mixture formed the basis of most of the Casa Lido's famous sauces. "Would you tell me more about Zio Roberto?" I asked.

"I will if you put that pen away and clean those carrots like you're supposed to."

I sighed and took a vegetable scraper from the drawer. As my brother Danny once observed about our nonna: *She don't miss a trick.* "Yes, Nonna," I said.

I watched her pour a generous helping of extra-virgin olive oil into the bottom of our biggest stockpot, heard the sizzle as the onions hit the hot oil. She talked while she stirred. "Your grandpa Giuseppe's mother was married very young and had Roberto right away. But then for many years, she had trouble having babies," Nonna explained. "Your grandfather was what we used to call a 'late life' baby. His mama must have been forty when she had him."

"So Grandpa and Zio Roberto had a big gap between them?"

"*Sì*. Maybe fourteen, fifteen years. Your grandfather barely remembered him. All he knew was that Roberto got involved with the wrong people and died back in Italy. End of story." She stopped stirring long enough to scrutinize the chopped garlic. "Did you take out all the sprouts?"

My grandmother was obsessive about garlic preparation. "Yes," I said, holding up my hands. "And I have the smelly fingers to prove it."

"Part of the job," she said shortly. "Use lemon juice."

"Speaking of garlic," I said, "Stink . . . uh, Mr. Petrocelli said that he 'knows things' that I could use in my books. Do you think he might have meant information about his brother and Zio Roberto?"

"Who knows?" She lifted one broad shoulder in a shrug. "He's an old man, and old men like to talk and make themselves important. He probably just repeats the same stories to anyone who will listen." She paused. "I suppose they could be about Alfonso. But he turned out bad, and, may God forgive me, so did your Zio Roberto."

"Yeah, you said that." *But bad in what way?* Could they have been mafiosi back in Italy? I imagined the two young men in Naples, dressed in suspenders and flat caps, looking like extras from *The Godfather: Part II*. Though my book wasn't a *Godfather*-type story, I couldn't help being curious. "So Grandpa's brother died young. What happened to Alfonso?"

"Last I heard he had emigrated here. But that was many years ago." She shook her wooden spoon at me. "I thought you wanted to know about your great-uncle Roberto."

"I do." I lifted a carrot high in my right hand, while my left crawled across the counter toward my pen and pad. But before I could grab either, my grandmother's words assailed my ears.

"You pick up that pen, missy, and I shut my mouth."

I let out a loud huff, prompting my grandmother to shoot me a look that froze my blood. "Okay," I said, resigned to the inevitable. "No pen. So, I'm supposed to just remember it all," I muttered.

"You're *supposed* to be working. Come to think of it, I have more important things to talk to you about than dead relatives. We have the anniversary celebration to think about."

I stifled a sigh. Nonna was obsessed with the Casa Lido's upcoming anniversary; it was clear I'd get no more family history out of her today. I briefly considered talking to Stinky Pete to find out what he actually knew about my grandfather's mysterious brother. Grimacing at the thought of a one-on-one with the odiferous Signor Petrocelli, I told myself I didn't have much time for writing anyway.

It was August, and we were coming to the end of a busy season, one which would be capped off by a celebration of the Casa Lido's seventieth anniversary and the last rush of Labor Day weekend. They were likely to be the restaurant's most profitable events of the year, and we were counting on that revenue to make up for our slow start in the spring. (A dead body in the tomato garden tends to keep the customers away.) As I thought about the events of the last weeks, it struck me that I'd been back in New Jersey for nearly three months—

almost a whole summer season. In that time I'd gotten myself involved with two men *and* two murders. That was some crazy arithmetic, even for me.

My thoughts were interrupted by a loud rapping noise and I jumped a mile. "I'm talking to you, Victoria," my grandmother said, banging her wooden spoon on the countertop. "Stop daydreaming. Hurry and finish those carrots; then bring me four jars of tomatoes from the pantry. And when you've finished that, you can write down the menu for the party as I dictate. It will be summer dishes—antipasto and bruschetta, cold salads, and maybe some shrimp . . ."

She was off and running. And in all the bustle of preparation for the dinner service and the plans for the Casa Lido's big day, Zio Roberto, his friend Alfonso, and Stinky Pete were quickly forgotten. Which turned out to be a mistake, because Stinky Pete was right: He *did* have a story to tell—one that nobody ever got a chance to hear.

Also available from
Rosie Genova

Murder and Marinara
An Italian Kitchen Mystery

Hit whodunit writer Victoria Rienzi is getting
back to her roots by working at her family's
Italian restaurant. But now in between plating
pasta and pouring vino, she'll have to find the
secret ingredient in a murder....

**"The tastiest item on the menu with
colorful characters, a sharp plot, and a
fabulous Jersey setting."**
—*New York Times* bestselling author
Jenn McKinlay

"So good I can taste it."
—*New York Times* bestselling author
Stephanie Evanovich

Available wherever books are sold or at
penguin.com

facebook.com/TheCrimeSceneBooks